VIR

MODERN

7

Rosamond Lehmann

Rosamond Lehmann (1901–1990) was born in Buckinghamshire. She was educated privately and was a scholar at Girton College, Cambridge. She wrote her first novel in her twenties, the best-selling *Dusty Answer*, and married Wogan Philipps, the artist, in 1928. Her reputation was firmly established with the publication of *A Note in Music* in 1930, and the subsequent *Invitation to the Waltz* and its sequel, *The Weather in the Streets*. During the war she contributed short stories to the notable book-periodical *New Writing* which was edited by her brother, John Lehmann. Rosamond Lehmann remains one of the most distinguished novelists of this century, and was created a CBE in 1982.

Also by Rosamond Lehmann

Dusty Answer
A Note in Music
Invitation to the Waltz
The Weather in the Streets
The Ballad and the Source
The Gipsy's Baby
The Echoing Grove
The Swan in the Evening
A Sea-Grape Tree

A NOTE IN MUSIC

Rosamond Lehmann

With an introduction
by Janet Watts

'But the present, like a note in music, is nothing but as it appertains to what is past and what is to come.'

W. S. LANDOR

virago

TO WOGAN

VIRAGO

Published by Virago Press in 1982
Reprinted 1992, 2001, 2009, 2012

First published by Chatto & Windus Ltd in 1930

A CIP catalogue record for this book is available from the British Library

ISBN 978-0-86068-248-6

Printed and bound in Great Britain by
Clays Ltd, St Ives plc

Papers used by Virago are from well-managed forests and other responsible sources.

Virago Press
An imprint of
Little, Brown Book Group
100 Victoria Embankment
London EC4Y 0DY

An Hachette UK Company
www.hachette.co.uk

www.virago.co.uk

CONTENTS

INTRODUCTION

Rosamond Lehmann herself calls *A Note in Music* 'a totally forgotten book'. She adds: 'It was even forgotten by me.' It stands separate and alone in the body of her work, and to its author herself, when she re-read it after fifty years, 'It seemed so not-in-the-canon that I could hardly believe I had written it.'

A Note in Music came out in 1930, some three years after Rosamond Lehmann's brilliantly successful first novel, *Dusty Answer*. By this time, as she recalls, 'a number of people were saying that *Dusty Answer* must have been my autobiography and that I'd never write anything else'. She was herself convinced that she was essentially a writer of fiction rather than fact – 'though the background of *Dusty Answer* was a good deal my own, that book was not my life' – and she set out to prove it in *A Note in Music*.

The background of this second novel was, however, also her own. Not long before she wrote *Dusty Answer*, Rosamond Lehmann had (like her first heroine) experienced the delights and passions of an Edwardian young womanhood in a charming riverside house; when she sat down to write *A Note in Music*, she had (like her second heroine) recently endured the melancholy and frustration of transplantation to the provincial north of England and an unhappy first marriage. But at this point, in the second as in the first novel, a new reality began to develop and depart from the one she had experienced herself: and an unknown story to emerge.

Miss Lehmann recalls: 'I wanted to get away from any sort of self-identification, and when I began to write about Grace Fairfax, I couldn't identify her with anyone I knew, and particularly not with myself — though later I grew very fond of her and felt very sorry for her.' As she points out, Rosamond Lehmann got away from her own hated northern exile, and her marriage. Grace Fairfax stays.

Dusty Answer had dropped upon the reading public as a bolt from the publishing blue, a *succès fou* from a young unknown. This second novel appeared in quite a different context. Rosamond Lehmann was now a recognised figure in the literary world: respected (but also suspected) for her outstanding first achievement; known as a clever Cambridge scholar, a social success, and a beautiful young woman. All these advantages helped to increase her vulnerability, and — true to publishing custom — reviewers who had been adulatory about her first novel responded dustily to its successor. For a reason Miss Lehmann cannot now recall or explain, the reviews for this book are the only ones she has preserved, though they were mixed, and included some of the harshest criticism she was to receive in her writing career. 'A disappointing second novel,' sighed *The Times Literary Supplement*; '*Dusty Answer* was a terminus, its very charms announcing, No road this way,' intoned *The Nation*.

There was, nevertheless, significant praise from

distinguished quarters. E. M. Forster wrote a personal letter to say that although he had not particularly enjoyed *Dusty Answer*, he considered *A Note in Music* 'an enormous advance', and especially commended its treatment of homosexuality. Harold Nicholson, reviewing the second novel in the *Daily Express*, expressed fears for its popularity for the same reason that he admired it – 'Miss Lehmann has now left the "thorny companionship of youth" and embarked on the forest of humanity.' Having written first of the tragedies of youth, she was now setting out to convey the tragedies of middle age; and while 'it is easy enough to awake an emotional response by the apt portrayal of young men and women bathing by moonlight', as Nicholson urbanely noted, 'it is difficult to succeed with the neutral tints of the unassuaged.'

Rosamond Lehmann is a writer of colour, passion and delight. Her language is lavish, graceful, rich with words; her subjects are large ones – the pleasures and pains of life. *A Note in Music* is no exception to these rules. Yet it is also singular within her work.

This novel is the most spare, sober, and severe of all Rosamond Lehmann's books: the starkest in theme, the most sombre in colour and mood. Its subject is the least remarkable, though not the least wretched, of the tragedies of middle age: loveless, lifeless marriage. Its setting is a northern provincial town where spring comes late in May; where the tidy paths of the municipal park offer meagre relief from a complex of streets, houses, factories and offices; where sickly prostitutes lend poor comfort to tired fat businessmen, and a wallow in a novel or a tram-ride to a film afford the only solace available to unhappy women with nothing but time on their hands.

Out of the shadows of this bleak world, a handful of people emerge. They look ordinary enough – positively dull, in fact. Yet as they come into the light of this book, they astonish us with the delicacy of their drawing, and they shock us with the tenderness of the characters they conceal. On a cold January night we steal upon Grace Fairfax and her husband, Tom, as they drag on their dinner clothes to consume a stodgy supper. Who could think, in this first glimpse of a clumsy, overweight, and dispirited couple ('slipshod' is Grace's own word for them), that by the end of this short novel our hearts would flicker with every hint of the odd smile that haunts the corners of Grace Fairfax's mouth? Or that Tom's portly pleasantries, as the pair of them take a wintry turn around that same town park, would cheer us into hope – and hope not only for our couple, but for ourselves? Yet so it is.

Compromise and resignation have become unconscious in the lives of Grace and Tom Fairfax, and of Norah and Gerald MacKay. Tom, the corpulent businessman, and Gerald, a nervy provincial professor, would have nothing to say to each other; but their wives – who meet only rarely – share a curious, intangible, powerful friendship. Both have been married for ten years; for both, it has been something of a decade of death. Dreams, hopes, longings, illusions, gaiety have receded almost imperceptibly from their outlooks and their lives. Grace's baby died, and so did her mongrel puppy; and the soft southern countryside and climate that she loved as a girl are as good as dead to her. So too, for Norah, is her sparkling young womanhood as a debutante in London; and the joy with which she hugs her two plain little boys does not close the wound of another death in the war, still rawly alive in her heart.

The two husbands wrestle in semi-blindness with their own private heartaches, and cannot comfort their unconsciously mourning wives. All four people are deeply isolated, and more or less unaware of their own and the others' unhappiness.

Yet glints of sunlight break through even the pall of clouds that sags over the gloomy north: and so does a catalyst visitor from the south. Hugh Miller is the great-nephew of the old man whose company employs Tom Fairfax, and he comes to try his hand at the family business as a last available scion. Hugh Miller has a certain grace of appearance, gesture and action that makes people feel glad to know him and sorry to see him depart. He also has a sister, Clare: polished, beautiful, a friend of Norah's youth and a covert fellow-sufferer of her old passion. She too, on her way to a Scottish sojourn, lights on our huddle of provincials like a bright butterfly on a damp clump of weeds.

The provincials turn to the southerners like shadowed primroses to the sun. Everyone – even the irritable Gerald MacKay – falls at least a little in love with one of them. Hugh Miller makes a string of silent and invisible conquests, which neither he nor anyone else ever notices. Grace, Norah, the little prostitute Pansy, even Norah's venerable old cousin Christopher Seddon – all are touched into feeling; the past passion of Oliver Digby, now separated in bitterness from Hugh, casts a long shadow; even the clerks in his office brighten in the radiance of his charm. To Grace, Hugh always seems unaccountably familiar: she cannot think where she has met him before. At the end of the book, she finds her answer, and the grace to share it with him: 'You were the person who was going to mean so much to me.'

Everyone we meet in this novel (and the company is limited, if rewarding) contains a world of pain, usually imperceptible to everyone else, and most of the time, to the sufferers themselves. Norah's stifled sorrow, Grace's loneliness and inertia, Gerald's tortured anxieties, Tom's disappointment – they are such ordinary pains, as they are such ordinary people; and who is middle-aged and not in mourning for something or someone or another? Hugh Miller is himself in pain, in his way, incapable of feeling the love he evokes in others. Only his sister is different. 'She was all right,' as Hugh notes with relief and approval. 'Not sad, not poor, not aged or altered.' If Clare's broken marriage has bequeathed her a legacy of distress or regret, it is part of her life's sentence to be allowed to share it with no one. 'She had perfected her art, if art it were; and continued triumphantly to present to the world the uncertain nature of her reality, to keep as her secret the nature of her honesty.'

There is pain in these people, pain in their lives. But is it real? How bad is it? Does it matter? These are the profound questions of this book. When Grace was a girl being courted by Tom, she fluttered between horror and comfort in his presence, and 'lazily wondered if all emotional truths were impermanent, only a matter of changing moods and circumstances.' Her creator seems to wonder, too. Her book's title is taken from a line of Walter Savage Landor: 'But the present, like a note in music, is nothing but as it appertains to what is past and what is to come.'

Rosamond Lehmann does not stop there. She investigates that nothing. *A Note in Music* is a study in nothingness: Grace Fairfax is its remarkable example, and the word echoes through the book like a refrain. Grace Fairfax has nothing to do all day, and she does nothing; embedded 'thick and flat' in her life, she feels as if 'nothing mattered, nothing would ever happen to her again'. She fears and shuns the prophesy of a fortune-teller who might say: 'A most curious case. There is *nothing* here: nothing in your past, nothing in your future'; and indeed, in the sharp focus of a single afternoon of beauty and happiness, her married life shrivels into 'ten years of nothingness'. (She is not alone in her plight. Poor Tom too fleetingly senses that 'there was nothing before him really – no one who cared about his troubles'.)

Nothing can come of nothing, and by the end of the book, almost nothing has happened. Two bright creatures have perched for a moment in an alien habitat and flown away again, their feathers more or less intact. Two middle-aged women have fallen a little in love, felt a little worse about their marriages. Two provincial husbands have felt the breath of freezing winds from the desert wastes beyond their comfortable cages.

Grace Fairfax is still struggling into her old black crêpe-de-chine and planning a supper of stodge for her comfort. Her husband is still dozing off in his chair. Norah and Gerald MacKay are still fighting their way out of the constricting tangle of emotions at the heart of their alliance. The northern landscape buttons itself tight in its winter uniform, as pinched and drab as if the bright south had never visited it with its warmth.

Almost nothing has happened. But something has. Within her life's perpetual nothing – and even on her holiday, Grace Fairfax (officially) did 'Nothing at all' – she has loved, and lost: for the first and undoubtedly the last time. Other things have moved and changed too. A needle of light has pierced the wadding around Tom Fairfax's head and heart, and his darkness will never be so complete again. Norah and Gerald have released their demons and faced them, and in their shared perception of the divide yawning between them is the hope that its space will be bridged.

It is the conquerors that have gained least. Clare

Osborne disappears over the horizon as opaque and unreal as when she came; and Hugh Miller, the pirate of hearts we have come to cherish, inspires our last wave of compassion. In this book we sense one young man touch the cold centre of the loneliness of life: but Hugh Miller has to face its frightening presence at his own centre.

There is no chance that he will ever have ears to hear the thunder he has sounded in one woman's life, that will continue to echo there until it ends. Yet a whisper has come through: which may in time become a voice of awareness. And Hugh Miller – who is, on his own admission, hopeless – has also the optimism that often accompanies that despairing condition. He will hear in the gulls' cries the reverberation of his final failure; he will think, 'Why live?' But he will also in the next moment involuntarily attend the first gusts of conviviality from below deck; and will note, quite without meaning to, that it is time for a drink and a chat.

There is laughter beyond the pain in this book; and it is not only Hugh Miller that hears it. Grace Fairfax absorbs her love and loss with an inward laugh, curious and remarkable as her outward smile: and her smile can linger in the air when there is nothing else left there at all. After Grace's summer of rapture, there will be new life in her house next spring – though it comes from an unexpected source; and that blossoming idyll has borne in her a rich fruit – of knowledge, humour, affection, compassion, quietness. After the rhapsody, one note lingers with a lasting resonance:

> Passing the open door of the kitchen one evening on her way to bed, Grace saw them all three sitting together in silence at the table. Empty plates and cups were set before them; and the light of one candle modelled the human group in tender masses of light and shade, and illumined their calm and empty faces. She was moved by the simplicity of their wants, the pathos of their elementary possessions . . . The child was on her lap asleep. There was not a sound, or a movement. Out of the luminous obscurity emerged the domestic union of their figures . . .

The same note sounds through Norah, striking out of her pain with a remorseless instinct for life.

> The secret was to look to the present chiefly, to the future a little, to the past scarcely at all; to let old days depart in peace, to break the last threads of irrecoverable associations, to give up trying to alter people who would be to their lives' ends unalterably themselves . . .

Do such words represent sound commonsense? Are they the counsel of despair? Might they even express a truth unalterable by what comes before and after? This quiet book makes us, unanswerably, wonder.

A Note of Music is written in a minor key. It is a story of human pain: it speaks of *ennui*, disappointment, grief; of loneliness, absurdity, failure. Yet a smile plays around its edges, like the smile at the corners of Grace Fairfax's mouth; and the note that it sounds is ultimately neither sorrowful or sad. In the shadows of this story there is something luminous; in its emptiest nothing, there is something alive. Within the veils of its loneliness and pain, there is love: a world of love. In the silence between what has been and what is to come, its note sings.

Janet Watts, London 1981

PART I

A NOTE IN MUSIC

PART I

She was dressing for dinner. Next door, she heard Tom splashing in his bath, and singing over and over again the refrain of one of his three tunes :

> ' *Oh, lucky Jim,*
> How . . . WI . . . EN-VY--HIM.'

Each time she heard the mournful bellow, the same memory cut across her exasperation. She remembered August, and her home, hundreds of years ago ; and the garden fête on the sunny lawn. She saw the Parish Ladies sitting on the imported cane Parish Room chairs, and sinking too far into the grass, for it had been a wet summer. She saw her father the vicar standing upon a platform and booming : '*Oh, lucky Jim* . . .' She had watched from her secret perch in the apple tree ; and suddenly, seeing that melancholy black figure, mild brow, open mouth, she had blushed painfully for him, had known he was being ridiculous, and wanted to giggle, to implore him to stop, to protect him from the Parish Ladies.

Since those days she had come a long way ; yet where were the milestones, or the turning-places ? There seemed nothing to look back on save a few freakish and capricious gleams assailing her at unexpected moments ; and certainly, she thought (pulling on her stockings), there was nothing before her.

At the Rescue and Preventive Bazaar last year, Norah had laughingly urged her to consult the fortune-teller, saying : ' She 's too uncanny, my dear. She 's told me the most astounding things. All my past.' She had refused with a scoff and escaped from Norah, and gone back quickly to her cake stall : for the truth was she was afraid of the fortune-teller. She had had a vision of the woman, scrutinizing her palm and saying finally :

' This is a most curious case. There is *nothing* here : nothing in your past, nothing in your future. As for character—lazy—greedy—secretive—without will or purpose.'

That was a year ago. And to-day she would be even more afraid . . . infinitely more afraid of one to whom the secrets of the heart might be laid bare. She paused in the buttoning of her old-fashioned cambric petticoat, and bit her nail, pondering this.

The song from the bathroom ceased, and she heard the tremendous roar, gurgle and bump which meant that Tom had heaved himself from the water and landed with a swoop upon the bath-mat.

He would be late as usual. Tom's unpunctuality was a curious phenomenon, considering how closely, in nearly all other ways, he conformed to type. She thought of his daily agonized, and sometimes vain struggle not to be late for the office, and her mouth relaxed in contemptuous indulgence. To the end of his life he would never cease to wrestle half-heartedly with his unpunctuality, and be vanquished by it.

They were a couple of slipshod characters, she thought, opening the cupboard and taking down her old black crêpe-de-chine from its peg. He hid behind precise attention to detail, behind unimpeachable personal tidiness, and the saving of brown paper and bits of string, and an engagement-book, and the multiple-column account book in which not even the weekly twopence to the pavement artist could blush unseen, but was carefully set down every Friday night under *Charities*. . . . And this dressing for dinner every evening—that was his idea. 'Keeps one up to the mark,' he would say.

His favourite word, she thought (plunging clumsily into her frock and hearing the shoulder-seams crack), was gentleman. A dinner-jacket, however tight and unbecoming, was the mark of a gentleman, and proclaimed nightly that he was a public-school man, had played cricket, was fond of a day's fishing ; and that but for these hard times since the war, and not being so young as he was after four years' service, he would now be in a very different position. The Fairfaxes had never been in business, he would say. But the family estates had passed most unfairly to another branch. He often said this when he met a stranger. The war had beggared all the old families, he would add : no money nowadays to fight a law-suit. Otherwise . . .

His pedigree was assuming alarming proportions in

his conversation, she thought (hitching up her petticoat where it dropped at the back). Her petticoats were always too long ; and yet, goodness knows, her skirts were long enough. She had ignored the short-skirt fashion when it came in, partly because she always did ignore the fashion, partly out of dislike for her legs ; but mostly because she could not be bothered to shorten her petticoats. These stout cambric ones with a border of *broderie anglaise* had been part of her trousseau. Nobody wore petticoats nowadays, Norah was always severely telling her—but that did not trouble her. Her lips twisted again into a half-smile, as she remembered how Norah had been forced to admit, at her suggestion, that a petticoat of this type was an integral part of her old-fashioned physical personality : just as, she thought, flesh-coloured silk stockings were necessary to Norah's contemporary form.

'A couple of slipshod characters,' she muttered, half aloud ; and noted that the habit of talking to herself was growing on her—just as all Tom's habits were growing on him. . . . How, without being both rude and incomprehensible, did one stop one's husband talking about gentlemen ?

As for her, she thought, attempting vaguely to hook her cuffs, she was a muddler, she cooked her housekeeping accounts, she mended neither her stockings nor his socks, she had forgotten for the past two days to ring up the plumber about the plug that would not pull (and Tom would be justifiably annoyed) ; she wallowed in novels instead of taking exercise . . . but . . . but . . . and she looked at herself in the glass . . . she was not weak ; no, she was not weak. She saw her neck springing strongly up from wide shoulders ; her deep bosom, her firm thick ankles. Motherly, she thought, smiling her crooked faint smile—solidly planted as a tree-trunk, imperturbable. She would not look so uncomely dressed in some peasant costume—round-necked, short-sleeved white muslin vest, black velvet laced bodice fitting snugly into the waist, bright-coloured ample skirts swinging out from her hips. It was these four-guinea crêpe-de-chines, with jumper tops accentuating her breadth at top and bottom, which were so fatal. She wished she were a peasant woman toiling all day long in the fields of some far country. When evening came the men and women would cry out her beautiful, mysterious, many-syllabled name, telling her to cease from her labours and come home ; and one would smile at her, and slowly walk beside her in the dusk, matching his long step to hers.

She took a deep breath and tightened the muscles in her arms. . . . No, she was not weak, and Tom knew it. Somewhere inside her there was power.

Her hat fell out of the cupboard, and she gave it a kick before picking it up. . . . With a shawl over her head, or a wide-winged bonnet, instead of these tight, counter-attractive felts—no, she would not be so uncomely.

She muttered : ' Oh fool, fool.' There was nothing to look forward to. Why could she not feel it as indubitably as she thought it, and so be done with this restlessness ? ' Skittish,' she said, quite loud this time, in her deep, rough voice.

Tom broke a prolonged pause in the bathroom by roaring '*Wi-i-ill ye gang* . . .' and then was silent again.

Part the hair, brush it, do the side-bits, then put on powder ; then coil the back hair into the nape. The side-bits were short. She had experimented with them one day when the periodical hatred of her hair assailed her ; but the result had not inspired her with sufficient zest to remove the remainder. As it was, it looked merely common, with those straight flaps over the ears. The truth was, Tom made too much fuss about short hair to make it worth while to put the matter to the test. He was that sort of husband. The *Daily Mirror* had once been full of letters about shingled wives from husbands just like Tom . . . *A Woman's glory*. . . . He had quoted the passage at her a hundred times ; for he was not sensitive about repeating himself, and brought out the stalest quotation, especially from Scripture, again and again in his loud, self-satisfied reciting voice ; as if he had thought of it himself, and were saying it for the first time.

And she went on letting herself look . . .—letting herself go, that was it—because every effort had become irksome. She was fairly comfortable, she told herself (putting in the last hairpin)—quite comfortable really, embedded thick and flat now in her life. Nothing mattered, nothing would ever happen for her again.

She wished for a moment that she were very unhappy—*a piercing pain*, she thought, or better still, *a blinding sin* : to feel as she had felt in her tenth year when she had violently wished to discover, in order to commit, the sin against the Holy Ghost ; or when she had called the garden-boy *Raca* because he teased her : to feel the sense of being set apart, alone beneath the shadow of the appalling dignity of certain doom.

But why not wish rather to be piercingly happy, transported with pure ecstasy ; or merely, gay as a lark ? How far indeed from gay was this life ! Contentment came in a warm sluggish tide of well-being when Annie drew the curtains, heaped the fire, and left her with a great cup of coffee and a toasted bun, and a new novel from the library ; or dreamily, wistfully, shot through with points of question and flickers of regret when Norah took her in her little car for a drive in the country.

And yes,—she had felt happy once looking after a mongrel puppy with weak eyes and a tender, foolish furry face bought for five shillings in the market. That puppy had been gay. His tiny spark of life had warmed her heart, and he had taught her to play games with him, and lain in very sudden sleeps along her shoulder, with his ice-button nose on her neck.

But in spite of all her care he had not thrived. Within a month he had sickened ; and after lying in her lap for a day and a night, dressed in a little flannel jacket, had died with unbearable resignation. It had been worse, more of a heartache than when the baby was born dead eight years ago. She had taken his death for a sign that nothing would ever come right for her now ; that whatever she touched would wither without blossoming. She had been, she supposed, very morbid. He had made everything worse, not better for her. His small person, stamped with the early neglect, disease, and suffering against which her love had been powerless, had become the symbol for the whole colossal ignorance and brutality of the town. Tom had not comforted her, and she could never confess to him her unconquerable dread of the streets on market-days—the men with an armful of puppies for sale, and all the anguish assailing her afresh. Tom had not comforted her ; but then she had not given him the chance. She had made herself like stone. She imagined Tom's face if she had said to him :

'I shall never get over this, Tom. I shall never try for anything for myself again.'

It was true ; but she could no more have said it, she thought, stabbed for one moment with a memory, than she could have asked him what he had done with that small form when he took it away, still clad in its unavailing jacket.

She shook out her powder-puff. . . . It was the

only thing left worth doing, she thought—to be like stone before the world; to tell no one 'I also suffer,' and by that admission be exposed to pity and the easy exchange of confidences. She was friendless, she supposed, except for the single odd relationship with Norah, who chaffed her and made rude personal remarks and looked in on her way to or from shopping; and treated her with something of the same brusque affection she bestowed on her two plain little boys.

Tom had no friends either, she thought: only people he went fishing with on Saturdays, or played golf with on Sundays. Mercifully he hardly ever brought them back to the house now: they were so boring. During the first year or so he was always bringing them. He had liked the feeling of keeping open house—of being the sort of chap people dropped in on without ceremony. And she herself, she supposed, had found them less boring in those days. There had generally been some trifle to laugh at, something one could say without much effort. Nowadays she could not be bothered with people to meals.

She supposed Tom felt the same. Or if not . . .

Do I make Tom happy? she thought, and paused for a second at her dressing-table while the words flashed through her mind and were gone again, leaving no tremor of question, but only a passing faint surprise; as if a trivial memory long buried had returned to her for a moment.

She brushed a ridge of powder off her chin. It fell on her skirt, and she left it there. Tom had views about powder too—declared he preferred a healthy shine. Not that her face ever shone, she thought, scrutinizing it in her ivory hand-mirror. She had one of those rather thick skins that always looked cool and dry, and of an even pallor. No colour ever came into it save when she blushed ; and that, she told herself with irritation, was all too frequently. One could not be like stone before the world with such a flush creeping up uncontrollably to betray a secret confusion or shame. At thirty-four, it was too ridiculous.

Now she was ready. She looked in the long glass, but, as usual, without seeing herself, because her figure, especially in this black shiny case, made her feel depressed and uncomfortable.

Seven-thirty. Fish pie and chocolate shape for supper. She had been looking forward to chocolate shape ever since ordering it this morning. There was no sound from Tom. He must be struggling with his collar.

She parted the curtains and leaned against the window, looking out. The January full moon stared down upon a back street, a row of back yards, blank windows and irregular patterns of roofs and walls. Nothing but town and moon petrified in the frozen night.

She thought suddenly of a smooth hillside crowned with a coppice of young beeches, and moonlight drenching the turfy slope; but where or when, if ever, she had seen this, she could not remember.

The country haunted her still, she said to herself: not a day passed without bringing some picture remembered or imagined. Dawn and sunset were not in these skies, behind the slate roofs and red brick chimneys of the residential quarter—but in her mind's eye, over country spaces; and spring and autumn still made her sick for home. How many times had she not thought of the summer evening when a bird had sung in the poor lilac tree in the front patch? . . . But that would never happen again, now that the trams came to the end of the avenue.

She let the curtain drop, and stood listening. A stillness had dropped suddenly upon everything. There was not a sound in the house, or from the streets.

She thought 'I shall soon be middle-aged'; and it seemed as if some one beside her had broken the silence to whisper the words in her ears.

The gong sounded. She opened his dressing-room door and looked in. He was cutting his nails.

'Ready in a moment,' he said. 'Go on down and begin.'

But she lingered at the door.

'I forgot about the plug,' she said.

'Mm. I reminded you three times this morning, I think.'

'I know.'

He gathered up money and watch-chain from the dressing-table.

'I might have known it wouldn't be done,' he said, 'I ought to have seen to it myself. But I should have thought you might have . . . Nothing to do all day and yet . . . However, it 's always the same.'

'I 'll ring up in the morning,' she said, thinking with loathing of the telephone.

She left him and went out along the passage. He caught her up on the stairs, and they went on down together, side by side, two strangers.

For ten years he had made a point of keeping up appearances by conversation on general topics whenever Annie was in the room. As a rule, when Annie went out, silence fell; but to-night he talked on, and she saw that with his usual aptitude for forgetting grievances, he was trying to put the evening upon an agreeable footing.

She thought how this facility, so admirable a quality in itself, did but make him contemptible to her. Everything that was difficult or disagreeable slipped off his consciousness. He would be clouded for a moment, and then shake himself and come back smiling, a little apologetic, appealing: 'Let 's all be comfortable and jolly again.'

And she would go on sulking, sulking—unresponsive, knotted inwardly like a skein of grey, harsh, tangled wool.

PART I

He said:

'There's a new chap come into the office. The old man's nephew, or rather grand-nephew. Come to learn the business for a bit, I believe. I should say he was just down from the 'Varsity by the look of him. Long hair and some queer sort of tie. More like an artist.' He laughed heartily, and added: 'Seems a decent sort of chap, though. I had a word with him: just shook him by the hand and told him I'd be glad to tip him the wink if anything stumped him. He thanked me very civilly.'

'Civil,' she thought: another of the words that did not match old family estates. She glanced at him—at the thick commonplace shape and texture of him, crowned with sparse oiled hair, and wondered for a moment how he had looked to the eyes of the old man's nephew, the artistic young man from the University. She wondered if Tom had already told him that his father's financial misfortunes had obliged him to renounce Oxford at the last moment, and start in business at the age of seventeen.

He told her he had had a slack day, and trade looked worse than ever. He told her he had arranged to play billiards with Potter to-morrow evening. He remarked that Annie made a jolly good fish pie.

How this room could still depress her! Though the curtains were drawn, the blank brick wall which was the view oppressed her to-night, as if it were visible.

The last tenant had papered the walls in dead blue

with an orange frieze. The electric light over the table glared out hideously beneath a contrivance of steel hoops, salmon-coloured frills, and beaded fringe. She had meant to change it all long ago ; but she had forgotten, or never had the money, or the energy.

'I wouldn't have made it any nicer,' she told herself.

Norah put on an overall and painted cheap chairs and tables in pretty colours ; other women redecorated their rooms with their own hands, for ninepence-halfpenny, they told you smugly ; adding that of course the only way to get the colour you wanted was to mix the distemper yourself. If she were to try she would only make a thorough mess of it. But at least, she thought, even if her house was dreary and impersonal—at least she knew it. She did not have a mauve and gilt drawing-room and rejoice in it, as some of them did. She did not express herself in royal blue with a frieze, or orange and black stripes, and feel aesthetic. It was only that . . . . only that she could not express herself at all, in any way—least of all through possessions ; through walls and pieces of furniture and ornaments, and all the incredible paraphernalia of household things. She hated possessions : so she did what was easiest, and then forgot about them. Besides, she was not here really . . . no, she was not here : not in this cage.

Annie brought in the chocolate shape and set it down in front of her. She came with her gentle, slow step, and lingered as usual, waiting for a word.

'Jolly good fish pie, Annie,' said Tom heartily.

'Thank you, sir,' she said softly. But it was never for Tom she lingered.

The eyes of the two women met over his head, and they smiled. They understood each other without speech.

Annie's gaze said soothingly:

'There. Cheer up. Your favourite pudding. Eat a nice big helping, and you 'll feel better, poor dear.'

She knew that she was the object of an obscure pity and solicitude from Annie—she was not sure why: perhaps because of her childlessness. She thought that Annie was the only person in the world whose sympathy she could bear. Annie had the gift of a perfect animal tenderness in her ample form, her voice, her gestures.

She had two helpings; and after that it was not so hard to unlock her tongue and answer quite agreeably when Tom asked:

'What about a movie? Feel like going out? No —too cold, I expect. Or would you?'

In his anxiety not to say the wrong thing he floundered, poor wretch, and contradicted himself.

'There 's a new film at the Imperial,' she said. 'We might see that.'

'Sure you feel like it?'

On the point of replying 'If I didn't, I wouldn't go,' she checked herself and merely nodded; then went upstairs to put on the ancient fur-lined grey cloth coat that had been his wedding-present to her.

As she pulled a hat painfully over the great knob of her hair, she thought that shingling might improve her temper. After all, Tom would probably never notice if she shaved off every hair on her head, or wore it in a reckless frizz. He never looked at any one much : only slight, unseeing, almost furtive glances. It must be years since he had looked at her.

And still, she thought, going downstairs again and seeing him below her in the hall, massive, red-necked, buttoning his overcoat—still she went on watching him, his presence remained a constant paradox : still, though she had taken him and marriage and all for granted long, long ago, she could not quite get used to living with this man.

They sat through the film in silence. He bought her some chocolates, and she steadily ate through them while she watched ; and, lost at once in the illusion, felt the familiar tide of well-being creep sluggishly over the mud-flats of her daily life. The heroine's fair wild crest, dramatic eyes and lips, slender limbs ravished and absorbed her. Tom faded in the darkness and became blent with the rest of the mass of dimly-seen forms, and with the fumes of tobacco smoke, and all the unreality of the cavernous pillared hall.

The lights went on, and at once the sphere of illusion crumbled beneath her feet and vanished, leaving scarcely a memory. She dragged herself to her feet as the tinted portrait of King George appeared on the screen, and the violins started to rasp out the National Anthem. Immediately Tom caught her arm and began to fuss and push, trying to get out before the rest of the crowd. As usual, she resisted, making herself a lump.

Suddenly he nudged her.

'Look,' he said, 'that 's young Miller.'

'Who 's young Miller?'

'The new chap in the office—the one I told you about. In the middle of the row there, sitting down. Funny, he must have been just behind us all the time.'

She looked, and by the dirty pinkish glare of the lights saw the solitary figure of a young man. She saw thick, untidy locks of light hair falling over a head thrown back and still. His face was in shadow. His hands were laid out on his knees, his body sunk deep in the chair; and he seemed in a deep abstraction.

'Wonder what he 's waiting for. . . . Shall we go up and have a word with him?' whispered Tom, trying as he passed to catch his eye.

'No,' she said sharply.

But he was not convinced.

'Don't suppose he knows a soul up here,' he said. 'Not much fun going alone to a movie your first night. I think I 'll just go up and say we 'd have asked him to join us if we 'd seen him before. It 'ud seem civil, wouldn't it?'

He looked dubious and self-conscious. She thought: ' He wants to make a good impression on the old man's nephew.'

' Let him alone,' she muttered. ' He 's all right.'

What had that imperturbable looking head to do with a provincial couple such as they? He was deliberately ignoring his surroundings, and he would resent any intrusion with cold politeness. She felt herself begin to blush, and she hurried Tom forward.

At the exit she glanced back and saw that he had risen and was lounging along the empty row towards another door. She noticed his height and his very broad shoulders, and it flashed across her for a second that she had seen him before. . . . Had he merely been waiting till the gangways emptied, and he could walk out at his ease; or (more probably), had he seen her and Tom, and deciding that she looked even worse than he, stayed behind in order to avoid them? The idea filled her with a sudden sense of humiliation. She had been all right once—her father had been at Oxford, he had taken her there several times, and she had seen how he harmonized with it, bore its stamp. The last time had been just after her engagement, when they two and Tom had made an expedition from London. That day had been a failure. Tom had looked quite out of place in Oxford, and she had suddenly felt that she did not want to be identified with him in any way—that the idea of marrying him had arisen in some state of mental distortion only now perceived . . . But when they got back to

London the angle had shifted again, and he, piloting them both over the crossings with manly and stern encouragement, had seemed more or less in perspective. She had lazily wondered if all emotional truths were impermanent, only a matter of changing moods and circumstances; and then drifted on.

They came out into the cold streets.

'There 's the tram,' said Tom. 'Hurry.'

He took her by the elbow, and they broke into an absurd trot. Running at any time was bad enough; but to be run with made her feel murderous. They arrived at the tram-stop to find a solid wedge of humanity struggling to get aboard.

'What was the point of hurrying like that?' she panted. 'You might have known there wouldn't be any room. I 'm not going to scramble in all that disgusting crowd.'

'Come on,' he urged. 'There 'll be room on top.' He caught the rail and swung himself on to the step; then held out a hand to pull her after him. But she dropped back and said sulkily:

'I 'm going to walk.'

She wanted to stay out all night; wanted to run away; wanted to . . .

He did not hear her. Arms and legs and bodies pressed indignantly against his form, swept it on up the stairs. The tram started; and the last she saw of him was his red face peering down and grimacing at her with puzzled anxiety.

The moment she was left alone, she felt the black

oppression drop from her. The street seemed all at once quiet and deserted. She buried her chin in her fur collar and walked on, feeling light, calm and solitary. Ahead of her, the great black outline of the cathedral cut into the purple sky, and beside it the Victory on top of the monument spread giant upsweeping wings. Yes, there was beauty here. But round the corner, the wind struck bitterly. After all, she thought, faintly smiling in self-mockery, it was too far to walk home. She jumped into the next tram and sat staring blankly in the middle of a row of blank faces till she was set down at her very gate. She let herself in ; and with the locking and bolting of the door behind her felt heaviness fall upon her again.

Tom had gone upstairs. She heard him in his dressing-room coughing and clearing his throat loudly. She sat for a few minutes by the whispering gas fire, glanced idly at a paper, ate half an apple ; then put out the lights and climbed wearily to her room.

'Tired,' she whispered to herself on each step. 'Tired, tired.'

How long since she had felt really well?

She undressed in the cold bedroom and got into bed, and lay moving her hot-water bottle up and down her as a shield against the piercing chill of the sheets. But she could not get warm all over. She hoped Tom would hurry : he would make her warm.

She heard the last tram come moaning down the

avenue and stop beneath the window; then start again with a wrench. It was the limping tram, the wounded one that screamed and faltered as it went. At first she had thought she could never sleep for the sound of trams trailing themselves up and down from dawn till midnight; and now, together with late footsteps and motor-horns, and the dustman's rumbling early cart, and Saturday night laughter in the streets, and the crying of the next-door baby before daylight, it was part of the sound of life.

A thought of the country came and she turned over, burying her face in the pillow the better to see a January sun on the fields. Along the hedgerows the tall ash and hazel rods thronged stiffly; they sprang up gleaming in the sun like lances of bronze and silver. The first lambs of the year were crying. . . . The light of the January fields was a pale shining violet. . . . But in this northern town the light had no colour. She thought of the little park with its deserted bandstand, hopping robins, struggling shrubs, keep-off-the-grass signs, silent nursemaids, dejected dogs on leads. None but the saddest, sparsest flowers grew in its beds; and even at mid-summer it never quite lost its look of grieving wintry sadness.

Ring up the plumber to-morrow, the damned plumber about the loathsome plug. Count the washing. Take a skirt to be dyed. . . . The film hadn't been a bit good really. What had that young man been thinking about, sitting alone and disdaining his surroundings ? For a moment she had thought she had seen him before somewhere. . . .

Tom came in and shut the door softly behind him. Without a word he switched out the light, got into bed, and turned over on his side. They lay with their backs to each other, far apart.

Soon she heard him begin to breathe deeply and evenly : and then he turned again with a sigh and came nearer to her.

' You 're cold,' he murmured.

' Yes.'

' Poor Gracie. . . . Soon get warm.'

He flung an arm over her and drew her close to him. It was a gesture almost mechanical—the habit of years.

After a bit he muttered indistinctly :

' Sorry about this evening. Whar on ear' happened ? . . . I couldn't help . . . Sorry. . . .'

' It 's all right,' she whispered. ' Never mind. It was me.'

He sighed heavily with sleep, making a little plaintive noise in his throat, like a child.

' There,' she murmured. ' There.'

She gave his hand a little pat.

They slept.

PART II

PART II

THE year slid imperceptibly from the first to the second month of its course.

In the southern counties February will come in with a sudden stillness, with mild blue watery air, with the ploughed earth mysterious in the dark fields, yielding to bear the young corn. From the lime tree the blackbird calls, one primrose dusk, a new call, and in the moment of that sound spring bursts upon the imagination, sealed buds have swollen, crocuses crowd the lawn, the swallows are over the river, stark branches swim in fresh mists of green.

But in the north there is no change. In February the wind-carved snow-wreaths still lie on the brown moors, old drifts heap the ditches. Should the rain unbind the earth for one day, an iron frost will lock it once again on the morrow

There is no change at all, thought Norah, standing on Grace Fairfax's doorstep and observing by means of a prolonged squint that her nose was red and besmutted. (Winter smuts were more deadly than the summer ones: they ground themselves into the rough cold-puckered skin.) The heavy sky sagged down over the roofs, and the wind blew bits of paper about the street.

A moment later Grace could hear Annie in the hall,

engaged in a conversation of her usual type, and saying softly :

'Quite well, thank you, madam. . . Oh yes, madam. . . . And the little boys, are they well ? . . . It was ever so nice when you used to bring them round to tea, in their prams. . . . Well, of course it 's quite a long time ago, now, isn't it ? I was forgetting . . . time does fly. It used to be a nice change for Mrs. Fairfax. . . .'

Norah's laugh rang out.

'Oh, Nannie's afternoon off ! My friends must have dreaded it as much as I did. I always dumped them on somebody. Do you remember when we left them in the kitchen with you, and went off to the Fair ? '

So they had ! thought Grace, listening in the sitting-room : put on their hats quickly and gone off giggling to ride on the merry-go-rounds while Annie minded the children : two cheerful undignified creatures making the round of the side-shows, then helping each other push the pram back, give a superficial scrub to the children and bundle them into bed a good hour past the proper time.

She saw an old self in a flash : an even-tempered young married woman with a hopeful outlook and the average activities of her kind. What in the world could have happened to her ? . . . It was all her own fault, for she had had no troubles, no real ones. It must be that she had been too unspiritual to keep a young heart : she had allowed the years, like a slow and fleshy vegetable growth, to stifle her. It was her own fault; or perhaps the fault of Tom—so coarse-fibred, drinking so many whiskies-and-sodas. . . But then, was it really to be stifled—to be thus packed inside with a gradual accumulation of brooding and critical thoughts? She was probably less stupid than she had been, if only people knew.

How like Annie to remember the Fair! She was always raking over the details of old times: she was the greatest bore in the world. There she was just outside the door now, droning on:

'Oh yes, madam, it was very nice. Little pickles! The big one, he would lock himself in the larder. And the baby—he was such an old-fashioned little soul, wasn't he? He gave me such a look, so solemn and majestic, when I jumped him on my lap. I nearly begged his pardon for the liberty. It seemed almost like . . . I told Mrs. Fairfax afterwards——' (Annie bent her head, overcome with respectful roguishness) 'I really felt for the moment I must have forgotten myself and was trying to jump Mr. MacKay. . . . That child was his living image when he gave me that look.'

Norah's chuckle came again.

'Little monsters!' she said. 'You should have tried spanking them, like their mamma.'

From Annie came soft sounds, murmurs of deprecation, of protestation, as who should say no better children ever existed, and—though she saw the joke—no mother less liable to spank; and she ushered

Norah into the sitting-room with an expression of triumph: for there was a treat in store for Mrs. Fairfax. Mrs. MacKay had come to take her for a drive in the car.

'Anywhere special?' asked Grace, as they drove off.

'Yes—to see the aunts for a moment. One of them broke her leg out hunting last week, and I haven't even inquired. Reckless old thing. But will anything kill her? No.' She sighed despondently. 'How am I to send Robin and David to school if they don't die and leave me their money? . . . But it 's no good hoping.'

Norah had relations all over the county: a couple of hard-riding, close-fisted maiden aunts in a stone barracks on the moor; a family of cousins, who, living on a large estate, sent sons into the services, kept daughters at home uneducated, moulded to their sagging tweeds, organizing girl guides, breeding Sealyhams, riding to hounds inelegantly, astride on comic ponies, or following the hunt in a derelict Ford; finally, a bearded elderly cousin who lived in a charming house in a green valley, collected first editions, prints, tapestries, and early English water-colours, and dwelt altogether in a certain haze of culture and mystery and tobacco-smoke: dwelt, moreover, in almost unbroken silence, for his wife was stone-deaf, and spent her days in the rose-chintz drawing-room, the world forgotten, reading the

French and German classics ; or in the garden, tending her rockery, looking at her roses and delphiniums.

Yes, Norah was well-connected ; her relations abounded. She had come often as a child from her home in London to stay with one or other of them, had ridden, walked, picnicked, and run wild with them. One of the naval cousins had madly loved her, and she had assisted the girls (in a spasm of yearning after personal embellishment caused by her presence) to do their hair. But when she grew up they lost sight of her. She had taken up dancing in London, they heard—or was it singing ?—and gone to a great many parties ; and nursed in France during the war ; and finally, after years, returned to the county, but not to the fold : returned married to Gerald MacKay, penniless professor at the University, of quite a different class, they said, able neither to ride nor shoot nor hold a rod ; very queer too : simply an ill-mannered boor, one would say, if it were not more charitable to think that early brilliance at Cambridge, or perhaps shell-shock, had unhinged him a little. It was quite disconcerting to find him there—if one came to call—restless and resentful, with the look of a trapped animal, only opening his mouth to dart a snub or a glance of blue fire at Norah if she attempted to include him in her remarks, or appealed to him, with her broad smile, for corroboration of some statement ; as likely as not snatching up a book suddenly and stamping upstairs to his bedroom. Whether or no Norah resented his behaviour it was hard to say. She was full of spirit, or had been once ; but one never saw temper in her eyes even, and she smiled on and never complained at all.

It was useless, then, to try to adopt or adapt Norah's husband ; and since Norah herself was for ever immersed in domestic matters, she too was dropped—or rather dropped herself : for she seemed to have lost all interest in country pursuits, and never went away without her husband.

Her relations hoped that she was happy. Combining duty with dentist or dressmaker, they paid her infrequent calls, and found her fresh-looking still and energetic. She had kept her slender figure, and still managed somehow to look better dressed than other people. True, her face was worn round the eyes and mouth ; but then she was well over thirty. Her hair was quite grey ; but it was that kind of hair.

When, after some years, she purchased a dilapidated second-hand Morris-Cowley, she occasionally returned their calls ; but more often careered past their very doors, going picnicking with her boys, or touring the moors with an odd-looking person from the town.

They left the tram-lines at last and the final straggle of pit cottages, and took the road which ran through flat pastures and great ploughed fields, and villages mingling old stone with new red brick and factory chimneys ; climbed gently to sheltered grassy uplands where the sheep grazed ; then more steeply over hill-roads to the tableland of the moors. Far away on every side stretched those dark historic contours, rolling to the horizon, line after line, like foamless deep-sea waves. All around were the stone walls, the shepherds' huts, the brown heath patched with the russet of old bracken, the sombre green of gorse, the coarse grass blowing yellowish and tawny in the wind, as if faint sunlight gilded it ; but not a gleam came out of the dun sky.

Norah slowed down and looked about her.

'What would it be like, I wonder,' she said, 'not to be always longing for this ?'

'You 'll have it in the end,' said Grace.

'No, no,' said Norah, still gazing into the distance. 'When Gerry gets a bit older he won't be able to stand these winters. . . . He can't now, really. We shall move on to Liverpool or Nottingham, or some such salubrious seat of learning. And we shall end our days in a *pension* just outside Bordighera. Gerry will sit like a fire-breathing dragon in a bath-chair, and I shall push him . . . or else be in my grave.'

But as she said this, she saw the picture too clearly : herself worn to death and lying under the earth ; Gerry's face when he sat alone or lay by himself wakeful in the dark watches ; the boys drifting about the house with no one to tell them what to do, their shirts grubby, frayed, outgrown ;

Gerry giving them too many lessons, hounding them on, enveloped with them in a black cloud of exasperation, misunderstanding, and dumb, tearless longing for her. She felt the reproach buried deep in their hearts against her, because she had abandoned them and ruined them : a core of anguished indignation in the three male hearts. . . . Gerry, who trusted only her (and her with such difficulty), swearing savagely to trust no one and nothing now, and the boys degenerating as they grew up, floundering in the bog of adolescence, among the urgent lusts of young men, whose bodies, in the first sap and vigour of manhood, drive them and betray them. Gazing across the moors, she told herself that she understood these things : she had been taught her lesson long ago when she had presented a spirit quivering with the malleability of first love, but smooth and light in texture as silk, to be petrified and graven for ever with the knowledge of the appetites of men . . of the appetites of Jimmy.

It had been her idea, not his, that they should keep nothing from each other. She had wanted to recreate for herself the picture of his childhood and boyhood in order to possess in some measure the wasted past before she had known him. She had been even more of an idiot then than she was now. For the thousandth time she asked herself anxiously, Could she have kept him ?—then checked the unprofitable train of thought ; for it did not matter now.

She had given him her trifling confidences, and he

in his turn . . yes, in the end he had given her his. He had shown her himself drunk, sleeping with harlots. All the mysteries that had been names merely, scarcely rousing her curiosity, the rhymes and stories she had laughed at with the others, but had not understood—all had slowly taken form and flesh : Jimmy's form, his debauched flesh, the mysterious forms, the bought-flesh of those who had tempted him.

For the loss to her of his chastity she had suffered —oh ! still suffered—a jealousy that pierced and strangled.

She remembered what had followed on her admission : that she had once before imagined herself in love (with a cousin)—permitted herself to be kissed.

Had *he* ever ? . . .

Poor Jimmy, so much of his confession had been unnecessary : for of such things as he had hinted at she had had no conception, and therefore no suspicion. He had had to enlighten her first as to the facts, almost from the beginning . . . poor Jimmy, saddled with the useless horror, the futile anguish of an ignorant fool. She had been very slow, painfully slow, to grasp his explanations. But he had persevered . . . yes, he had persevered.

After that, she remembered, she had become quite obsessed, quite nasty-minded about sex. She had thought of nothing else. She had passed through parched days, inflamed and sleepless nights. No matter how the conversation opened she had had to work it round in spite of herself to the one subject, torturing herself and him with questions and answers. He had laughed at her, he had been gentle with her—sheepish, bored, evasive, remorseful, angry, all in turn. And at last he had cried out 'It 's no use. You 'll never understand——' and she had heard in the words an inexpressible weariness and misery; as if he needed her and knew she was inadequate to help him; longed to rest in her, and she would not give him peace. Then in a moment all was clear and calm. At the last moment she had not failed him after all. The mist before her eyes had cleared and she had recognized the man she loved, and loved him with truth and passion; casting away the false and empty form of his ideal image. Jealousy was gone; shrinking and pain, misunderstanding and outraged pride all vanished. She had taken his hand and embraced all knowledge in serene perspective, from the erotic curiosities of schooldays to the habitual indulgences of young manhood. She had accepted the fact of lust in him divorced utterly from love. That had been the hardest; but she had managed it.

Poor Jimmy, he had been very wretched—just that once. Yes, perhaps it was he who had been the more wretched in the end. His self-loathing, frenzied and fantastic, had been one more violent initiation for her; but she had triumphed. At long last she had become solid to the core, invulnerable—a hearthstone in an old house, scrubbed clean (but worn a little with ancestral steps) over which a husband might walk securely into his house.

It was such a great love, she whispered to herself: how could it be (for the thousandth time) that it had not availed to save him? That was his fault . . . so like him . . . just as everything was coming right at last. In spite of her, he would not, could not care to save himself. To her passionate feminine instinct for life he had opposed his masculine indifference; and somehow, in the general destruction of mankind by man, he had disappeared with a smile and a shrug, and defeated her.

And unfortunately, Jimmy being long since dead and herself having for husband Gerald MacKay, this bitterly-won understanding was rather wasted; for she had married a creature of extreme innocence and chastity, quite uninterested, one would almost think unaware of the difficulties of his sex: absolutely no use to growing boys.

But why worry, she thought, after all? The boys would get through all right, as other boys did. Perhaps, too, things were different in these frank, enlightened days: perhaps girls did not get such shocks. Perhaps it was true (though appalling) what one heard: that they too were beginning to take their experiences casually, promiscuously, before marriage.

She became conscious of Grace sitting silent beside her. There was a woman on whom no one had ever made demands. Quite certainly Tom and she had never tortured each other with feverish intensity, or bound themselves together and plunged headlong into deep waters to sink or swim. The very idea was comic. Grace, now, had no important human relationship, occupation or interest—nothing real in her life ; and yet she herself was in some way a perfectly real person—that is, one capable of experience. She had a humorous smile ; one could not help wondering what she was thinking about. It was curious that they never talked together about love and marriage, as women generally do. They were topics on which Grace seemed to have no views : as if she had not been married at all : had not, after all, shared a double bed for years with a husband : one, moreover, who trod heavily by day, sniffed firmly, sang in the bath, drank, smoked, wore plus-fours at the week-ends, and was altogether most unmistakably a man. But she never so much as said he snored.

Once some time ago Norah had inquired :

'Were you in love with Tom when you married him ?'

She had laughed first, either in mockery or in embarrassment, and replied after a pause :

'Well . . . I knew I was going to marry Tom,' and said no more, leaving Norah to consider whether the words were to be taken as fatalistic, or referred to some parental arrangement or coercion.

It was a pity, thought Norah, drawing up before a

pair of wrought-iron gates that headed a sweep of drive, that Grace had wasted her life.

She took a paper-wrapped object from the back of the car and tucked it under her arm.

'I 've brought her a hyacinth in a pot,' she said. Rather a moderate specimen. Why waste a good plant?' She addressed Grace vigorously. 'While I 'm in here you take a brisk walk. It 's what you need. Come back in a glow or something.'

She glanced at Grace's colourless cheeks. She herself had lost her complexion after the birth of the children, and now used, with great secrecy, a little rouge.

Grace crossed the road, and wandered up a grassy track that led to the top of the moor's slope. The light was failing already. In the west a mass of darker clouds marked the defeat of the battered and struggling day. It was sad on the moors, and the wind blew with a chill whistle. The wild birds cried and flew. There was a gull from the sea, flying high up, with the wind, on motionless wings. At the top of the slope she looked far out over shadowy dramatic wastes of land, and saw the sea, laid in a dark line along the horizon. She thought of the coast road that wound beside low, blond sand-dunes; and of the grey-green coarse sea-grasses sprouting over them like tufts of sparse and bristling hair. She remembered the day when she and Tom had taken a train to the coast, one Sunday, soon after their marriage. They had found a lonely bay, and stayed there all day paddling, scrambling over slippery rocks, lying on the beach. When evening came, a flood of blue light, blue as the inside of a wet oyster-shell, gleamed in the damp sands, and all the air was liquid and lucent with the reflection. Far away at the end of the rocks, a lonely child was bowed over her shrimping-net ; her small figure, lost almost in an immensity of space, was moving and significant. The North Sea breakers, quieting with evening and the ebb of the tide, collapsed with a soft explosion. And as she lay watching, all had become fixed, crystallized into forms absolute and eternal. Earth and sky mirrored each other in a blue element half air, half water, the lonely child bent for ever above her net, the breaking wave spread itself at the edge of the unmoving fields of the sea like a long bank of flowering marguerite daisies.

She had promised herself to come often to the sea, but from that day to this she had scarcely seen it. It had needed too much ardour and energy to come alone : and Norah said the coast depressed her. She had wanted to spend a summer holiday there ; but every August had seen them departing for a fortnight in Cheshire with Tom's mother. It was one of the very few things, she thought, that Tom had always been firm about : his holiday must be spent with Mother because she counted on it. It was all right for him : he played golf and she gave him his favourite puddings and fawned upon him. Every year he declared with a shake of the head that poor old Mother was ageing rapidly ; but though looking each year more purple, mottled, and puffy, more lewd, more like a decaying plum, she had contrived to remain on the branch and so husband her resources as to be able to greet Tom's wife each year with unimpaired malevolence : until last winter when she had suddenly dropped off, and Tom had buried her with deep filial feelings and returned from the funeral quite pale and broken.

But the emotion she had had, had been of a different kind : a simple one, in fact, of overpowering relief, such as a prisoner might feel at unexpected acquittal. Next August she would be free. The thought leapt in her mind now, as she started to walk down again over the wet heather. She could go where she liked ; and at last she would go alone. Yes, she would suggest to Tom that they should separate for their holiday, and he would be shocked at first, but soon acquiescent. . . . Where should she go ? Far away, right in the south somewhere, but inland, not by the sea. The sea was often ugly, and sad except when the sun shone. The place she wanted must be sheltered and green, with a smell of hay and clover in the air, and thick hedgerows, and cottage gardens packed with flowers. Yes, she would find it.

She quickened her pace : she was almost running, a thing she hated.

'But do I hate it ?' she wondered ; and now she was definitely running, slowly, springing rather high over the heather, smiling to think how odd she must look—large, clumsy, in a long mackintosh, ambling downhill on matronly limbs, and rather enjoying herself.

'Home, now, home,' said Norah, climbing into the car, and her voice, which was clear and firm, not sad, seemed to ring mournfully, inhumanly, like a voice of the moor, through the wind's clamour and the grey failing of the day. The half-light made her pallid and insubstantial, and took the warmth of colour from her crimson coat and hat.

'Can we race the rain ? ' she added, looking round her with a dubious grimace.

After a few miles she took a short-cut down a narrow lane, and as she turned the corner, a patch of red flashed suddenly against the shadows ahead.

What 's that ? ' said Norah, peering. 'A pink coat. . . . Oh, the hunt ! I wish we 'd seen them.'

A young man in a pink coat and muddy breeches was walking down the road in front of them. He paused in his slow, loose stride when he heard the car and stood still in the middle of the lane, as if preparing to ask for a lift. But when he saw that the car held two women he hurried on, staring fixedly in front of him. Grace recognized from afar the old man's nephew. She had not seen him since the night of the cinema, three weeks ago.

'Oh, it 's that boy, I do believe,' said Norah, slowing down, 'Hugh Miller. He came in to play bridge the other night, and Gerry liked him. He actually talked to him. It's funny—I knew his sister in London years ago. She wrote and asked me to look him up.'

She came up beside him and stopped the car.

'How d' you do,' she called. 'Like a lift?'

Forced to stop and look at her, he recognized her with a smile in which spontaneous friendliness and reluctance were mingled: the smile of one who liked his fellow-creatures but who would just as soon—perhaps rather—be left alone by them. He stood and continued to smile, attractive, polite—wondering, thought Grace, how he could escape from these women.

'I didn't recognize you for a moment,' he said. His voice too had a mixed quality, diffident and careless; and very quiet. When he spoke he gave her a firm gaze, and then looked away again.

'Would a lift be any good to you?'

'Oh no, thank you. Don't bother.' He seemed to draw back. 'I was just on my way to the station.'

'To the station? It's miles away, and you'll be soaked before you get there. Are you going back to the town?'

'Yes,' he admitted.

'Well, do get in, then: if you don't mind the dickey.'

Idiot Norah, thought Grace, and worse than idiot to press him. She saw herself and Norah, two wind-battered, red-nosed married women, accosting a reluctant young man, coaxing him to drive with them. She experienced again the feeling that had assailed her in the cinema, of a humiliating difference between her and him, deeper than difference of sex, something secretly, perhaps unconsciously aloof in his personality. She felt afraid of him, and wanted to obliterate herself from his sight. She said awkwardly, with a blush :

'Perhaps he 'd rather not.'

And at once she felt him stiffen obstinately, sensitively to deny her words, as if she had rudely exposed his secret boredom ; and he said with alacrity :

'Thanks awfully then, if you 're sure you don't mind. I 'd love to.'

He climbed in, drawing up his long legs as best he could in the narrow space.

'Splendid !' he said. 'Terribly comfortable,' and sat huddled together, heroically smiling.

'Had a good day ?' called Norah over her shoulder.

He leaned forward swiftly to reply.

'So-so. A good morning. But then my horse went lame, and I had to take him home. But it was nice to get some exercise after a week of that office.' He added politely : 'Do you hunt ?'

'Used to,' said Norah.

After a while she looked round again and said :

'You must be frozen. You ought to have a coat.'

'Lord, no !' he shouted back.

She smiled faintly, observing the glow of colour in his fair skin and the clearness of his eyes. He looked so full of fresh air, so well exercised. He was the sort of boy who would throw away the undervests his mother sent him at school, and declare on the coldest day that he was boiling. It was quite extraordinary how pleasant Gerry had been to him.

In half an hour's time they were at Grace's door. He tumbled out to open the door of the car for them, looking, in his bright coat, against the fading greyish-brown of street and houses, startlingly tall and vivid.

Grace said, blushing :

'Won't you come in ?'

A timid desire for him to accept struggled with a desperate hope that he would refuse ; and she anticipated already the way he would quickly say 'Thanks awfully, I must get along,' and smile and escape from them.

'I never introduced you,' said Norah. 'Mrs. Fairfax, Mr. Miller.'

'How d' you do,' he said, looked at her firmly for a moment, then looked away again ; and they all stood nervously waiting.

'Well, won't you ?' said Grace ; and this time she felt amused ; it was ridiculous that three human beings should stand together on a doorstep and cause each other such a waste of anxiety and embarrassment. She lifted her eyebrows faintly, and the corner of her mouth twisted.

His quick and grateful response to an amusement he did not quite understand twinkled in his eyes.

Now he would come cheerfully in, she knew, to have tea with her.

'Come on, Norah,' said Grace with authority, opening her front door.

'Well, just for a few minutes,' said Norah, impulsively abandoning her family to unsuperintended bread and butter. 'I 'm perished and famished.'

The trio disappeared, the door was shut; from its frame of brown paint and ornamental glass, a number engraved in bland white china stared out once more upon the darkening street; announced that here, securely enclosed in a brick case, flanked on each side by a row of similar cases, family 37, of the human race, concealed themselves to eat, to take off their clothes and lie down to rest; to speak to each other those words, memorable or trivial, that are withheld from strangers' ears; to observe each other, safe from the world's observation, with unhooded glance or gaze . . or, without speech or look, to turn apart, each in his equipment of the common body of the species, each to his one unshakeable faith and foundation; to the abiding solitude and secrecy, the perpetual assurance, of his separate and individual spirit.

Grace drew the curtains, poked the fire to a bright blaze, lit a red-shaded standard lamp. The room came to life in the glow: the dead-leaf colour of the walls gave back a feeble reflection, the faded brownish-orange pattern of the chintz melted into dim warmth.

PART II

'Lovely,' said the young man, and he sat down at once on the fender-stool and spread his hands to the blaze. 'Please excuse the mud on me. I took a toss. . . . Nothing.'

Annie came in with the tea-table, opened eyes of astonishment and delight, and remarked gently:

'Would the gentleman care for a boiled egg?'

She had been with a hunting family once, and she knew what pink coats meant at tea-time. Mrs. Fairfax, poor soul, would never have thought of it.

'If—if you 've got one,' said he, flippant or awkward—it was hard to know which. He added, turning to Norah: 'One does get an incredible hunger.'

'I know,' she said. She lay back in her chair, watching him for the intermittent likeness to his sister. He reminded her of Clare Miller; and vaguely of something else: of a host of other things youthful and forgotten.

She questioned him about his hunting. A friend of his uncle, he said, an old Colonel James, had mounted him. It was frightfully nice of him: didn't she think so? Norah knew Colonel James. He must have approved highly of his riding, she said, or he would never have trusted him with one of his precious horses.

Oh well, of course, he admitted, he had ridden all his life.

'I remember Clare riding,' said Norah. 'Does she still?'

'No, not for years,' he said, 'not since her marriage': and a pause succeeded the last word, for Norah knew that the marriage had not been successful, and that Clare lived apart now from her husband.

Then, remembering the loneliness of his figure walking in the dark lane with no companion, she asked him if he had met people yet, if he had joined the racquets club, whether he had friends to go to for week-ends.

'Oh yes,' he said swiftly. 'Every one 's terribly hospitable and nice—don't you think so? There 's my great-uncle, you see—I can always go to him for week-ends,—if I want to. And then somebody 's asked me to a dance. . . . I don't know who. I got the invitation this morning.'

He felt in his pocket and pulled out a crumpled and muddy card. 'Must have fallen on it,' he said, and read out, 'Lady Forbes.'

'Oh,' said Norah. 'Already? . . . She 's got a lot of unmarried daughters.'

He smiled and stuffed the card back in his pocket.

'Perhaps I 'll go,' he remarked. 'Anything for a change from the office.'

Annie brought in a heaped tray and set it down.

'Coffee or tea?' said Grace. These were the first words she had spoken.

'Oh, coffee! How marvellous,' he said with enthusiasm.

PART II

'I always have it at tea-time,' said Grace. 'I have far too much.'

'We all have too much something and flourish on it,' said Norah. 'Mine 's tea. Very vulgar.'

'Mine 's . . . neither of those,' he said; and they all laughed.

A spark of memory flashed on Norah. She heard Jimmy say, rather defiantly, in answer to some protest of hers: 'I *like* drink—almost any kind. I never refuse it. As for champagne, everybody knows it 's the best tonic in the world.'

He cracked his egg, and remarking 'I must do this,' dipped bread-and-butter fingers into it and ate with relish.

How he seemed to fill the room, thought Grace. He gave out a sense of clear colour, even apart from his clothes; and his head, modelled with a strong outward curve above the nape and covered with heavy straight yellow hair, was finely proportioned and arresting. But his features, she decided, were plain. More like an artist, Tom had said. What characteristic nonsense to apply a label simply because he did not shave his head and oil the stubble, and generally take precautions against a certain appearance of individuality.

'Do you mind a pipe?' he said, looking at her; and his shyness came back like a recurring motif in the theme of his behaviour.

'Goodness no,' she said. 'Tom—my husband—always smokes a pipe.'

A realization came suddenly into his eyes. . . . The red-faced chap in the office whom the clerks called Uncle Tom. . . .

'Is your husband the Mr. Fairfax who 's—who 's in my great-uncle's Company.'

'Yes.' She blushed. 'He 's been with them for years.'

Now, she thought, he had placed her: the wife of one of the company's most typical underlings: *his* servant probably in a few years' time, supposing he inherited the business and Tom's time-worn machinery continued dependable.

But all he said, in his quiet voice, staring into the fire, was:

'He was frightfully nice to me when I first arrived. Frightfully helpful.'

'I 'm glad,' murmured Grace.

He lit his pipe and got up to go.

'Oooh!' he said, stretching cautiously and laughing. 'Terribly stiff. To-morrow it 'll be agony.'

'Did you know you 'd torn your coat?' asked Norah. 'Under the arm.'

'What a bore.' He twisted his head to examine it. 'I thought I heard a noise there. Lord, the whole thing 's gone. . . . It looks rather serious, doesn't it?'

Norah chuckled.

'Don't despair,' she said. 'It 's only the seam—easily mended. Is your landlady obliging?'

'Not frightfully.'

PART II

He remembered with distaste the surprising occurrence of last week-end. He had been away, and had returned unexpectedly on Sunday night to find a strong smell of spirits pervading his bedroom, his bed tumbled, and a pair of fierce, ancient, and insanitary corsets mysteriously reposing between the sheets. Since then he had suspected that he was not comfortable in his lodgings; and that his landlady was something more definite than an old trout. He wondered for a moment whether to mention these odd but boring facts. But no. They might offer to find him another place, or make some sort of fuss.

Grace had a prophetic vision of him, sitting in his horse-hair armchair with set jaw and huge borrowed needle and thread, stitching his coat together an hour before the next meet. . . .

'I 'll mend it for you,' she said. 'It won't take a minute.'

'No, no. Please don't.' He withdrew into himself embarrassed, surprised. 'I can easily get it done, or do it myself. I sew beautifully. I often sew on buttons and things.'

But Grace had already got up and said at the door, over her shoulder:

'I 'll get Annie's work-basket. There 's only one needle in mine.'

When she came back he had flung his coat on the sofa, and was sitting in his shirt-sleeves talking gaily with Norah. He looked up with a beaming smile and said:

'It 's frightfully nice of you. I took it off. I thought it would be easier for you.'

'You know you can't sew a stitch,' mocked Norah.

She got up and pulled her hat on again over her short rough curls. The young man noticed her hair with approval: the silver streaks in its darkness were attractive.

'I must go,' she said. 'I strongly feel I 'm needed at home. Good-bye, Grace. Do you know how to thread a needle?'

'Go away,' said Grace. 'I shan't start till you 've gone.'

The young man shook hands, murmuring, stilted and polite again:

'Thanks so much for the lift.'

'Come and see us again some time. Gerry and I so enjoyed the other night.'

'So did I. It was such fun,' he murmured.

'You must come to dinner or something.' Her voice and smile invited him cordially, but she sighed involuntarily, thinking what a horrid meal Florrie would cook, and how she had nothing amusing to offer to this boy, Clare's brother.

The rain had begun to fall heavily before she got home. The garage door stuck, and she struggled with it while wind and wet drove unkindly against her in the dark.

The boys had thrown down their coats on the floor in the hall. Florrie had as usual left the kitchen door open, and the smell of onions came forth undaunted. She picked up the coats and then stood clasping them to her for a moment ; and the jangling of her nerves subsided, replaced by the sudden tender feeling that her little boys' garments gave her. What did it matter, after all, if they flung their coats down when they came into their home—gay and careless, running upstairs ? Must they not be free as much as possible from the irksome checks and constraints which the mere fact of urban existence, besides education and, worst of all, Gerry's caprice, imposed ? It was her duty to see that they were allowed their high spirits. And anyway, she thought, hanging up the coats and going to shut the kitchen door, tidiness was not a noble quality—one might almost say unmasculine ; in their hearts, women did not value it in men, despite its convenience.

She went into the sitting-room. Gerry was in his armchair by the fire, reading from a large volume and making notes on a sheet of paper. He glanced up with a preoccupied expression which she guessed to be deliberate, and resumed his work.

She pulled off her hat and sank into a chair opposite him.

'Hullo, darling,' she said. 'Busy still ?'

He did not reply at once; and then said grudgingly:

'I 've been busy since tea-time. I had to send the boys upstairs.'

'Poor chaps,' she said. 'I must go to them. I 'm sorry I didn't get back to tea.'

He shrugged his shoulders slightly. Though his eyes were lowered on the page, she divined their expression from the slant of the lids, the way they swept up to narrowed corners beneath the prominent oblique ledge of the temples. He was in his knotted mood because . . . probably because she had stayed our longer than he expected; because he knew he would not give as good a lecture as he wished to; because the boys had had buttery fingers at tea . . . something of that sort. Now he was asking her to come and untie him—and defying her to try. Why should this vampire family so prey on her and pin her down that even one afternoon's freedom became a matter of importance, to be regretted afterwards? Why should she let him for ever drain her to sustain himself?

But she thought swiftly: No, no! That was not how it was. It was no virtue in her, but a law of nature. To grudge him what she had within her to give him was as if one born with the power of healing by the laying-on of hands should refuse the sick a life-giving touch.

Electricity, vitality, spirit—call it what you would—the supply was not to be exhausted by one demand, however ravenous and perennial. No, rather, perhaps, it was dependent on this for its replenishment. Only, to-night she hated the active life, wanted to have rest from this perpetual crumbling of the edges, this shredding out of one's personality upon minute obligations and responsibilities. She wanted, even for a few moments, to feel her own identity peacefully floating apart from them all, confined and dissolved within a shell upon which other people's sensibilities made no impression. But this was not possible, never for a second, in one's own home.

What it is, she thought, ceasing with a jerk to indulge in self-pitying reflections, to be an ordlnary domesticated female!

She started to hum a little tune, checked herself at a convulsive movement of Gerald's shoulders, and said:

'Aunt Ethel 's making a record recovery, I 'm afraid, darling. It was so dark and drear on the moors. We met that boy you liked on the way back. He 'd been hunting. I gave him a lift.'

He lifted his eyebrows and inquired, rather disagreeably:

'What boy I like?'

'Hugh Miller. You know you thought he was nice when he came last week.'

'I fail to remember his making any particular impression on me,' he said, turning over pages. 'But then I don't boast your unerring intuitions . . . or your spontaneous enthusiasms. However, if you say so . . .'

'Well, anyway—— ' She could not help laughing a little, he was being so characteristically impossible. (How he loved to make her feel a fool!) . . . 'The boy *I* liked . . . Grace threw all her complexes to the winds and invited him to tea. By the time I left she 'd offered to do plain sewing for him, and he was sitting beside her in his shirt-sleeves.' She looked hopefully for a gleam ; but observing rather the reverse, finished lamely : ' He 'd torn his coat.'

What a blunder indeed ! She felt his mind working busily on some tortuous underground track, snatching food for suspicion from her idle words. ' So that 's it,' she could hear his tense silence shout at her. ' You neglect me in order to enjoy the company of a strange young man.' Heaven knows what scenes of gaiety and licence her innocent account was suggesting to him ; for in his imagination she indulged in orgies of unbridled conviviality, once safely away from the restraint of his presence. ' Probably,' she decided, ' he sees me dancing on the table, and all of us taking off everything.'

Alas, she thought, he nourished against her a constant jealous reproach, whose essence was roughly : ' You enjoy yourself in a world that I hold to be joyless.' It was true. His dark could not permanently influence her light. Natural cheerfulness would reassert itself again and again ; and unfailingly she found herself responding to the mild pleasures which life offered.

But these were not for him. The most one could hope for, youth once gone, he said, was that age might gradually blunt one 's perception of the miseries of existence. And in the bitter times he whispered to himself, looking with a faint hope to the years ahead : *Calm of mind, all passion spent.* But in the worse he knew that he would make a desert around him and call it peace.

She left him and went upstairs to her boys. They were very quiet in their little room, once the night nursery, now their inadequate play-room. Her heart gave a twinge to see them sitting so still in their chairs, one at each end of the red-clothed table, heads propped on hands, each absorbed in his occupation. She should have come back and played the piano to them. She saw them suddenly grown up and independent of her. . . . Were they quieter than other children ? Were they at all crushed ? She remembered with relief the coats in the hall and the basketful of their woollen stockings to repair.

How their darling ears stuck out. . . .

Robin, who was nine, was poring over a glass of water in which dangled a thin bit of string.

'Hullo, mum !' he said. He had a piping little voice which annoyed his father by sounding perky.

She bent over him and looked at the water.

'There 's alum in this water,' he said. 'I bought it myself at the chemist. It 's a thing I found in my experiment book. This string 's going to get all covered with crystals. But I 'm afraid not before morning.'

'Thrilling,' she said.

He wriggled round and threw himself against her, putting grubby paws on her, rumpling his scrubby crest of hair against her shoulder. He was an affectionate child: apt lately to follow her about in a dogged, silent way, to stay awake until she came to bed, and to lavish abrupt demonstrations on her: unlike David, she thought, looking across at her second-born. David at seven had impenetrable reserve. He looked out from his own world with calm but intent gaze, and loved only his brother.

'What 's David doing?' she said.

He was laboriously doing something with a pencil in a black copy-book. When she spoke he quickly shut it and covered it with his arms, faintly and suspiciously smiling at her.

'He 's doing a drawing of some horses for me,' whispered Robin.

She nodded and said:

'Your supper will be here in a minute, my fellows. Don't come down and say good-night: Father 's busy. Undress, and I 'll come up and look you over while you wash.'

She gave Robin a pat, and, passing by David, lightly smoothed his head.

Was it fond and foolish to imagine, seeing the white embossed moulding of his forehead and his dreamy eyes, that he was going to be different from other little boys? If David were to be an artist, his father would understand and cherish him; Gerry would be appeased in his long gnawing grievance against the world.

But she sighed. Robin had asked her yesterday whether it was at all likely that he could ever have a pony, and she had not been able to give an encouraging reply.

She went down again, to the little sitting-room in which her treasures—her piano, her old embroidered screen, her walnut tallboys, her Chinese plates and bowls—were perforce huddled together in the small space among more necessary objects, and did little more than serve to make the room look overcrowded.

Gerald had put aside his books and was lying back in his armchair. She went to him and whispered, close to his ear :

'Relax. . . . Relax. . . . Relax.'

She put her hand on his contracted forehead and he closed his eyes. After a moment he put up his hand and gripped hers, and she felt some of the tautness begin to yield and flow out of him.

She took her work-basket and sat opposite him and began to sort stockings and wools.

He would be all right now. There would be no scenes, no explanations after all. After supper she would ask him to read aloud to her, and they would sit one on each side of the fire, looking what they were—a harmonious couple.

Yes, she thought, hidden deep beneath the discord, known only to each other, was the place of union where husband and wife could still pluck from each other the essential note. Her marriage was a reality, a success, in spite of all.

The secret was to look to the present chiefly, the

future a little, the past scarcely at all; to let old days depart in peace, to break the last threads of irrecoverable associations; to give up trying to alter people who would be, to their lives' end, unalterably themselves; to fill up every day with a variety of practical occupations; to remember, with harshest self-discipline, that Jimmy was dead and God knows where, well out of reach, probably nowhere; and that her concern must be with the living. . . .

Yes, he had reminded her, that boy: not really in the least like, of course, but he was the same sort of person. . . . What about *his* morals, she wondered: he was so debonair and independent; it would take a lot to cramp his style. What could he and Grace have made of their *tête-à-tête*. . . . It really had been funny to see Grace sitting with his coat on her lap, and him sprawling beside her at his ease.

What joy, what utter bliss if one had come suddenly upon a young man walking alone, ahead of one in the dusk, and he had turned round and been, not that one, but Jimmy. It would not have seemed so overpoweringly, insanely impossible—not for a moment . . . quite, quite natural: simply the instantaneous, long-deferred re-establishment of sanity, faith, truth. She would have cried out 'Oh! . . . I *knew* . . .' and then she . . . what peace and . . .

She took up a half-knitted stocking and carefully counted the stitches.

'Thanks most awfully,' said the young man.

'That 's marvellous.' He bent down and examined the mended coat with admiration.

'It isn't,' said Grace with a smile. 'But I think my enormous stitches will hold it together.'

He put it on again and straightened himself.

'Splendid,' he said.

There was a pause; but she did not feel uncomfortable, she told herself, in spite of this phenomenal event of a strange young man in the house.

'Well, good-bye,' he said, and he held out his hand.

She wondered if she would ever see him again.

'Are you going to be long here—in this town?' she said.

'Oh, I don't know . . . not very long. . . . Perhaps just till the autumn . . . . it depends.'

'I hope you won't have to stay if you don't like it,' she said impulsively, and blushed.

He leaned on his shoulder-blades against the mantelpiece, and looked down at her with a kind of humorous guardedness in his expression, as if to say: 'Now why should you be interested in what I do?'

'Oh, I probably won't stay if I don't like it.' He repeated the words with a little laugh.

'Be warned in time,' said Grace.

'Don't you like it, then?' He spoke awkwardly, as if the question had been forced out of him against his will.

'Oh, I . . .' she said contemptuously, shrugging her shoulders.

He vaguely noticed that her eyes were pretty—

long and narrow and in colour a blue-green ; and he wondered more vaguely still what dissatisfaction or unhappiness her laconic answer might imply. She was rather an unexpected wife for old Fairfax to have. Perhaps they did not hit it off. She was not nearly such an easy, cheerful person as the other woman, Clare's friend.

He said with faintly defiant gaiety :

'Oh well, I generally manage to enjoy myself. I rather like being in a strange place.'

She nodded.

He added, preparing to go :

'Besides, spring 's coming on, thank goodness, and summer. One can't be bored in summer.'

'Tennis, you mean, and fishing and——' she murmured.

'Yes. And then one can always get out into the country in the evenings and walk or bathe or something.'

Her heavy eyes were quite wide open this time as she looked at him and said eagerly :

'Oh yes ! I used to do that.'

He glanced down at her, and said rather reluctantly again :

'Not any more ?'

'No,' she said, walking with him towards the front door. 'But I miss the country.'

Her voice faded on the last words, and she stood still in the hall, staring dreamily ahead of her. They both waited.

PART II

Odd woman, he thought—she embarrassed him. He wanted to be gone, and she seemed to be keeping him here ; and he could not help a flicker of curiosity about her. He felt the weight of the things she had not said.

At length he said awkwardly :

' I suppose you 're fearfully busy always.' For perhaps the trouble was that she had a lot of children to look after, and never any free time.

' Oh no ! ' She looked as if the idea of her being busy amused her intensely. ' I do absolutely nothing at all.' She added after a pause : ' I go to cinemas.'

' I do that,' he said. ' I go to them all.'

' So do I.'

They laughed together.

No, he thought vaguely, she could not be a mother. Her large-boned frame was clumsy and somehow shapeless and immature, like that of a great girl in her teens. She moved as if she had not yet quite learnt how to manage her limbs. Yet one might imagine finding something restful about her appearance, something suitable to a mother ; and her voice came out of her throat in a deep amusing way.

Hearing the young man's voice in the hall, Annie pressed forward from the kitchen with majestic speed, with solemn alacrity, to accord him the ceremonious showing-out due to such a young man, accustomed no doubt to the best houses ; and to gladden her eyes with another look at him. But

Mrs. Fairfax had already opened the door and was standing beside him, looking out and exclaiming:

'Oh, the rain! What will you do?'

'I like it,' he said.

'Should we lend the gentleman an umbrella?' inquired Annie earnestly, stepping forward.

'Yes, an umbrella,' cried Grace. Of course Annie would turn up and expose her helplessness.

'No, no, no!' he cried in disgust. He ran down the steps and stood in the downpour, looking up and laughing at them both. The light from the hall lamp was on his face, and the rain enfolded his head and shoulders in a wreath of long silvery needles.

'Lovely,' he said. 'I've never used an umbrella in my life.'

'Nor have I,' she called. 'I haven't got one.'

So much, she thought, for Annie, who retired with a pensive smile to the kitchen and there meditated on the reckless endearing folly of young men; and asked herself unhopefully if Mrs. Fairfax had had the sense to ask him to come again.

'Well, good-bye,' he said.

'Good-bye.'

The iron gate creaked after him, and he had disappeared.

The rain seemed to increase as she stood listening to it. It came with an enormous whispering hurry, with a solid rhythm that prevailed above the noises of the town, flattened them out, drowned them almost.

PART II

The street lamps were like a row of blurred incandescent chrysanthemums, and beneath their light the wet tram-lines gleamed sleek and serpentine.

Tom would be back soon now. He would be fully equipped with umbrella and burberry, and he would remove his shoes at once and put them to dry by the fire, and altogether take every precaution. . . . What a good thing they had not met on the doorstep. Tom would have been too pleased and surprised, too cordial. He would have talked about the right things in not quite the right way, and striven a little too hard to create an atmosphere of good chaps together.

That boy now . . . probably he had never told himself that days must be got through, life must be lived to the end. He had never known that feeling which, like a dread familiar, dropped down each morning upon the waking pillow. His heart had never sunk as consciousness returned.

It would upset him a little to know that a person was unhappy : he had a kind face. But of course he would be puzzled too ; perhaps a trifle scornful. He would think there must be some simple remedy.

If only she could find out from him. . . . He seemed to have a secret of mastery, of confidence, of being at home in the world. He would disregard inauspicious detail, and be lucky, and know how to manage his life as he wanted it.

What past had shaped him, what experiences defined him so clearly ? He was a creature compact of youth, but he was not a boy.

Had he ever loved a woman, she wondered, or been loved ?

It had given her extraordinary pleasure to mend his coat, and to have him sitting there beside her. It had seemed somehow natural : a moment of saying peacefully to oneself : 'this is what life is.'

Anyway, he had enjoyed his coffee and his egg. He had been very appreciative.

Just as he stood there in the rain, the moment before leaving, she had been brushed again with a sense of sudden but dim recognition. Now where could she have seen him before ; or of whom did he remind her ?

That feeling of fear he had given her had soon passed off ; but she could imagine feeling it again just as strongly next time she saw him.

But perhaps—quite probably—she would never see him again.

By the time he reached his lodgings he was dripping wet. He took off his clothes and flung them on the floor. No hope of a bath, of course ; but he must have at least a can of hot water. He rang for Mrs. Veale, but there was no reply. And she had let the fire go out. Hateful room, he thought, looking round it : foul expression of Mrs. Veale's festering soul. He put on his dressing-gown and crouched by the hearth, stuffing newspaper into the grate and applying to it match after match. No, it was no good : too much paper, no wood, damp coal. He desired fervently to break up all the furniture and make a roaring bonfire and burn the place down.

All the fire-irons crashed down, and he collapsed with a smudged face among the knobs and lumps of the one armchair, and swore obscenely, aloud.

What next ?

No, it was no good, he could not stand it, he would chuck up his chance and go. He would go abroad again, back to South America, or perhaps India this time. This was no life for him. It would be easy to go if the old man were not such a dear old boy : if his two sons had not been killed, so that there was nobody—as the old man so often tremulously said —but himself to carry on the name and inherit the great arduously-built business.

Yes, but he had had quite other ideas for himself. He had told himself he would only stay if he liked it : and so he would. He had only come back because there did not seem any immediate chance of getting the capital to start out there on his own (and he must be on his own, could not stand being under authority) ; and because the old man kept on writing ; and because . . yes, really because he had been homesick, had missed England and his friends, and, chiefly, Clare. For he must admit it to himself : he was not proof against the appalling onslaughts of loneliness. Why had he come back to this damned town on a Saturday evening ? Simply on the chance of finding some letters waiting. He had had none all the week except for one wretched invitation, and it was unbearable. Everybody had forgotten him. He had pictured the envelopes on his table—one from Clare, one or two from friends in London, and one other . . . the one he still expected by every post, although the likelihood of its arrival had long since vanished. Now he must wait in suspense till Monday.

If there was no letter from Clare on Monday, he would wire to her and tell her off. Yes, he would. He could not stand these lodgings any longer. She must come and stay for a bit, and help him find something else. And he would buy a car somehow; and a gramophone. That would help. And he would send for his dog: it would be a rotten life for the poor chap by day, but he would smuggle him into the office or manage somehow; and have him for company in the evenings.

His spirits rose. Now, what was he to do with himself? Saturday evening, no fire, no food.

He would go out to a hotel and get a bath, and afterwards have a quiet dinner there. He would take a book and read while he ate. He glanced over the volumes of his library: *Moby Dick*, *Mr. Sponge's Sporting Tour*, *Tristram Shandy*, *The Life of Dr. Johnson*, *War and Peace*, *The Oxford Book of Prose*, one or two modern anthologies of poetry, a Shakespeare, the translation of Rabelais, Milton's Poetical Works. Oliver had read Milton aloud to him one long vacation. He remembered the voice of Oliver and the sound of *Paradise Lost*: he had revelled in it. Then there was *South Wind* and *The Journal of a Disappointed Man*, and a novel called *Jacob's Room*, and a paper volume whose title haunted him, *A l'Ombre des Jeunes Filles en Fleurs*. These were Oliver's. They had got mixed up with his own books long ago, and he had meant to return them, but he never had. He would some day—next time he saw him. He opened a cover and saw his signature, *Oliver Digby*, in a minute hand. Lastly there was Oliver's own poem, just one, *Transmutations*, in a black and white futurist paper cover, inscribed on the fly leaf (in Greek) from the author : but the poem, unfortunately, he had never been able to understand.

No, he did not want to read. He wanted entertainment, distraction. He would go to the Palace Hotel for a bath, and then perhaps look into the bar—gathering-place, so he had heard, of the clerks and the tarts—and see what was to be seen on a Saturday night. Then after dinner he would try a music-hall, or possibly a cinema.

That odd woman who had asked him to tea ! . . . Really, she and the other had looked a comic couple, sitting bolt upright in their incredible car. He had been absolutely aghast when he saw two women instead of some solitary male as he had hoped. But it had turned out all right. They were rather fun, and kind too, smiling away, giving him eggs, mending his coat. And he had got away all right, without any fuss ; though Clare's friend had come pretty near another invitation. Once was all right: Clare had asked him to be polite, and he had been. The queer husband had talked to him about travelling, and it had all been quite easy. But once was enough.

So Hugh Miller went down to the Palace Hotel, and there, in the lounge, met Pansy, who decorously agreed to drink a glass of sherry with him.

Afterwards they went to a popular café and dined to the strains of a jazz band so loud that conversation was mostly out of the question. He liked her small mask of white china, her mouth painted bright red, her eyes as empty, stainless, and pretty as little blue flowers, her rounded delicate miniature figure dressed plainly and neatly all in black. He was glad of the band, for her voice was rather awful. In between the tunes he solemnly teased her, and felt very cheerful.

Afterwards he took her to a music-hall, and laughed at the funny man; but she considered him vulgar. During the intervals, he listened with an expression of mild benevolence to her inconsequent chatter. He could not help yawning now and then (for the day's exercise had made him sleepy), but he nodded his head encouragingly while she told him about the cup of coffee that got spilt all over her new costume, and the pneumonia she had had last winter, and the moving dummy she had seen in a shop window rinsing clothes as an advertisement for washing soap.

And after the show, feeling by now positively

drowsy, he raised his hat and bade her a polite good-night.

'I 'm afraid I must go,' he said. 'Can I get you a taxi or something ?'

He saw her contented expression alter. He felt in his pocket for his note-case, and then held something unobtrusively out to her, and said, with his mixture of shyness and assurance :

'Sorry. Please take this.'

She glanced at his hand. There was a pause. Then 'I don't want it,' she said, low and hurriedly. She stood and stared up at him from her tiny height, with her sad blank face of a doll, as if there were something more she wished to say.

'Well,' he said finally, rather embarrassed, 'thank you for your company.'

'Thank you for yours,' said she, and walked away.

He went home and was sound asleep five minutes after he got into bed.

The next day was a fine blowing blue and white day, and he went out of the town and tramped all day alone upon the moors, wearing his oldest tweeds, and singing, not always quite in tune, all the songs he knew.

PART III

PART III

Now it was the middle of May. Spring had come in three days and nights to the North, and the last traces of the May snowstorms had vanished. Even in the midst of the town some stir from afar of orchards breaking into blossom stole upon the senses. With the evening light, spring came into the houses from streets that wore a fresh and happy air; and housewives mending their fires bethought themselves that soon might come the brief warm weeks when fires need not be lit till dusk; perhaps a brief surprise of summer heat when even after sunset an unlit grate would not seem frugal and comfortless.

In the residential quarter Norah's acquaintances inquired of each other 'Have you seen Mrs. MacKay's striking-looking friend?' Speculation was rife. It was not customary to keep one's importations to oneself. If one's means did not permit of dinner-parties, one entertained at tea; one telephoned round to one's circle, saying (if not in so many words) 'Come and have a look'; and one expected immediate return invitations—a full social programme. Indeed, a kind of civic welcome was prepared: an almost civic responsibility felt for the degree of hospitality enjoyed.

But Mrs. MacKay was ignoring all customary usage. It was the first time, so they believed, that she had ever had a friend to stay ; and the appearance of her guest confirmed the rumours they had heard of Mrs. MacKay's dashing Society life in London in the days of her youth. She herself never referred to pre-marital times ; but one had a suspicion in conversation with her on any subject that she was not . . . not local, not identifiable with the community in spite of her willing and capable association with the kind of activities which had their expression in bazaars and committee-meetings. She was a well-bred woman ; one distinguished her indubitable County blood ; her detachment was intangible and unspoken : unlike that of Mrs. Fairfax, that disagreeable woman, snobbish and exclusive without any justification whatever, and presuming on what appeared to be some sort of friendship with Mrs. MacKay. It was no good ringing her up to get information : she would only affect non-comprehension ; and one would feel in her voice the peculiar quality of her smile at the other end of the telephone. Yet, if any one were to be considered worthy (they thought sarcastically) of an introduction, it would probably be she. But so far nobody had been seen to enter or leave the front door except that young Mr. Miller—a brother, so it seemed ; and there was a suspicion among Norah's acquaintances that it was young Mr. Miller (who had more than once, when expected to dine, dance or play bridge, sent feebly-manufactured last-minute excuses, and had, besides, recently declined to join the tennis club) who was responsible for the concealment of what looked like an interesting novelty.

But they wronged him. It was Clare herself, who, pausing here for a few days on her way to pay a Scottish visit, had refused all entertainment, saying (with perhaps the faintest overtone in her voice) 'I only came to see you, Norah—and Hugh'; and it was impossible even for one so little prone to morbid reactions as her hostess not to feel a kind of anxious and apologetic desire to thank her for the favour conferred by her presence; not to fear that, as a luxury she was incongruous, as a decoration, wasted; not to know that Clare was realizing the circumstances of provincial life not so much with sympathy, as with increasing disapproval. All she said was, 'My dear, I never could have stuck it'; but, in the midst of the odd assortments of her mental processes—thoughts suggesting a preoccupation with self, but stated with dry detachment, fitted with an impersonal application—she would drop a comment or a question which produced in Norah mingled feelings of inferiority, yearning and defensiveness. For, after all these years, Clare still dined out and danced in London, bought Paris models, went abroad, and gave the illusion that these delightful things, these nothings, were real; tacitly assumed that the essence of life was, and should be still, as it had been in their youth.

No, it was a mistake, of course, this eagerly-awaited

visit; they were too far parted now; and there was no flavour after all in the long-anticipated *Do you remember?*

It does not ease the burden of the past to share its recollections; for with each plunge into it, each withdrawal, something is left behind that weighs more heavily than the memory; something that can never be shared or imparted—a sense of accumulating unease, surprise and contrast, of going alone, in unsuspected isolation, on one's way; and worse, a comfortless suggestion that the way—life, in fact—is without continuity. Is it possible to look back from the present as if one watched the reel of a moving picture wound smoothly the reverse way from its close: to say, that time and that hour brought one inevitably, with only apparent deviation, to this hour, this place? No, as one rushes headlong, flying with Time, portions of life split off and float away, one little world after another; and looking back, one sees them behind one as stars and constellations. Old burning pieces of experience shine now from their fixed places with unimpassioned ray; perhaps that fragment torn apart with cruellest wrench and most shattering concussion now hangs there, close indeed, but cold, all fires extinct, like that dead star the moon. And between these little lights lies trackless darkness: chaos and old night close up on one's heels, swallow the path for ever.

Yet, though one never can recapture, turn in one's

course and revisit, there come now and then—at a sound, a scent, a word—intimations from the past; live threads waver out, throwing feelers after hints of affinity. Misgiving comes, bewilderment, hope, surmise—a host of witnesses, striving to shape the spiritual shape of what has been; till it seems in a moment all will be linked, gathered up into unity and purpose.

And if memory had lost its savour, thought Norah, it had also lost its sting. It was through Clare that she had first met Jimmy: they could both recall the time when he had been the chief part of her daily life; and, trying his name aloud in the ears of another for the first time in a decade, she had felt the easing of a secret strain. It was easier than she had feared. Somehow, because Clare knew he had once been so violently an individual, so fiercely a factor in reality, it was less hard, in her company, to think of him from a great distance, almost as a symbol now for first love, first grief.

It is true that we grow older, as Clare said; we can mark the very day when we cease to suffer vain longing to torment us; and then the thorny companionship of youth is at an end. It might be, thought Norah, that with the return of Clare, this process, long deferred, of shedding the last vestiges of girlhood was going to take place. Clare despised her youth and all its storms. The better times were all ahead, said she. One goes by oneself, one is free, one enjoys oneself without fear of other people's opinions ; one sees to it that no relationship shall sweep one beyond the balancing point where possession of oneself ceases and suffering begins. Yes, said Clare, she could be happy now.

No, she declared, she would never marry again. She dropped a hint of past wretchedness, seemed to have been unhappy in her marriage, to have been under a cloud for years ; said vaguely that of course it was ridiculous not to change one's life if one was dissatisfied with it : one must persevere until one's true individual focus and centre was established. One must never let one's past actions bind one with remorse or regret, she said : but pass on at once and shape the future.

It sounded wise, thought Norah : but easier to adopt as one's philosophy when one has abandoned not only minor ties but the more solid results of past actions (such as husband and home), than when one's whole endeavour is to lie, till death, as gracefully as may be, in the bed one has made

But it was as difficult now as it had always been, Norah told herself, to see Clare except under a haze, in a glamour. She lay now stretched upon the sofa, dressed in a short black pleated frock and a little coat embroidered in many colours ; and a strange air stealing in the room, stirring live colour in the blue curtains, touching the bowl of daffodils to a luminous transparence, washed over her too, made her head rare and remote, her quiet hands delicate as polished stone.

She had grown slenderer, sharper with the years. Her reddish silken hair was cropped short to show a pair of ears like white coral, small and flat; but over her forehead it waved back in loose soft waves. No wonder her young brother was proud of her, thought Norah: she had something that was not common: not dignity, neither grace nor charm exactly. . . . There was no physical type to which she approximated. She gave the impression of being a unique experiment in material, line and colour.

And the quality of her mind was a constant source of perplexity. She was not well educated. She could be banal enough; and yet even Gerald came back from the lecture-rooms with expectant eyes, washed his hands before dinner, and talked to her during that meal—stranger still, listened while (now, as in old days) she threw off sparks, was for a moment witty, illuminating; seemed to have read, to be familiar with music and pictures. But were these fragments proof of a knowledge and understanding which she kept to herself?—or, as it were, the reflections, the shallow lights and shade in the polished surfaces of alabaster, jade, cornelian, and such ornamental stones (cool, hard, yet in a way rich and yielding) whose texture her appearance suggested? It was hard to tell. She had perfected her art, if art it were ; and continued triumphantly to present to the world the uncertain nature of her reality, to keep as her secret the degree of her honesty

Hugh came into the room, accompanied by a large black spaniel with frilled ears and paws of magnificent proportions.

He greeted his sister with a kiss, grinned at Norah and subsided in a sprawl on the window-seat, where the sun fell full on him and shone with an iridescent glitter on his yellow hair. He had dropped in in this way on each of the evenings since Clare's arrival. He was quite at his ease.

' Clare, come out,' he said. ' I 'm going to take Grock in the Park.'

The seven years between brother and sister was not noticeable. They looked roughly of an age, and that age belonged somehow datelessly and with a suggestion of permanency between youth and maturity. There was all the unlikeness in the world between the easy smiling play of his features, his look of one with an external habit of mind, good-humoured yet obstinate, and her still, veiled face, at once watchful and uncommunicative. But when she spoke, her eyes broke up her impassivity with a lively light ; and then the kinship was plain. They resembled each other too, thought Norah, in a certain lordly and careless demeanour, as if they were accustomed to some sort of natural privilege from life.

PART III

Carefully, in front of the mirror, she put on a little black hat, and wrapped herself in a black coat trimmed with light, silvery fur. Hugh gave her an approving glance. He always noticed her clothes ; her good taste flattered him.

Gerald came in by the door which they had opened to go out.

'Hullo, Gerald,' said Clare.

She was very nice to him, took trouble to draw him out. She told Norah that he had an interesting mind : that he was very amusing.

'Going out ?' he said in his swift, sharp, whispering voice. He stood against the door in a characteristic attitude, defensive, shrinking, as if he had suddenly got lost. His eyes flickered from one to another ; he thought he detected a kind of unease in them, as if his entry had checked them in their natural talk and laughter . . . as if his presence, he told himself, dried up the springs of normal humanity.

'Darling, you are back early,' said Norah tactlessly.

At these words, a wave of pure hatred for her closed over him. It was she who made it impossible for him to be unlike himself ; to respond and expand as he wished in the society of this young couple. But for Norah, he could have made friends. There she was, as usual, anxiously guarding now him, now them ; subconsciously persuading them to conspire against his inclusion.

This young woman was both friendly and beautiful.

Left to themselves, they would get on splendidly, he felt sure. She treated him in a sort of mysterious, teasing, attentive way, so that he felt himself an unusually entertaining host. . . . And the boy—he was nothing, of course, a young fool. Yet he had something . . . a quality one envied him and wished to seize for oneself. It was a compound of his gay and active nature, the way he had travelled, roughed it all over the world; and chiefly his youth, his youth! . . . like a quickening fountain of water running over one's own aridity.

'Excuse me,' he whispered rapidly. 'I merely came in for some books. I have to work.'

He made a dart for a pile of books and vanished, shoulders hunched, without another look. They heard the door of the dark little box which was his study shut with a bang.

'Oh . . . and I haven't dusted in there to-day,' murmured Norah.

Clare and Hugh went out. She lightly took his arm, said something silly and suitable to Grock, and they walked briskly down the street together.

Over the slopes of the great town park the wind blew fresh and strong from the sea. Sunlight poured out of the west in a full flood. The sparse crooked-jointed trees were in new leaf, the brown grass wore a faint veil of green, and, in the green, a sprinkling of daisies. Through the noise of the wind and the far-away clamour of the traffic came the sound of children's voices raised in their play, of women's laughter, of barking dogs. Men walked in quiet groups from their work, raced their whippets, lay on their backs in the sun ; or wandered singly, hands thrust in their threadbare pockets, the unmistakable stamp of the degradation of unemployment in their faces, their shoulders, their gait. Shop-girls stepped two by two with a swing, eyes alert beneath the brims of their new spring hats. Children and dogs chased each other, quarrelled, ran after balls, tumbled in the grass. In the distance kites were flying.

Movement flowed in all directions, without pause ; till it seemed to Grace that the bench she sat on was the only fixed object in the ferment of the circling world. It must be the weakness of convalescence that made one so quiveringly sensitive. Forms struck one's eyes as if for the first time, sound pierced too keenly, colour and light were too living, too exquisite. The greys and browns had vanished, swept away before a torrent of blue and golden light, submerged beneath a spate of green.

She sat wrapped in her old grey coat in the shelter by the pond. It was her first day out after an attack of influenza. Huddled on a bench, she felt her own breath mysteriously come and go. She heard herself cough : it was the cough of a real person. She looked down and saw herself moored to the seat as firmly as the stout old lady sitting opposite her ; yet she felt the wind lift her, whirl her like a straw, a feather, in its wake.

But it is hard enough, even in health, she thought, to remember one's own solidity : it is at any time a shock when some chance brings home to one the fact of possessing, like everybody else, a face and body visible to others, a voice that makes an audible noise. . . .

She watched the ruffled pond in its dismal cement basin ; the children on the brink, kneeling to sail their model yachts.

Along the asphalt path which girdled the water, accompanied by a spaniel swinging jaunty flanks, came Hugh Miller and a young woman. How confidently she held his arm, with what full measure of life they held on their way ! The people on the benches stirred as they passed, turned their heads to look after them : they gazed—a row of drab watchers, shadow-like—the ill-clad, the unmemorable, the human mass whom none would ever pause at in passing and distinguish face from face.

She saw them a long way off. She wanted to get up and go away, but she could not. They would not notice her, she thought. She watched them.

The spaniel jumped suddenly, in a great flutter, into the pond, and started to swim after one of the yachts. A child screamed, the dog seized the boat, the two stopped. Grace heard Hugh call imperatively, then laugh : she saw the young woman finger her hair, examine her shoe. . . .

Sun and wind seemed to leap up with wild spring vigour to envelop them ; they were rapt away where they stood, dreamlike images in the midst of light, echo, movement. . . .

The dog swam back ; Hugh bent down and pulled him out of the water, by the scruff. Grace heard him say ' Shake yourself ! ' and then ' Look out ! ' as his command was obeyed with more goodwill than discretion.

Now they were going to pass her. Hugh was looking straight at her, and she could not drop her eyes when she saw his expression alter and fix slightly as if with an effort at recognition. She would not greet him, she told herself—she would give him every opportunity not to acknowledge her ; but the colour swept up into her face. He tentatively raised his hand to his hat, and then, seeing her faintly smile, smiled charmingly in response : hesitated, murmured a word to his companion, and came lounging up to her and said in his quiet, half-diffident, half-confident voice :

' I haven't seen you for ages.'

She moved as if to get up, but instead only looked up at him, giving him all her face, and said :

' No—not since the winter. It 's really spring now, isn't it ? '

She felt suddenly weak, and controlled with an effort the first onslaught of a nervous shuddering.

' Can I introduce my sister ? ' he said, rushing awkwardly over the formal words : and then smiling again and swiftly touching Clare's arm.

Lovely she was, thought Grace, lovely. . . . She

tried to look at her clearly but her eyes seemed blurred, and she grasped but an impression of looks vivid yet delicate in colour, tenderness of contour, clarity of finish. She turned again to Hugh, and said, faintly twinkling at him :

'Not gone yet ?'

'Not yet.'

'How are you getting on ?'

She could not take her eyes off him. He had a look of gaiety and good fortune about him that amused and delighted her.

'Getting on pretty well.' He gave her a quick glance, as if he were beginning to recall the sort of footing they had reached last time—those moments of a vague, rather humorous private understanding.

'How are the cinemas ?' he said, suddenly remembering.

'I 've missed some. I 've been ill, this last fortnight.'

'You don't look well,' said Clare. Her voice sounded solicitous, and Grace blushed.

'I 've had influenza. I seem to get it every year, and it 's always rather awful. I don't think this is a good place to get well in.'

'I should think not,' agreed Clare.

'I used to live in the South. I think if you 're born and bred a southerner you never quite get used to the climate—or anything—here. You may get to love it, but it 's almost like living abroad, I think. . . . You want to go home.'

They nodded, looking at her with serious faces.

She thought: 'Why don't I stop talking and let them go?'

'I 'd never want to settle here,' said Hugh.

Clare gave him a glance which seemed to say: 'As if you 'd want to settle anywhere!'

'It 's all right with the sun,' went on Grace. 'I 've been thinking, if all the people could get drenched through with sunlight *once*, the expression of their faces would be different ever after. But there 's never enough. . . . The winter 's been very long, hasn't it?' She looked up at Hugh.

'I suppose it has,' he said.

'If only this will last now. . . . The country must look beautiful.' She addressed Clare: 'D' you live in the South?'

'Yes.'

'How lovely. I suppose it 's been spring there for a month now—real spring. Here it gets mixed up with summer all in a week or two, and after that it 's autumn again.'

They laughed.

'Well—we must get along,' said Hugh.

The dog was running hysterically up and down the edge of the pond, hovering with wails on the verge of another plunge.

'The old idiot,' he said; 'I must go and collar him.' They watched him striding away.

'Are you staying with Norah?' Grace said.

'Yes. . . . Do you know Norah?' She sounded surprised.

'Oh yes. Norah and I—started here about the same time. We went to a cookery school together.' She laughed and added: 'She told me you were coming some time. I haven't seen her lately. I don't want to see any one when I'm ill.' She smiled.

'She's such a dear,' said Clare with composure. She took a little gold box from her bag and carefully powdered her nose.

'I suppose he doesn't mind her doing that,' thought Grace anxiously, as Hugh came back with his dog. Powdering in public derived from indecency in the male code to which she was accustomed. Years ago, on expeditions with Tom, Poudre Nildé had burnt a hole in her pocket. She had given up carrying it now.

'He's a nice dog,' she said. 'He's got charming paws.' She held out a hand, and the paws were planted effusively in her lap. 'You clever, you noble swimmer,' she said. She kissed the top of the black satin head. Something warmer broke through the pleasant politeness of Hugh's smile.

'Have you got a dog?' he said.

'No.' She paused, and added, colouring: 'I've seen him before. . . . I've seen you sometimes in the evening going down the road to the Park with him. . . . You pass my window.'

'Oh, have you seen us?' he said, rather awkwardly. It embarrassed him to realize he had not given her a second's thought, going down the avenue. He had quite forgotten where she lived. 'Yes, I give him a run when I get back from the office. And before breakfast too : we run round the Park. Very good for us both. Luckily my new landlady 's lost her heart to him. But it 's a rotten life for the poor chap.' He broke into a broad smile. 'At first I tried smuggling him into the office. I thought he might sleep under my desk. But it didn't work. He let out a yelp in the first half-hour : the clerk next to me stepped on his toes. There was the hell of a row.' He relapsed into sudden shyness—remembering Tom perhaps, she thought. Tom would certainly not have been amused. 'Well, good-bye,' he said quickly.

'I do hope you 'll soon be quite well,' said Clare.

'Thank you. . . . Good-bye.' She blushed ; her eyes shifted nervously away from them and then back to them as they turned to leave her.

Hugh looked back suddenly and said :

'This weather 'll soon put you right, I expect' ; and his voice was so encouraging, his enthusiasm for the weather so whole-hearted, his appearance, with the sun on his bare, ruffled head so engaging, that she almost laughed aloud, and called 'Yes ; oh yes !' and put up her hand in a swift gauche little gesture of farewell.

They walked away down the asphalt path, and she watched them go—charged already with that excess of mystery, that weight of meaning which they were to bear for her henceforth, for ever after.

Tom would be back soon from his golf club committee meeting, waiting for supper. She must go home. She got up, feeling new life in her limbs. The ache was gone from her back and the sickly, dusty feeling from her mind. They had refreshed her, she told herself. . . . What had they said?

But it was she who had talked nearly all the time, not they. . . . Nervousness had made her chatter. . . . No, it was not that: to her own surprise she had not felt shy or self-conscious after the first few moments. It was the way they had looked, as if they had come bearing gifts . . . she mused over the expression. . . . Yes, that was it: bearing gifts. They had fed a spring inside her, the words had bubbled up from a source long dry. She had been filled with a sense of momentary adequacy as a person; had been enabled to give utterance to little things which were her own. And again she had felt herself thinking cheerfully: 'This is what life is. . . . What I am like.'

They had such good manners, both of them: easy, delightful manners from the South. . . . She warmed herself again at the thought that he had taken the trouble to stop and speak to her.

What did they talk about together, the brother and sister?

She would be gone out of their minds for ever by now.

PART III

It had all been a dream.

She walked along, past the bandstand, between the railed plots of lawn with their careful beds and groups of evergreen shrubbery. More than the trams, more than the gasworks, and the shops and the smoking chimney-stacks, was this garden wont to speak to her of the town, the town. But to-day, in the borders tall tulips were unsheathing the faint-tinged petals of their sculptured heads ; and there, above a bed of variegated laurel and privet, was a little almond tree in full flower, shaking out its rosy branches with simple prettiness on the blue air. After all, she thought, one blossoming branch can call up spring. Here was the essence of the season. The country ways could only play variations on this theme.

There was a small boy kneeling on the path in front of her, examining a red wooden engine : a nondescript child in a white sweater and blue serge knickers. He looked up a moment, then down again at his toy, and said in a preoccupied voice :

'I 've lost something off this engine.'

'What have you lost ?'

'A bit of wood.'

She said :

'What a beauty! It's enormous.'

He said :

'It goes as fast as anything. Look.'

He seized the string and rushed with it a few yards,

looking back at it over his shoulder with some anxiety.

'Very fast indeed,' she said. 'I should like a ride.'

He threw her an appraising glance, and said carelessly :

'You 're too big.' He made another examination, sighed deeply and added : 'Besides, the back wheels are wobbling. I must find that bit that 's lost.'

He picked up the engine in both arms and started to walk away ; then stopped to say :

'If you come to-morrow I 'll show you my motor.'

'Thank you,' she said. 'I 'll look out for you. Good-bye.'

''Bye.'

This time he stood and eyed her gravely as she went away.

No doubt, she thought, children could be amusing. She had never had such an encounter before ; and certainly, on the assumption that mutual boredom and embarrassment could be the sole reactions, never attempted to seek one. But he had accepted her after one glance as equal and fellow, and they had shared a few moments quite complete, in the essentials of companionship.

Now she had turned into the avenue. It was quiet almost as a country lane. One or two couples strolled ahead of her ; there was not a tram in sight ; red brick, yellow brick melted and glowed tenderly in sloping shafts of sunlight.

'It 's all right,' she whispered to herself ; and she went in through her front door and left it wide open to the air.

Tom was not in yet. Annie's voice came from the kitchen ; subdued and yet insistent it sounded, with its north-country lilt ; and a man's voice answered her briefly now and again. 'It was my friend, madam,' Annie would modestly reply, if questioned. His voice had suddenly begun to haunt the house a year or so ago. Since then the aural manifestations had been regular ; but Annie had not revealed him to the eye. Perhaps she would marry him some day. What would they do without her ?

She went into the sitting-room and stood at the window. Several times, standing there, she had seen him pass. She was ashamed to realize to what extent the hope of seeing him had become interwoven with her old habit of looking out of the window. He had come swinging along with his special stride, idle and powerful, a noble stride, and it had given her pleasure to watch him : pleasure and a kind of ironic pang to be so certain he would never glance in her direction, remembering her.

It was foolish to have told him : it had stressed something—some tremendous contrast—in public, which should have remained her secret. . . . Besides, he would not like to feel himself watched.

Now that the sun had left the street, the colour of the air was hyacinth-blue ; and oh ! . . . she saw suddenly the lilac tree was in full leaf, and there, at the top, were two or three clusters of whitish buds. It was years since it had flowered.

In her neighbours' gardens grew, on one side a may tree, on the other a laburnum. Lilac, laburnum, may, none of them had ever had any nature. They were nothing ; they did not grow from roots in the earth ; they were emblems of the town, dismal imitations, like the feather and shell flowers everybody had nowadays. But now all at once she saw with emotion a small white lilac tree, struggling to grow after the manner of its kind—a starveling with crooked trunk and brittle haggard maze of leafless twigs, and a crown of grubby leaves : and see, it had laboured to put forth a few new shoots, tender and bright ; it was going to have a flowering. It was awake, alive : it revealed itself to her, and she loved it. She dreamed, as she stood there, that it grew, covering the house, blotting out the street, climbed till it rose above the roof. She saw it in sunlight, cool and vast, a bountiful tower. The heart-shaped leaves swelled full, in cloudy masses, the profuse cones of blossom hung heavy and lambent in the green ; and with a somnolent tremendous humming the bees came to the fragrance.

She thought of a line in the little anthology Norah had given her last Xmas :

' *Come down to me, O my lilac among women.*'

What evocative beauty ; what words for a lover ! She knew all that the poet meant.

She fell into another dream, of the vicarage in the

Sussex village where she had lived till her seventeenth year. The walled garden bore a great old tulip tree ; and by the gate a judas tree, that flared out each May in violent-coloured, unfamiliar blossom, seemed to cry danger and alien passion to the passer-by. She remembered interrupting a lesson in her first school-days to inform the teacher 'We 've got a tulip tree *and* a judas tree in our garden.' (It had seemed, still seemed, too much richness.) But later a schoolmate had remarked 'I shouldn't have thought a clergyman's daughter would boast about a judas tree': and she could still hear corroboratory murmurs, still feel her shock and shame.

What a garden that had been—how cherished by her father ! She saw his long thin back stooping over a tiny magnolia tree which he had planted under the south wall. Like a seven-branched candlestick in a church it had looked, the second spring. The stiff, pale, upward-pointing flower-buds were set along the boughs like wax tapers : formal and holy it was, a little ecclesiastical tree.

Why was it, she wondered, that all her endless day-dreams went back to that vicarage and its associations for their background ? They had moved to the Isle of Wight when her ailing father resigned his living. She was nearly seventeen then, she had left school in order to look after him. They had lived at Freshwater for five years ; the only events of her life—the war, the first appearance of Tom (in naval uniform), her father's death in the month of the armistice—had taken place there; but she scarcely ever thought of it, and the images it summoned to her mind were few and dim.

'Really,' she thought, 'leaving the vicarage was the beginning of my going to pieces.' The further she had emerged into the world from that loved shelter and protection, the more her essential weakness of character, her reluctance to deal with responsibilities, her inability to cope with daily duties, had become manifest; and little by little, in her idleness and stagnation, the visual sensibility which had inspired her childhood had petered out.

There was Tom now, opening the gate. She smiled to him from the window, and she saw how his eye lightened, his step hastened at her greeting.

Funny old Tom, she thought, kind Tom: he had been very good to her lately, given her her medicine and rushed home from the office at lunch-time to see that she was all right. One ought to be thankful for a good steady husband.

He came into the room quite eagerly, saying:

'Better?'

'Much, much better.'

'Oh, good for you! I am so glad, Gracie.'

He put his arm round her shoulder and gave it a cheerful squeeze, and she did not have her usual impulse to move away from him.

'You 've had a rotten time,' he said sympathetically. 'But this weather 'll soon put you right.'

The same words, she thought, in almost the same

tone. She wondered what the spring meant to him, what thoughts were in his head ; and all at once she had an impulse of pity for him. He was forty-five.

'Yes,' she said. 'I went out and sat in the Park. It was delicious.'

'That 's right. You must get out as much as you can.'

He thought to himself : 'She ought to get away into the country.'

'Look here,' he said. 'What about our holiday ?' He took out his engagement-book. 'Let 's see. I 've got a whole lot of fixtures these next two months. Meetings, etcetera. Golf—cricket club. . . . You know they 've put me on the committee now.' He turned the pages with a frown. 'But after the first week in August I might . . .'

She interrupted with a sort of cry :

'Oh Tom !' She coloured a little and went on almost impetuously : 'I want to go away by myself.'

His first thought was that he had not heard her say a thing in that tone of voice for years.

And in the end, after he had looked blank, felt hurt, proposed various south-coast resorts to which he would willingly accompany her, stressed the expense of the journey, suggested that it would 'look funny,' he had to say that of course she must do as she liked.

But what, he wondered, what in the world was *he* to do ? He could not imagine.

He was going to miss Mother very much this year; but he would not, could not tell Grace this. Sympathy was not her strong point. . . .

He dreamed sometimes of an ineffably tender, womanly woman, some one who would ever listen, admire, console. Mother had not been that exactly, but she 'd always stood up for him, been proud of him: she 'd been a good mother to him. . . .

He was getting old. There was nothing before him really—no one who cared about his troubles.

But by the time they went in to supper he was restored to cheerfulness. It was not such a bad idea of Grace's, after all—a bit of a holiday on one's own might be quite enjoyable . . . a bachelor again . . . not so old after all—not so bad-looking either. He might wander round—look up some old pals. He might . . .

Over the fish pie he considered several possibilities.

'My dear,' said Clare, as they walked away, 'what nostalgia.'

'What what?'

'*Heimweh*.'

'What?'

'But I really thought you were introducing me to the housemaid—till she spoke. Her voice was nice. Why must people wear such misbegotten clothes? She wasn't bad-looking really. . . . Poor thing.'

'Mm. She 's rather a comic, isn't she? Her husband 's a manager in the office—a bluff old fellow with a paunch. Enough to make any one take a gloomy view, I should think.' He added : 'Lucky I didn't cut her. Can't think how I managed to recognize her. I haven't seen her since the winter.'

And he described his tea-party with a grin.

'Do you mingle much in society ?' she asked.

He laughed.

'Not much. I've dined out a few times—met some of the local snobs and magnates—Uncle Lionel's friends—played bridge—that sort of thing. . . . And I've attended several football matches on Saturday afternoons. And I go to the movies with one of the clerks in the office : when he's feeling the devil of a chap he takes me on to the local dancing-hell, and we pick up a partner apiece and drink lemonade and dance divine waltzes with all the lights dimmed.'

He thought suddenly of the little creature Pansy whom he had seen there once, sitting alone, very lady-like, sipping coffee. She had looked at him hard, unsmilingly, out of her minute white face. He had thought 'I'll go and dance with her soon.' He had been in good form that night. When next he thought of looking for her, a burly foreign-looking gentleman had claimed her. He saw them going out together.

He added :

'It's a rotten life. Still, one manages to get some amusement out of it. And I generally get away week-ends. . . . Let's take one more turn round the Park.'

'Don't let me be late,' she said. 'Norah has a meal at seven-thirty.'

'Oh, that 's all right. They 'll wait,' he said airily; adding, as they set off again: 'You know, I suppose I ought to do something about all these people.'

'Do what?'

'What indeed? Oughtn't I to give a dinner-party or something—take 'em to the theatre—polish 'em all off in a lump? I thought it would be a good opportunity, while you 're here.' He looked at her out of the corner of his eye, teasingly.

'Right you are,' she said. 'Only you must let me select the guests. I bar all local snobs and magnates. I bar all the matrons with marriageable daughters. I bar the daughters even more: all local young maidens absolutely barred; also all the cheery young men. Norah's husband barred, for his own sake as well as mine. Who 's left? Norah. And I bar taking her to the theatre. She 'd only fidget and wonder if the back door was locked or if the boys had gone to bed in their boots. She 's utterly hopeless now. She never opens a book. She 's so *dull*. When I think what she used to be like—such good company—terribly pretty too, in a conventional way. I suppose he 's done for her. She never had any judgment about men.'

Clare thought of Jimmy, that spoilt imperious male, that handsome and faithless lover: thought how he had twisted her round his finger—simple, innocent

Norah, staying at home always, just as if she were married to him, and waiting for him to come back when he felt like it.

He had treated her shockingly : everybody except herself knew that : but as she was too stupid to realize what was going on, it hardly seemed to matter ; in fact it served her right, one could not help feeling. The odd thing was that he had come back to her, apparently, every time : perhaps really would have married her in the end.

All the women had lost their heads over Jimmy. He had had a way of making one reckless . . . so that one offered oneself to him unreservedly . . . for a night or so . . . or longer if he would.

But these old matters should be buried deep, out of sight even of oneself. At least he had been honourable enough, or discreet enough, to keep one secret.

She said :

'I suppose she enjoys being victimized.'

'I suppose so,' said her brother vaguely.

They walked over the grass, with the sun and the now dying wind upon their faces.

'Saturday to-morrow. We 'll motor out into the country,' said Hugh. 'There are some marvellous places you really ought to see. I 'll take the morning off.'

'Yes,' she said. 'I couldn't stand this place another day.'

'I suppose I 'd better ask the MacKays to come,'

he said. ' We 'll have lunch at an inn somewhere. It 'll be a way of paying back—easier than a theatre And perhaps they won't come—or, he won't.'

They planned their expedition.

' What about asking that woman too ? ' he said suddenly.

' What woman ? '

' The one in the Park just now. If the others come, we might just as well have her too. She 's always talking about the country. Do her good.'

There was, thought Clare, a streak of kindliness in the boy's nature. She remembered with amusement his reputation for kindness during his dancing days in London, before he went abroad : how charming he was to the plain and neglected, how attentive to dowagers. He was like that ; he indulged in little acts that made for popularity. To be liked was a need of his nature.

' Well, if you can bear it,' she said. ' I don't mind.'

' I rather like her,' he said. ' She might be good value, given a chance.'

It was, she thought, the sort of non-committal answer that he always made.

They were back now at the gate by which they had entered the Park.

' I suppose I must go back now,' she said.

' Oh, pooh to that,' he said. ' You can't go back. It 's after seven-thirty anyway.'

' Their domestic is so appalling,' murmured Clare.

'She and Norah have painful asides all through the meal. And she blows on my head when she hands things.'

'Ghastly. Don't go back. Come along with me.'

'But they expect me. Isn't it too rude? After last night—and the night before . . .'

Last night he had driven her out to dine and play bridge with the parents of an Oxford friend rediscovered in the hunting-field. The night before, the evening of her arrival, she had pleaded fatigue and gone to bed before dinner, and Hugh had come in to chat with her, and Norah had brought up her tray.

'Come on,' he said. 'You can ring them up from my digs, and then we 'll go out and get something to eat, and look in at a low music-hall or something. There are always one or two good turns, and the rest is so incredible I think you 'd be amused.'

'I 'm sure I would be,' she said. Her eyes lit up. 'I love a low music-hall. Oh, Hugh!—you shall show me night-life in the provinces. We 'll go on to the dancing-hell.'

'Hurrah!' he said.

He whistled to Grock; she took his arm; gaily they went off together down the street towards his lodging.

'It is fun to be with you again,' she said, looking up at him out of her greenish-yellow eyes.

He squeezed her arm and his smile broadened. No one was such good value, no one looked so well.

He felt proud and confident, going about with her. She never interfered with him. Her life was lived apart from and unknown to him eleven months out of every twelve; her pursuits, her thoughts were a mystery, had it ever occurred to him to call mystery what neither vexed his mind nor engaged his imagination. They never grew to know each other any better, he might have said, had the possibility of a progressive relationship ever struck him. He knew enough about her. She was all right: not sad, not poor, not bored, not aged or altered as he had vaguely, uncomfortably feared she might be by the abolition during his absence of a husband he had scarcely known. She had written to him: *I have decided to leave George. Too complicated for a letter. I'll explain when I see you. No divorce at present.* By the time he got home the new order was established, she never spoke of him, all rumour of the affair had ceased in London. She had a delightful little house in a mews, and some sort of mild half-time occupation, decorating lamp-shades or selling old furniture or painted wastepaper baskets (he forgot precisely what) in one of those new smart little shops. She had a small fast car and went away for week-ends.

Sometimes when he was alone, and the surprising, the uneasy, the lonely fit came on him, he thought of her: thought that, if she were there, he would really talk to her and feel better; thought that she was his only sister, dreamed of some undefined, all-understanding relationship which should exist between them, supposed that he was very fond of her : suspected, indeed, that he dearly loved her.

' Of course, my dear,' said Norah on the telephone, ' it 's quite all right. It doesn't matter a bit. . . . No, we 've hardly been waiting for you a minute . . .' (the fish, she thought rapidly, was the only thing quite spoiled). She listened, then said : ' Tomorrow ? . . . Well, it would be lovely, but I don't know if I could leave the . . . Well, all right, perhaps for once . . . I 'll tell Gerry, but he never goes out, you know. . . . He hates motoring. Still, I 'll ask him. . . . Terribly nice of Hugh to think of it. . . . Wouldn't he rather just have you ? . . . Who ? What woman who said she knew me ? . . . Oh, Grace Fairfax ? . . . Oh, but how terribly nice of him. She 'd love it. I 'll ring her up. . . . Thank you so much. Have a good time. No, we won't. I 'll leave the key under the mat.'

She opened the door and called through to the kitchen :

' We 'll start now, Florrie. Mrs. Osborne won't be back after all.'

In his study, Gerald heard her.

Of course, he thought, of course : it was that boy again—strolling in and out as if the house belonged to him, so sure of himself, with his damned grin ; taking her off—their guest, *his* guest—without a word of apology, seeing to it that no one else had a chance to get to know her. . . .

Norah put her head in.

'Supper, Gerry. Clare 's not coming. She 's just rung up to say Hugh wanted her to go out with him.'

'Oh,' he said, 'a remarkable display of good manners, I must say.'

'She might have let us know a bit sooner,' conceded Norah equably. 'However, she said they forgot the time. She was very apologetic.'

For the hundredth time it occurred to her that she never had known when to give herself the luxury of taking offence. She had no dignity—was only too willing to smooth things over. She added :

'She 's his sister after all, darling. She really came to see him, I suppose. I 'm sure I don't mind what she does so long as she isn't bored.'

Yes, he would only bore her, he thought bitterly : she had not been able to face the thought of his company, and so had stayed away with a lame excuse. He shrivelled. He desired to turn on Norah.

'I fully realize,' he said icily, 'how tedious my society must be. By all means let her use my house as a hotel.'

And a temperance hotel at that, she thought : but he would not think that funny. . . . A regular glass of port would be so mellowing ; but if she were to urge it, the result would be a biting commentary on the cost of maintaining two boys whom she had (so the suggestion was) insisted on bringing into the world to plague him.

But she wanted to tell him how sorry she was for

his disappointment. He had hoped, she knew, for a little success with Clare. She—and in a lesser and more distorted degree, the boy too—had awakened in him an almost unprecedented impulse to struggle towards a personal relationship. She longed for them to encourage him, grieved to see him dashed and defeated. She put a hand on his shoulder.

'And, darling,' she said, 'they want us to motor into the country for the day to-morrow. I thought I'd ask Mrs. Thompson if she'd take the boys for the afternoon. I would so love to go. I told them you didn't care about expeditions.'

Blundering, foolish creature, he thought with exasperation. . . . He said curtly :

'Did you refuse for me ?'

'No, darling—not exactly.'

'Because I'm quite capable of answering for myself.'

'You'll come, then ?'

'I might.'

'But, darling, that's splendid.' She was discomfited : he was more determined than she had thought. 'Only I was thinking of ringing up Cousin Christopher Seddon to ask if I could bring them to tea. I thought we might play some tennis.'

For there, perhaps, was something they would appreciate, she had been thinking—something she was able to offer them that might not bore them. But for years Gerald had refused to accompany her there.

'Would you mind?'

He made no answer, but gave a kind of snort, expressive, she feared, of cynical amusement, and shrugged his shoulders. . . . 'As if it was I,' she thought, 'who's the snob—not he, poor dear.' Inverted-snobbery complex, Clare would have called it.

'You could browse in the library,' she said hopefully, 'if you wanted to escape.'

But perhaps, she bethought herself, Clare and Hugh were going to perform a double miracle: perhaps they were going to deliver him at one blow from the twin demons with whose disastrous manifestations she had wrestled for years in vain: from his particular form of snobbery; and from that inner voice which, crying to him under social stress 'Escape!' was no sooner heard than, alas, obeyed.

They went in to dinner. Stertorously breathing, red-pawed Florrie moved about the room.

They ate in silence, brooding, dreaming.

The roast chicken, thought Norah, reproached her from its dish: specially ordered for Clare, an extravagance, wasted now.

She dreamed of to-morrow: saw the long avenue of beeches through which they would drive, the deep radiance of mossy grass, the daffodils blowing; saw them all at tea in the great hall. She anticipated the anxious responsibility she would feel in bringing them beneath that roof, the fear lest they seem incongruous, discordant (as she had often felt herself) in face of the something rare, eccentric, haunted with the frustrations of age, with sterile grace, in its inhabitants.

But Clare's beauty would make a harmony : and Hugh had such charm. . . .

Grace would be dumb, of course, but silence never mattered in that house. . . . How extraordinarily nice of Hugh to think of her ; but, also, how queer ! . . . She must ring her up. She would probably get panic and refuse.

He would show them to-morrow, thought Gerald —he would show them. . . .

And he thought, rather extravagantly, of golden lads and girls coming with song to meet him : and everything renewed ; and himself laughing—teasing Clare back, and throwing up his head, like Hugh, to laugh aloud.

The clocks of the town chimed ten o'clock. Tom answered the telephone and brought the message to Grace's bedside.

'Asleep ?' he said.

She did not move or open her eyes.

'Yes,' she said.

He repeated the message. There was a silence. It could not be true.

'I told her I didn't suppose you were up to it,' he said.

'Oh yes.'

'It means a long day. . . .'

'Say I 'd love to come,' she said, lying quite still.

Folly, madness. . . . But one could think it over in the night, and send an excuse to-morrow morning. For the moment, it was such a pleasure to say yes.

'She asked us both,' he said at the door (at least, would have, she 'd said, if only there 'd been room in the car . . .), 'but I told her I 'd arranged to play golf as usual. Pity.'

'Yes. What a pity!'

'I was to tell you particularly that it was *their* invitation.' His voice was questioning, self-conscious.

'I met them this evening in the Park,' she said, buried in the pillow.

'Oh, did you?' he said quickly. 'Have a talk?'

'Just a little one. . ' Bulky and stolid he stood, waiting to be told more. 'Mostly about the weather.'

And the weather, the blessing of the sun, had worked as a kind of charm perhaps; had made them like her—could it be?—like her and wish to see her again.

'Oh, *go!*' she whispered into the pillow.

He went down, repeated his wife's message, exchanged a few pleasant remarks with Norah, and rang off.

Of course, it would do her a world of good, a day in the fresh air. She was so keen on the country.

Their invitation. . . . Young Miller, that meant,

and his sister. Quite a surprise. Well. . . . Probably he 'd have felt a bit uncomfortable with them himself, a whole day like that. Still, it was unfortunate he could not go. Grace might have shown a little more plainly that she thought so. He would have liked to meet the young chap in a friendly way, had often thought of throwing out a casual invitation to dinner ; only Grace was always against any entertaining . . . and of course the circumstances were different—education, position, and all that—awkward to explain properly. Still, this invitation only proved there were no superior 'Varsity airs about him : after all, it was a compliment (though a suitable one) to be asked to meet his sister.

But as he stood by the telephone, a wave of doubt, of envy and unease, rose darkly in his breast.

The clock struck eleven as the audience at the Queen's Theatre ceased to stream out into the streets.

Packed into the last seats in the circle, half-choked with the smell of people and of Virginia tobacco, Clare had been amused ; had marvelled at the kind of jokes with which the low comedian (from Lancashire) brought down the house ; clutched Hugh's knee while the leading lady strained an unyouthful throat and the chorus waved nude mauve dimpled legs ; applauded the acrobatic patter dancing with genuine delight ; had indeed derived entertainment from the whole crude, threadbare, yet in a way vital production, fair sample of the kind which passed through the town and vanished, week after week

'That was an eye-opener,' she said, as they came out into the crowded street. 'Now on, Hugh, on!'

'Right,' he said. 'We 'll do the thing properly and take a tram.'

While they waited for one beneath a lamp-post, they practised a patter dance upon the pavement; and the passers-by stared . . . stared . . . with the bulging, uncompromising stare of the north.

The dancing place was a long, low-ceilinged, ill-ventilated room, lit with a sickly light from lamps enclosed in art shades of coloured silk—orange, red, and purple, elaborately painted with representations of fruit. There was diffused within it a kind of hypocritical decorum, a furtiveness suggesting the repressed and dismal lasciviousness of British non-conformist imaginations. It was vulgar, said Clare, without being funny. She was bored.

'I told you it wouldn't amuse you,' he said.

'Does it amuse you?'

'N-no,' he said. 'Not much. Once in a way one can get some fun out of it—if one 's in good form.'

The term expressed an indefinite state, and was also capable in his vocabulary of a more exact interpretation; not that there was any fixed boundary between the one state and the other, or any appreciable difference. One didn't always need alcohol in order to be at the top of one's form. He added:

Some of these girls are damned good dancers.'

'I never saw such an unamusing collection,' she said. 'I don't see how anybody *could*——'

He laughed with a trace of embarrassment. . . . After all, with a sister one did not refer to these matters in a really personal way.

'They 're not exactly my taste either.'

He thought of Pansy again. She was not here to-night. She was different, with her neatness and pallor, and her curious prettiness of a little animal: an animal at once tame and savage. Like a pretty little monkey she was, with a monkey's pathos. One of these evenings he would find her again.

Clare peered at some length into her pocket mirror, used lipstick and powder-puff, and said:

'Well, let 's dance once, anyway.'

Gracefully, skilfully, they danced the blues. The sight of them gave a momentary spur to the band; but they left the floor at the first encore, without clapping; were seen to eat a ham sandwich apiece at the buffet; and went out.

He heard the clocks strike twelve as he started to walk home after dropping his sister at Norah's door.

He whistled because he felt dispirited; decided to take the longer way home and let a good dose of night air clear his head.

He walked down two little streets and turned into the avenue.

Perhaps he would not see these streets much

longer. In the taxi, Clare had said to him: 'My dear, this is a terrible place. Shall you stay?' And then teasingly: 'Don't the great open spaces call any more?' Little did she know what went on inside him sometimes, the restlessness, the bothered feeling. . . . If only Oliver were to write from wherever he was, abroad, lost, and say 'Join me,' he would be gone to-morrow. . . .

Well, it was no good realizing now how much one missed him.

Now, where was it that woman lived? . . in the middle, somewhere on this side.

With a feeling of discomfort, he pictured her standing alone at the window, watching him go past. And he had never so much as given her a thought. She was a nice odd woman: he wouldn't mind a bit if she turned up to-morrow. It had suddenly seemed such a shame to know she felt like that about the country and not give her the chance of a peep at it.

She had been nice about Grock.

He quickened his pace. The dear old boy would be waiting for him.

The clocks struck one.

Pansy left a dark back street in which shone out, with ambiguous emphasis, a solitary hotel lamp. She walked past the barracks, turned into a street of mean little red-brick and stucco dwellings, and let herself into her brother's house. He had left a candle burning. She took it, made a cursory inspection of the kitchen, raked out the ashes, sniffed. Coming in one night she had smelt burning. Will had thrown a cigarette end down, the edge of the rug was beginning to smoulder. He tried to be tidy, but he hadn't much sense.

How her legs ached ; what a shame it was to have to work as she did, nine-thirty till six on her feet, endlessly shampooing, cutting, waving ; and the tips next to nothing ; and not a good class of shop, she knew that—a nasty cheap little place, a common class of people. . . . It must be months now since she had seen *him* going out of the gent's saloon, the other side of the shop. What a shock that had been! She had felt her heart jump. To think of him there! She had watched for him since in vain. Probably he had found a better-class place now—had been in a hurry that first time, or had nobody to tell him the best place for a gentleman to go. Most likely he went to Louis' now in South Street. She had often thought of trying there for a job in the ladies' part. It was quite the most select in the town. Probably they wouldn't take her, though : she had Enemies in her place, nosey-parkers, who might speak secretly against her. That morning in the shop was the first of the times he hadn't noticed her. Then there was the evening in the Palace Galleries, when he had sat with a crowd of young fellows round him, laughed and danced so gaily, not with her ; and then to-night, coming out of the pictures with a beautiful girl on his arm. . . . Ah! It gave her a kind of pain in the stomach to think of those times when he had not seen her ; or pretended he hadn't. If only she could chance on him when he was alone, and she dared go up to him.

She was dead tired, dead tired. To-morrow she would get home early and have a good long sleep. She went slowly upstairs, past Will's door, heard his heavy regular breathing, trailed on to her own bedroom.

She set the candle on the high deal dressing-table and peered into the mirror. How pretty she was, how pretty ; what a lovely shape were her red lips ! That one to-night in the hotel had told her she ought to go on the films : he had said she could do anything she liked with a face like hers. Ah, but they all said the same sort of things, specially the fat, smooth-spoken, elderly ones. Ugh ! . . . Funny, she never could remember them half an hour afterwards—not their looks, or anything, thank God. One didn't need to think it over : it was all wiped out as if it had never happened, except for the money. That was solid, luckily. But him—she 'd have remembered him all right, and not cared about the money. He had left her there in the street (she thought, anxiously, for the thousandth time), and she saw him offering the money, looking, not green and awkward, but kind and shy, haughty and very polite. Her refusing it, quick, on an impulse, must have shown him she wasn't just an ordinary . . . But was it that she hadn't pleased him ? She gazed at herself again. Like a flower, she thought. Surely nobody could think her bad with a face like hers. Perhaps that 's what he had thought : too frail, too flower-like to touch. She heard him saying, very gently : ' How I hate this for you, Pansy—an exquisite refined creature like you.' He would ask her why. . . . She would explain to him how she 'd always had to struggle, how different she was really, how unhappy. He would understand.

Perhaps he was engaged to be married to that girl : perhaps that was why he hadn't . . . . They made a splendid couple : but she looked hard, not good enough for him, nothing like.

She was seized with a fit of coughing. Yes, she was very delicate, she never got rid of her cough now : far too delicate to go on the films—to do any work really. Supposing she had the pneumonia again next winter. . . . The doctor had ordered her to wear good thick combinations. . . . Was it likely ! She would have liked to tell *him* how seriously the doctor had warned her. Sometimes she wondered if she wasn't in a consumption already. . . . And the face she stared at hung mournfully in vacancy—(like a flower, thought one ; or another, a little monkey).

She started to undress.

Then what would Will do without her ? Only one little job he had had in ten months, and now out of work again and not a hope of anything this summer. It wasn't only that the building trade was in such a bad way : it was poor Will himself : simple he was ; nothing actually wrong, of course, but a bit silly, poor fellow. Nobody wanted to employ him. The very last thing Mother had said was that Will would always need looking after. It was true. Here he was, close on forty, and quite like a child. He was snoring now. . . . Good old Will : he was good to her, he cleaned up the house, cooked his own dinner ; he thought the world of her, never asked questions —hadn't the sense to, thank goodness.

She dropped into her creaking bed, blew out the candle, and, sinking into sleep, saw *him* as she saw him always, in a huge gold and pink ballroom, coming towards her, noble in a tail-coat, a flower in his button-hole, bowing over her. The band struck up. She laid her white ringed hand on his shoulder. Round and round they went in the waltz ; her frock swung out, glittering with diamanté. 'How beautifully you dance, Pansy,' he murmured. 'How delicious your hair smells.' He clasped her to him, and on they went, round and round, dreamily, for ever and ever.

PART IV

PART IV

THE car drew up before the porch, and they all sat still for a few moments, dazed with forty miles of torrential moorland air upon their faces; for Hugh's was the kind of swift, flapping, manly car whose broken windscreen engulfs its occupants in a perpetual gale from the four quarters.

The house was a white stone Georgian block, symmetrical, ample, dignified, with a massive carved and pillared porch. A low stone wall bordered the terrace in front of the house, and a shallow semicircular flight of steps dropped from the centre of it to a sunken garden set with a pattern of formal beds, bright now with wallflowers, primulas, and bordered with low clipped hedges of beech in fresh leaf.

The central paved walk ran down through lines of tall, crowding, rosy tulips to the small circular basin of a lily-pool; and by the water's edge upon an ancient bench of carved Italian stone sat a dark masculine figure. Presently it rose and vanished on stealthy tiptoe into the shrubbery. Norah's heart sank at glimpse of Cousin Christopher in flight from his guests. Perhaps now he would not appear again till after they had left. If Cousin Mary also were to remain *perdue*, as was likely, what was she to do with all these people?—How answer to all of them for her rash and ridiculous action?

They were all climbing out of the car now. Hugh stretched himself, smiling ; his yellow hair stood on end, his face was flushed with wind and sun ; his dog pranced round him with triumphant shouts.

That dog, thought Norah, would be the last straw for Cousin Christopher ; and would Cousin Mary look with indulgence upon Clare's cigarette, and the lips that held it, whose brilliant colour and shape required and received constant public renewal ?

Gerald was striking a match for her. He looked happy. Something both dreamy and eager was in his face—something of youth—and his hair, too, was ruffled, boyish-looking. He had his own charm, thought Norah ; perhaps, if Clare was nice to him, he would continue to forget that he had been brought to visit his wife's county relations.

The air had whipped no colour into Grace's cheeks. She was standing apart from the others, in her special way, solidly planted, still, lonely-looking, a faint smile in lips and eyes as she gazed out over the garden. She had taken off her hat ; and above her drab frock her face was arresting in its waxen pallor. By what happy accident had she lit on that queer greyish dress with its long full skirt, its defined waist-line, its white puritan collar and cuffs ? For once her obstinate indifference to fashion had led her to achieve a personal design. If one were seeing her to-day for the first time, one might think the funny old thing almost . . . what might one think her ? . . . interesting certainly . . . almost a plain beauty.

PART IV

'Let 's wander down the garden,' said Norah; adding without conviction: 'They 're sure to be pottering about somewhere.'

Their footsteps echoing on gravel and stone seemed, thought Grace, to break into a timeless peace. Below the white, gleaming house, the blossoming garden lay spread out within its green hollow, enfolded in girdles of old trees, with the harmonious unreality of a garden of the imagination.

They went through the paved garden, down another flight of steps to a stretch of lawn and a tennis-court. Alone beside the net stood a tall, dark youth. He wore a peach-coloured crêpe-de-chine shirt, open at the throat, and a broad crimson silk handkerchief carelessly knotted in place of a collar; and a pair of flannel trousers of softest grey.

'Who is this vision?' murmured Clare. 'Son of the house?'

'No, there isn't one,' said Norah. 'I can't think who it is.'

He came forward and said in a rich and musical voice, articulating in a clipped, emphatic way:

'How do you do. Which of you is called Norah?' He looked at none of them.

'I am.'

He glanced at her for a second out of a pair of thick-fringed, deep-set, dark eyes, and said, looking away again:

'I 've *just* been *marking* out the tennis-court for you.' He waved his hand towards the marker.

'They *thought* you might want to play.' He dissociated himself from the suggestion with a shrug.

'We did bring racquets,' murmured Norah.

'You 'll find it very soft. Also uneven. However '—he smiled with sudden charm—'I 've made you some beautiful straight lines.'

He did not let one help him, thought Norah, out of his shyness, if shyness it were. Standing with his head down like that, in utter repudiation of their presence, he made one feel clumsy and tongue-tied.

'I *don't* know what you want to do,' he said. 'Will you amuse yourselves? You were to *fish*, if you *wanted* to, the old gentleman said. He was *somewhere* about, but he 's disappeared. I *don't* think he wants to see you at present.'

'Are you staying here, then?' asked Norah.

'Yes,' he said. 'I often do. I 'm their grandson.'

'Their *what*?' Her mind made rapid incredulous darts and remained blank.

'My name is Ralph Seddon.'

'I am—I was Norah Seddon—I 'm a cousin.'

'Really?' He looked at her without interest.

She had a sudden flash of memory.

She exclaimed 'Oh!' remembering some rumour of an only son, vanished or dead—some old grief or disgrace, never referred to—a story long finished before the time of her youthful visits.

'I 'm *quite* genuine, if that 's what you 're wondering,' he said briefly, surveying them all beneath his lids.

'I didn't know,' murmured Norah. 'I—— '

'Why should you?' he said lightly, turning the corners of his mouth down in a pseudo-smile. 'Is it important? I as*sume* you 're *some*body's grandchild yourself, though I don't know whose. . . .'

There was general, rather uncomfortable laughter, in which she joined, feeling herself snubbed.

'Well—— ' she said, hoping to appease him with a friendly smile, 'we 're relations, then.'

He bowed abruptly from the waist.

What an awkward situation, what a difficult young man! . . . She turned to the others for assistance, and was confronted by a variety of unhelpful facial expressions. Only Hugh had remained apparently unimpressed: he seemed not even to be listening. He had picked up the tennis balls and was juggling with a skill that might have roused envy in a professional breast.

'Take anybody on,' he cried.

They all looked; and the tension thus eased, he added, after a moment, still juggling: 'Did anybody say fishing?'

'Yes,' said Norah eagerly. 'The lake is full of trout.'

'I shall go and stir 'em up.'

He sent all the balls up one after another to a last record height, let them drop, and said, turning rather shyly to Grace:

'Shall we try for a trout or two?'

A flush of pleasure swept up into her cheeks, and she replied swiftly:

'I'd like to watch you.'

'What about you, Clare?' said he.

'I'll fish,' she said, 'if there's a boat, and somebody to row me.'

Perhaps her eyes slid for a second towards the romantic youth. But he said with an air of deep relief:

'That's all right, then. The rods are down in the boat-house. I expect you know the way.'

And he went away, without another look, up the garden, walking with bent head and stumbling, uncertain stride: the gait of one accustomed in his walks to look within himself, rather than at the path he follows.

'I'll row you,' said the voice of Gerald, a voice so new and strange in quality that '*Well—*' said his wife, emphatically, to herself, and got no further, caught in a general tangle of surprises.

She conducted them to the lake-side, provided tackle, helped Clare and Gerald to embark, pushed off the boat, watched Hugh for a moment while he whipped out his line and started to cast from the bank with nonchalant skill, waved to Grace—then sat down on the grass in the sun, took book and half-knitted stocking from her bag; laid down first one, then the other; stretched herself out and sank into a peaceful doze.

PART IV

Little by little and in silence they had reached the farther end of the lake. Grace sat down in a little clearing where a few bluebells mingled with the fresh young grass, and a fringe of larches made a shade. Happiness stole over her.

Some essence of the spirit of the spring day seemed to hover, brooding and shining, upon the long, sunny stretch of water. The lake was girdled with trees and bushes, and wild song welled out as if from the throats of hundreds and hundreds of choral branches. The unfolding leaves covered the boughs with a manifold variety of little shapes. Knots, hearts, points, clusters of rosettes, dots and tapers of budding foliage, made up embroideries of infinite complexity in jade, in greenish-silver, in honey-yellow; but some were tinged with a russet flame, haunting the eye with an autumnal prophecy.

He stood in front of her at the water's edge casting this way and that with easy, graceful movements of wrist and forearm. He fished with the unemphatic assurance, the careless rightness, which were the special qualities of his whole physical being. How satisfactory, she thought, to be made thus, clear and unambiguous, and not as most people were, in a muddle of conflicting features and indeterminate results: with the eyes of a poet and the hands of a butcher, the frame of a prize-fighter and the lined brow, the spectacled eyes of a scholar.

The thought of Tom came to her; how he would have enjoyed this day's fishing. Tom was a fussy and ungainly angler and a malign fate ordered his expeditions disastrously. But again she thought, almost guiltily, how he would have enjoyed it and talked about it afterwards.

Gentle birth, property, family, the stately homes of England—she told herself that Hugh's appearance suggested such terms. He was "above her station": he knew it, and was taking special pains to make her feel at ease. . . .

At this moment he turned round, smiling with the greatest friendliness; and an exclamation of poignant pleasure and surprise arose within her as she received in a flash, through all her being, the impress of his essential self. She saw him with overpowering clarity, a being of unparalleled individuality, set apart from everybody else she had ever known or would ever know.

'Poof,' he said, 'hot!'—and he threw off his coat. 'Not even a nibble yet,' he said. 'Aren't you bored?'

'No. I do like to watch you fish.'

He laughed, and said with a quick, amused glance: 'Funny thing to like.' He added: 'Cigarettes in my coat pocket. Help yourself.'

'I don t really smoke.'

But she took up the coat and felt in the pockets with a warm sense of the intimacy of the action. It gave her pleasure to touch his possessions.

Soon he glanced round again and said, smiling

'Remember that coat of mine you mended?'

'Yes. Did it split again?'

'Rather not. It was splendid.'

Her happiness rose and entrenched her more firmly. She took out a flat, gold cigarette-case engraved with a monogram.

'What a lovely case!'

'Yes, it was a twenty-firster.'

She opened it and read the inscription: *Hugh George Miller, Esq., Presented by the Tenants of the Willowfields Estate on the occasion of his Twenty-first Birthday*; and she felt the certainty of her happiness waver and thin out. The imposing words opened a window into a world closed to Grace Fairfaxes.

'Is that your home, Willowfields?'

'Mm.'

'It sounds nice.'

'Yes, nice country. I don't go there much.'

'Don't you like it?'

'Love it.'

She was silent while he moved a few paces and cast again far out into the lake. He was an adept at withholding personal information; perhaps it was natural reserve, perhaps he was bored with her questions; perhaps, since it was never safe to judge by appearances, he had a past of secrets and sorrows to conceal. But he continued of his own accord:

'Only, I always seem to be somewhere else. Abroad, or somewhere; all over the place. I'd like to get down now for the fishing: but I don't know how much more the office will swallow. I 've already tried it on a good few times since the season started.'

He grinned, and then tried to check himself—remembering Tom again, she supposed.

She said, fingering his cigarette case :

'Are your mother and father alive ?'

'Rather.' He seemed to imply with amusement how particularly alive they were. 'Father, mother, two young brothers, and sister Clare, all alive and kicking.'

She could not picture him in his family character : there was something peculiarly unattached about him. It seemed unlikely that he was a dutiful son.

'And you 're the eldest ?'

'I am.'

'And when you were twenty-one, were there great rejoicings ?'

'Oh, well'—he looked surprised and embarrassed—'there was a sort of beano. Of course, it 's all rot, but they expect it, you know. They enjoy it.'

The silence that ensued was uncomfortable. The little rift in her security seemed now a vast and ragged breach through which she beheld him dwindling and disappearing from her down alien vistas. There seemed now nothing more to say.

Suddenly he was tense, winding in a taut line. She saw the leaping fish come up and watched him unhook it and lay it on the grass.

'A good two-pounder,' he said. He looked up and smiled contentedly.

'Poor little fish,' she said, 'enjoying its life a moment ago. Now, where is it?'

'Gone to glory.' He turned a laughing eye on her. 'Does your heart bleed for the poor little chap?'

'It does, rather.'

'Cheer up. No more murder for to-day. This grass looks too inviting.'

He put down his rod and came and stretched himself at full length on the ground beside her. He lit a pipe and lay back, puffing and staring at the sky. He did not suggest moving: he did not seem bored at all.

Far away she saw the boat move into view and pass across the landscape: Gerald straining at the oars, Clare standing up in the bows, her head bare and bright in the sun. Silently as figures on a screen, they disappeared again, behind a little island of trees. She smiled to herself. They too were an incongruous couple. He said:

'This is extremely pleasant. I do like water. I must have water. Wherever I end up it will be by a good bit of water.'

Her mind leapt ahead and saw him older, in some strange place of his own choosing, some strange woman by him, his chosen wife . . . the chance acquaintance, the commonplace occasion of such an afternoon as this, long, long forgotten.

He said: 'I shall never make a good business-man.'

'I'd rather you didn't.'

'Why not? It 's as good as anything else.'

She caught a hint of something new and unexpected in the words and the tone . . . boredom, discouragement: what he would call being fed up. What had he had in his life?

After a silence he said, dreamily:

'Where 's old Grock? Rabbiting, I suppose, and won't be back for hours. Silly old idiot, he does enjoy a day in the country.'

'Yes, it 's lovely for him.'

'Haven't you got a dog?'

'No——,' she paused, and added with a deep flush, 'I had a puppy, a little mongrel I bought in the street. But he died.'

Something in her voice made him say swiftly, abruptly: 'Bad luck.'

She had an impulse to tell him that never before had she been able to speak to any one of that ridiculously disproportionate little tragedy; but the words would not come. He said:

'I wonder if our host and hostess will turn up before we go?'

'Yes; it was queer about the grandson, wasn't it?'

'Mm. It was bad luck on that chap.' (There was something about him that had given him a queer feeling of Oliver: a trick of the voice—a gesture.)

'I wonder what it was all about?'

'Don't know, I am sure, but you could see he thought it was none of our business.'

So he had been conscious of the situation, sorry for the boy: deliberately helped him by feigning indifference to his predicament.

'He 's handsome.'

'Queer-looking chap. Bit too aesthetic-looking for my taste.'

So there was a limit to what was aesthetically permissible. He himself wore becoming colours and let his hair wave; but the other overstepped the bounds presumably, with his crêpe-de-chine and his pretty scarf.

'I thought he was posing, rather,' she ventured. 'He needn't have made us all so uncomfortable.'

'Mm. A bit conceited, perhaps. It 's a phase. I was the same at Oxford.' He chuckled. 'I thought I was the hell of a chap.'

After a silence she said:

'I think these people must be nice to leave us to enjoy this without any supervision—instead of plodding round everywhere with us and making us see they wished we 'd go. . . . I think this is true hospitality.'

He nodded.

'Some gardens give you a special feeling. It 's when they are made by people who—I don't know —who have a sort of affinity—just as some people have with birds. Or it 's the difference between a work of art and a clever exercise. You can tell at once. This is the special kind. It was the same where I used to live in Sussex—my father's garden.'

'Whereabouts did you live?'

'A tiny country village, just under the downs.' (The turfy, tender-looking down-shoulders, pasturing the dark flocks of the juniper bushes.) 'My father was vicar. I'm still homesick,' she finished, with a smile.

'Sussex is nice.'

She looked down at him. He seemed to be reflecting: he leaned on one elbow, and his clear eyes stared unblinkingly ahead of him . . . his shirt-sleeves were rolled back to the elbow, and she saw the muscular forearm and the strong blue veins running beneath the white skin. She was conscious of his length and grace, of the fine shoulders beneath the thin white stuff of his shirt. Seen thus in repose, the rather untidy lips folded, the eyes thoughtful, his face and form were memorable. Comely was the word for him . . . a comely young man.

He stretched out an idle hand and picked a bluebell, sniffed it and put it in a buttonhole of his shirt.

She said: 'Where I lived, the beech woods were full of bluebells. You never saw such a sight. They almost made your eyes ache with the blue. I've scarcely seen a bluebell since I left my home. And the primroses—I think of them every spring . . . you simply can't imagine. . . . I wish I could show you.'

She was back again, walking up the steep, chalky

lane that wound up behind the village to the beech wood. The thorn flowered in the hedges and the grass beneath gleamed and foamed with the moon-coloured profusion of the flower which she called milk-wort or Star-of-Bethlehem. She went into the wood and saw the first wild flash of the bluebells. They ran away into the shadowy distance on every hand, flooding the ground with urgent blue—with a blue that cried like the sound of violins. She sat beneath the smooth, snake-striped, coiling branches of her chosen tree, and saw beneath her a creaming tide of primroses, clotting the mossy slopes, brimming in the hollows.

But these experiences could never be imparted: one could never explain to any one their supreme importance; say that bluebells made a musical outcry; that primroses, with their warm, faint, sweetish smell, were the milk of the earth. These disjointed words to this young man were all she had ever spoken aloud in praise of her memories.

He looked at her surreptitiously out of the corners of his eyes, noticing her for the first time that day. She was staring ahead of her, and he felt a kind of dreaming intensity in her expression and her pose. He saw her full firm breast outlined in the grey stuff of her frock as she sat above him; the strong modelling of a white and graceful neck. He wondered how she had looked as a young girl: quite attractive, perhaps. He supposed she was getting on now. He said to himself that she was a rum 'un; rather intriguing, rather nice; and somehow he kept on feeling sorry for her. He said:

'Do you go back sometimes?'

She opened her narrow eyes.

'Where? Home? Oh, no, I couldn't.' Her voice was vehement. 'Besides, the expense . . . we only have one holiday a year.'

She stated this not plaintively, but as a simple fact; and he had a moment of uncomfortable perception of the lives of those compelled by circumstance to remain in one place year in, year out, whether they liked it or no.

She continued:

'And up till now I have always had to go—somewhere I didn't want to . . . my mother-in-law, in fact.' She made a confidential grimace. 'However, she's dead now.'

The triumph in her tone made him burst out laughing. She was like a child, half ashamed of herself. She clasped her hands together and cried:

'And this year—this year I'll go where I like . . . by myself . . . where I like.'

He sat up and watched her, highly amused.

'Where's that?' he said.

'I'm not sure, yet. I'll find it.'

She felt in the depths of her being a thrill, a rush of expectation. She stared at the water and saw, as if upon its shining surface, the summer months stretching out before her, bearing a promise as rich and strange as any in the years of youth.

PART IV

' It 's going to be a glorious summer,' she said.

She saw in dim, chaotic vision, what she would seek, and find : a southern landscape : cottage gardens crammed with flowers ; cornfields bordered by great elms ; dog-roses and bryony in the leafy lanes ; gentle slopes crowned with copses ; clear brooks set with iris plants and bulrushes, running between plumy willows through the pastures.

' Tired ? ' he said, after a pause. ' Want to move ? '

' Oh, no.'

' Sure ? I was forgetting you 've been laid up.'

She flushed swiftly at such proof of his thoughtfulness.

' No, no,' she said softly. ' I 'd like never to move. . . .'

They sat on. He watched her again. She sat so still she hardly seemed to breathe. She was the most quiet person he had ever known ; she made a sort of peaceful feeling. . . .

At last he stretched himself and said :

' Where 's everybody ? '

As if in answer to his words, the boat slid into view again, with Gerald rowing towards the opposite shore and Clare winding in her line ; and Norah emerged from the trees and came down to the landing and cried across the water : ' Tea, tea ! '

After tea they played tennis. Norah and Hugh

played against Clare and Gerald ; and Grace sat on a bench by the edge of the court and watched them. They made a well-matched four : Norah played a steady, feminine game ; Clare was graceful and erratic ; Gerald re-discovered an exasperating skill with cuts and top spins ; and Hugh was all over the court, smashing furiously at the net, volleying from every position, running at top speed to the back line to send a wild lob backwards over his head, cursing himself, laughing, applauding his partner.

After two sets he came and threw himself down by Grace.

'Gosh! Out of condition. . . . Can't serve for nuts.' He wiped his brow, patted his diaphragm, and turned a bright eye on her. 'Now you must play.'

'I can't play.'

'Rot! We 'll take 'em on and win every game. I 'll do all the running about. You stand in one place, and if anything comes near you I 'll yell "leave it," and you just duck. Have your shoes got heels? Take 'em off and play in your stockings. I often do. We 'll get on splendidly. Come on. I 've eaten too much. Must work it off.'

Grace found herself on the court, racquet in hand, shoeless, giggling, while he encouraged her and leapt about her.

The game was resumed.

Norah stood by herself and looked at them. She said to herself, 'I am left out again.' There was no doubt she was not wanted at all. Gerald had forgotten her and was so happy. He had rolled up his shirt-sleeves and was vying with Hugh in boyish zeal and good-humoured shouts. Lucky that nobody had suggested that husband and wife should play together this time . . . still, nobody *had* suggested it . . . no, she did not mind in the least. Her thoughts flew to her children, and she wished she had brought them : such a treat for them, and they would not have bothered any one : she could have taken them off to the quarry to look for birds' nests. They liked to be with her. She heard in her mind's ear Robin's pipe, anxious and frequent : 'Can we come with you, mum ? Mum, will you play too ?' Yes, they preferred her company . . for a little while longer they would prefer it.

Was she a successful mother, she asked herself—did she really exert herself for them as much as she should ? How differently, how spectacularly, she had imagined her children ! But that was in the days of Jimmy, when she had wanted a son who should really be Jimmy himself, re-created through her, her own possession from the womb : so that the ache about his past should be appeased. Actually, motherhood had proved in anticipation chiefly a physical process ; in realization—not overwhelmingly glorious : an enormous worry and responsibility, an enormous hindrance to liberty : a hot and cold perspiration when they shrieked, nervous terror mounting to panic and something like hatred when they went on shrieking, and an acknowledgment to oneself that they were quite ordinary babies : and then month by month, the growing feeling of being bound to them in one's very bowels, so that if they had a pain one had a pain oneself.

She looked again at the players. What had Gerald and Clare made of their afternoon together ; and the other two, what could they have found to say to one another ? They seemed all to have made such progress during her absence. She thought suddenly : 'Something is happening to everybody in this place except me. . . .' Some influence was at work, rapid and mysterious. Perhaps they were all falling in love . . . what an idiotic idea . . . or perhaps they might all be a trifle tight. Supposing Gerald were to come and tell her he had fallen in love with Clare . . . she hoped he would not. Apart from the imprudence and general upset, no happiness could come from loving Clare. Jimmy had said that long ago. She roused a perpetual sense of expectancy ; in a moment, one thought, she was going to give something that no one else could give : and always, she gave nothing. These were Jimmy's words : though fascinated (one suspected) he had not liked her much.

Where were the old people ; and that curious, rude, offended boy, where was he ? Their absence seemed almost sinister. It was as if from their hiding-places they were busy casting spells over all except herself. The boy had started the plot, the dream, with his unreal statement ' I am their grandson '; now the excitement grew. As for herself, she was left out; but—her heart gave a jerk at the thought—left out, perhaps, on purpose, and so given her part, drawn into the unreality. For one afternoon, no ties, no dependants. She was free as a ghost.

She turned her back on the four, and escaped to find an old self among remembered haunts.

Down through the wood where the path was slippery with mud and moss, now, as in old days; (she had fallen down inelegantly, flat and sprawling, and Cousin George in the Navy had picked her up and then kept his arm round her—to make sure she did not fall again). Along the lake path, over the little bridge at the farther end where the burn ran out again, into the cow pasture, up the hill to the birds'-nesting quarry. She was free and seventeen years old, swinging along. She wore a white, floppy, crêpe cotton blouse made by herself and smocked in red silk, and a pleated red skirt and a black patent-leather belt tight and trim round her waist. What an extraordinary costume . . . it had seemed all right then, very becoming. ' What a pretty figure,' Cousin Mary had said, patting her. ' You 're as pretty as paint,' said George. She had had just the right looks for a cousin in the Navy. Jimmy had transformed her through pain and passion into something more suitable to him, more interesting. Now, though her figure was still nice, her face was ageing. Gerald was not the kind of man one stayed pretty for.

Here was the quarry, looking just the same, smothered in brambles. How strange to come back here alone to find it, and to think of old days : to be caught at the quarry's edge by the knowledge of time and change. She looked back at the girl in the white blouse and saw her so different, so unconnected with her present self, that there seemed no link at all. But from now on, whatever of change life held, there would be no new way for her to live it, no new experiments or experiences. She would feel the same inside now, till she died . . . and there was that nuisance Gerald, skipping about on a tennis lawn, falling in love. . . .

Agile, sure-footed, leaping down through the prickly bushes, tearing her stockings. . . . George had called 'Mind out,' and lost his balance, and come slithering down on top of her. Grimacing and feeling himself carefully behind, he had remarked (he had a slight lisp) : 'Thtill got the theat of my panth, hooray.' That had seemed a pretty daring remark, and she had giggled, as was fitting. Also he had said, to frighten her, 'Look out for thnakes,' when of course there weren't any. Then they had sat in a comfortable, scooped-out shelf, draped round with long, leafy tentacles of bramble, and he had explained to her his theory of the fourth dimension and spoken highly of the works of Mr. H. G. Wells. He was one of those enlightening cousins—not only in an intellectual way. He had suggested kissing her, just to see what it was like. She had told him it was all right. After that, he had kissed her a few more times (what shy and innocent kisses !) and given her, at parting, a naval button made into a brooch.

He had gone down with his ship at the battle of Jutland. But by that time Jimmy had come, and gone for ever ; so that no other death, not even poor George's, seemed particularly important.

But she saw him now very clearly—his sturdy form, his cheerful sailor's face, touched by transfiguration in the distance : as much alive—or dead, poor George—as the girl beside him.

She walked on, savouring her solitude, treading with light and supple movements over the rough turf. When she was a young girl she had danced with such a particular, swimming grace, that she had actually thought of embarking on a professional training. The war and being a V.A.D. had put a stop to all that. Pity. It was her one claim to distinction. But Gerald, from some twist of puritanism or jealousy, disliked even a reference to her dancing days. Yet sometimes, when she tried to see through his eyes, it seemed to her that it was that very happy rhythm in her, the simplicity of response to life that perhaps it expressed, which had made him need her and say so pitifully, almost directly after their first meeting—two worn-out relics of war service thrown up by the Armistice—that she must marry him.

And ever since he had tried to do her down.

She stopped, and said aloud: 'Why should I live with my enemy?'

She would go on walking and walking, and perhaps she would never come back.

The whole of Christopher Seddon's collection of clocks struck seven o'clock. They sounded from every part of the house with a variety of voices, harsh or musical—a few chiming in unison, most of them treading on each other's heels. The friendly voice, the warning voice, the jocular, the nervous, the complacent, the exasperating, the malicious one that woke you in the night—all awoke and gave tongue. Last of all, from the centre of the house, came the huge and weary one, summing up (thought Ralph Seddon, listening in his room) with an absolute pessimism, subduing the many different voices of humanity with: *All is vanity.*

Subject for a poem, he thought; or a symbolical poetic drama in one act. But rather trite. He whispered: 'I must write, I must write.' He must justify now, this very summer, that faith in him which the letter in his pocket expressed. He took it out again and read the last lines:

I shall never write anything now, but it's obvious you will; especially since you survived your time at Oxford without publishing—and without wrecking yourself with a hopeless love affair. I advise you to stick to people of your OWN sort, because whatever they do to you, you can talk about it to them—explain yourself—use their own weapons against them—and that 's a comfort. It doesn't matter to be hurt in your own way—in fact, though I hate to admit it, it may profit a man. But NON-UNDERSTANDING—the hoof unconscious—that's too brutal and too bloody.

You ask me if I am happy. I don't know yet. *Meanwhile be you happy in your ancestral retreat : but don't stay in it too long. Art does* not *thrive upon a cloistered virtue, whatever you may think now. See everything, try everything. You have the natural integrity to stand no matter what. That 's (partly) why I love you and (chiefly) why I have faith in your future. Some learn honesty when parents, schools, etc., have done their worst : but you, I feel, were born with it,—though of course your lack of parents has given you an advantage. You are the first person I have believed in since Oxford, when I believed—in myself, I suppose. Write to me.—O.*

Underneath was scribbled, in a hurried, irregular hand: *Forgive all this sermonizing etcetera. I am not like that really. Thank you, Ralph, for being so sweet to me that evening at the party. It made my visit more pleasure almost than pain. When may I see you again? Will you come to Italy in June?*

He put the envelope back in his pocket. He must answer it at once, and then, how time would drag until his answer arrived! No excitement was so curiously penetrating, so concentrated and instantaneous, as that caused by the sight of the letter one awaited, lying sealed and pregnant upon the dark table.

He looked out of the window and saw those people still on the tennis-lawn. Now and then their voices came up to him. When would they go? How he loathed them! They had forced him to explain his presence, and then gaped at him and tied him up with self-consciousness and then expected him to join in their jolly fun . . . thought him rude, probably, for making no pretence of joining in. Yes, he had been exposed by an idiot of a woman, helpless in his ghastly shyness. How like a woman! He had seen one of them, the pretty one, smiling: laughing at him, no doubt.

As he watched, he saw the long, bowed figure of the old gentleman going down the steps, moving with his odd, stealthy stride towards them. And then his grandmother came out of the house, dressed in a flowing, flowered lilac silk, and a vast beribboned straw hat, perched quivering on her white hair. She went down to the garden and wandered among the beds, pausing and stooping now and then over the flowers.

Ah, she was the only woman who was all right. She was impregnable in her tower of deafness. She would go on stooping over her flowers, and nobody would know what she thought about, and nobody would try to recall to her the old days; (for you could not shout at the top of your voice about them: he knew enough to know that they were not that kind).

And when he looked at her he thought her so accomplished, so rare and beneficent, so wise with so few words, so courageous (bearing, as it were, the last fruits of some long-past necessity for courage) that it seemed miraculously fitting that in her old age it should be granted to her to stoop in unbroken silence above her flowers. . . .

He sat down and wrote his letter and addressed it in his neat Oxford hand. It lay on the hall table ready for the post: *Oliver Digby*, *Esq.*—with a London address.

The shadows lengthened on the lawn. White-bearded, pallid of eye and cheek, unsteady of stride, Christopher Seddon crept towards his guests.

He offered his hand to them each in turn, limply, in silence, averting his eyes. He summoned no social smile. He made them feel nervous.

'Have you enjoyed yourselves?' he said at last. His voice was faint.

It was Clare who answered, composedly, while the others murmured corroboration.

'We have, indeed. We 've fished and played tennis, and eaten the most delicious strawberries. They 're the first I have had this year. I suppose this lovely weather has brought them on.'

'Hot-house.'

'What did you say?'

'Hot-house.'

He closed his eyes rapidly as if to dismiss her from his field of vision; then addressed Gerald:

'Norah's husband, aren't you? Where is she?'

Nobody knew.

Hugh said shyly, but with an engaging smile:

'I caught you a fat trout for your supper, sir.'

'Thank you.' A gleam shot for the first time from beneath his hollowed brows.

'I hope we haven't been an awful bore, rampaging all over the garden. It was frightfully nice of you to let us come.'

'And now,' said Clare, 'we must find Norah and be off.'

'You must all stay to supper,' said Cousin Christopher, faintly but distinctly.

'Oh, good,' cried Hugh, covering any silence there might have been. 'Then I can fit in a bathe. May I bathe? I saw there was a diving-board.'

'Ah, yes, a bathe. . . . Are you equipped?'

'Am I what?'

'Equipped . . . with a garment?'

'Oh! no. But anything will do, I don't mind.' (He seldom gave his attention to equipment.) . . . 'We might all bathe if we could get fitted out. What do you think?' He turned to the others.

Gerald and Clare thought they would like to bathe. Hugh turned hopefully to his host. The bounty of a house that had provided fishing-tackle, tennis-balls, and hot-house strawberries could not, he felt, find bathing apparel a stumbling-block.

'I seem to remember,' murmured Mr. Seddon, almost smiling, 'in times past, lakefuls of nephews of my wife's. I dare say there are garments put away. Nothing for ladies. . . .' He winced.

'Oh! I can wear any boy's thing,' said Clare, observing her hips and thighs complacently.

Hugh turned to Grace.

'You oughtn't to, I 'm afraid,' he said doubtfully, 'not on top of 'flu.'

'No! No!' She shook her head vigorously, laughing. At his instigation she had run about hitting at tennis-balls and missing them, but not even he should make her step into the lake, her Edwardian limbs encased in a one-piece male swimming suit.

He swept them all after him as he led the way back to the house, talking easily, abolishing difficulties, unconcernedly mingling incongruous elements by dint of sheer enthusiasm for activity. She heard him inquire of the silent and peculiar figure at his side if he were sure he wouldn't have a quick dip too; if he ever got any duck or snipe over the water; telling him what kind of fly he had used for his trout; saying how absolutely topping the garden was—and weren't there some Roman remains somewhere near? . . .

Soon the faint voice of his companion gathered a little strength, floated back to her in fragments.

'Much bothered' . . . she heard . . . 'a rapid growth of water weed coming up again this year . . . thinking of getting an expert . . .'

And soon : 'The history of the county I am engaged on . . . some difficulty . . a few illustrations and maps . . . might care to see the kind of thing . . .'

By the time they reached the house, they were pacing shoulder to shoulder, talking as men talk once they have recognized in each other the mutual background of country landowners. Grace caught the expression on Christopher Seddon's face: a sort of dawning liveliness was touching its mournful clayey contours, so that he began to seem very nearly (but not quite) what Hugh—probably owing to the beard—certainly thought him : simple and kindly, a dear old gentleman.

When the sun was setting, the dark and serious young man walked out of the house and down towards the lake.

He listened. They were still about, those people—bathing now. Their loud voices called and hung on the windless evening air. A woman cried out, with an ascending inflection : 'Icy ! Icy ! Icy !—' and laughter followed ; and in silence he heard the crystalline splash of a diver. He took the lake path through the trees, where already there was twilight ; and blackbirds were singing. When he came to the lake's edge he peered round a tree-trunk and saw the fair young man standing solitary upon the bank, gazing into the water. The others had disappeared. He was a shape of beauty and repose : leaning his weight slightly, easily, upon one foot, the other thrust a little outward, a hand on his hip, languid but firm —a pose for a sculptor.

A pose for a sculptor ; and yet, thought Ralph, the attitude was curiously individual. He had seen it before. Somewhere in the past he had seen that form—not in the flesh, but in representation, drawn or photographed. . . . His mind flashed suddenly to Oliver's album that they had looked through together that day in London . . . among the many groups and places of Oliver's undergraduate days, a page of rocks and sea-coast and bathers, and somewhere on that page this figure alone, looking down into the water. He had noticed it specially, because Oliver, contrary to his custom, had written beneath it neither name nor initial ; and because something that seemed romantically significant in the look of him, lonely, and turned away, had called to mind that poem, *On An Athlete Dying Young*. . . . 'One of my hearty acquaintances,' Oliver had said in answer to his inquiry—and that was all.

The figure stirred suddenly, as if roused from musing, dived, cutting the water clear and deep ; emerged, dried itself vigorously with a small towel, rubbed its hair up on end, put on shirt and trousers, started whistling, and lounged away.

Should he run after him, thought Ralph—approach this other walking by himself in the garden ?

But no . . . better to be alone: to indulge the lonely mood, to wait for image and phrase to arise and take shape in the teeming mind.

Empty now was the landscape, air and water steeped in the same nacreous essence of draining light. The last of the sun still hid among the tree-trunks. Light in the evening woods stands still, stands still in golden shapes of semi-transparency. (Remember this.) . . . See beneath the glass-still, silk-skinned water, the reflections, solid-seeming, another world. *O World intangible, we touch thee*. . . . Lean down and see your own face looking back at you, floating wraith-like among roots and foliage. *And your own footsteps meeting you, And all things going as they came*. . . .

It had all been said. . . . Be more complex, more elaborate. Consciousness is a cut crystal with a million million facets: how to apprehend and discriminate and gather together: problem.

There were once two lovers who wandered by a pool. They kneeled by the brink and looked down and saw their own reflections. He held her with his arm; she turned her face to his. But, as their lips met, a shoal of fish came darting through the water and shattered their image into a thousand pieces; and when the surface was still again, it was empty of their faces: they were gone.

So, in that moment, out of one image of reality,

three were born: three worlds, or dreams, were made. There was the dream of two happy lovers; and in the pool another dream, where human shadows made symbols of love and life: love wavering and frustrated at the very apex of fulfilment: life scattered and fleeting. And the third was the world of the fishes: beings sentient in their own element, darting from the dark alarm of alien lives into their own separateness again.

Something might be made of that, in an irregular, wandering rhythmical pattern. This might be the line to pursue: to see one reality and turn it inside out again and again, making of one many, and all conflicting; and ending with a question mark. . . . But Pirandello had done this, and Oliver said it was tiresome.

Write a play. Revive the poetic drama, but on new lines: no Elizabethan pastiche. Let the age speak. Catch the complex and subtle rhythms of speech and action peculiar to modern consciousness; and yet be universal, be simple and direct. Leave symbolism alone. It has no guts—transforms live flesh and blood into a sawdust parcel of tainted literary and cinematographic devices.

Yes, one must live first, go everywhere, explore everything: then suck out the life-blood of experience, lay bare the quick of joy and pain on paper.

'I will wander over the whole world.

'I will keep a notebook of extraordinary wisdom and beauty to be published after I die young.

'Besides writing poetry I will know everything about music, painting, sculpture, architecture.

'I will go nowhere, but retire from the world now and live as a hermit, absorbed and dissolved in nature; with no human contacts to blur and hinder the intensity of my concentration.

'I will be in love for ever. . .'

He pressed his hand against the envelope in his pocket. . . . Yes, but was it this one? Sometimes it seemed not this one but another, an unknown. Sometimes he felt as if he could never love, did not want to love, was not capable of it. Sometimes it seemed that if the emotion within him was not to suffocate him, he must fling off all restrictions, burst through all local habitations and names, and be free, and be in love with all things, and embrace the whole of creation at once.

'I am all air and fire, burning, burning. . . . I am dark and secret, capable of every vice. . . . I am too young, too old. . . .'

Down the lake-path came a woman running. She was the one called Norah, who had been so enraging. She was flushed, panting; and her eyes looked dark and wide-open. She caught sight of him as she ran past, and stopped with a startled exclamation.

'I must hurry, I must hurry,' she said. She looked round vaguely, and seemed to be speaking to herself. Like the white rabbit, he thought.

'Why?' he said, leaning against his tree-trunk and feeling that this time the advantage was his.

'I went a long way, a fearfully long way, much farther than I meant, and then I suddenly realized I must go back. I don't know what the time is, and they 'll be looking for me, and—all sorts of things. We must get back.'

'Back where?'

'Back—home—back to the town.' He thought she gave a quick shudder. 'Where are they all?'

'They 're all right. You needn't worry about them. They 've been bathing and goodness knows what. I expect you 've been asked to supper.'

'Oh! . . .' She reflected, and then, with a curious expression: '*Gerald* bathing? . . . And Grace? I shouldn't be surprised. . . . How funny!' She started to laugh, but not mirthfully. 'Well—what it is to have young ideas! I dare say they haven't even missed me. Oh, dear!' She took a deep breath. 'And I 'm dead beat.'

She seemed to wake up suddenly and gazed at him out of bright brown eyes—(rather nice eyes).

'Tell me, who are you? Why does everything seem queer to-day? I 'm sorry I made you cross, but you needn't have been so nasty.'

'I 'm sorry,' he said, flushing a little. His voice sounded for a moment young, sincere, distressed.

'Is it true you are their grandson?'

'Yes, it 's true. At least, in point of fact, *her* grandson. My father was her son.'

'Was she married twice, then ? Fancy my not knowing ! '

'I think not. She had lovers, I suppose you know : or at least a lover.'

He threw all the nonchalance at his command into his tone and expression : for most likely she was the sort of woman who would be shocked. But she did not wince at all ; she only went on looking bewildered.

'Lovers ! Oh, was that it ? . . . Didn't Cousin Christopher mind ? '

He stared at her, laughed, and shrugged his shoulders.

'Oh, I think not. He 's quite civilized.' (So that was the way modern young men talked.) 'I dare say he followed her example. They were quite figures once in London, you know—in whatever corresponded to Bloomsbury in the naughty 'nineties.' (Now what on earth did he mean by that ?) 'I don't know how they arranged the offspring question, but I presume they had an understanding. At any rate, my father was reared under the label of Seddon.'

She said, a little uncertainly, feeling that no matter how broadminded she tried to be, she was bound to arouse his scorn :

'They always say love-children are the best.'

'Oh, my father was no good at all,' he retorted airily. 'He was shipped off to the Dark Continent when he was sixteen. Women and wine, you know, in the good old style. I must say I admire him.'

'And were you born out there?'

'I was born there—in circumstances over which time has drawn a seemly veil. Anyway, he carried on the splendid tradition of unmarried fatherhood. It 's a great advantage, don't you think, to spring full-fledged out of nowhere? It helps me to be a romantic figure.'

'Yes.' She looked at his dark, expressive face, the pride and passion in the lines of every feature, the strong wide structure of the brow, and the rough locks falling over it.

'Is he dead, your father?'

'Oh, rather. He drank himself to death. He wasn't really a nice character, but he sent me to France and Germany to be educated, which is more than any teetotaller would do for his son. He left it in his will that I should make my grandmother's acquaintance when I was ready to go to Oxford. And so I did. And here I am.' He made his little bow. 'I 've been working for my finals and came here for two days' rest.'

'I see,' she said rather blankly; and checked a facile remark on her good fortune in coinciding with his visit: for probably he held the reverse opinion.

What a queer young man! . . . There was something about his point of view and way of expressing it which made her conscious not only of uncleverness, but of the fact that she dated badly.

'Well,' she said, 'I suppose she 's very fond of you.'

He shrugged his shoulders.

'She 's quite remote. We all get on excellently. We don't converse much. But now and then she lets fall a shattering remark in that way deaf people have. She told me once I looked like my grandfather; but I didn't ask her who he was—and she didn't tell me. Naturally, it 's none of my business.'

He finished on an offhand, challenging note. She said nothing, and he continued more agreeably:

'She doesn't speak of my father, but simply, I 'm sure, because she feels he 's such an unimportant character. So he was.'

'Then this place will be yours, some day, I suppose.'

'I don't know. Did you want it?'

No question could have been couched in more casual and unambiguous a tone. He might have been asking the time. But she coloured, surprised in her inmost thoughts: *one hope less for Robin and David*; and answered in a swift, hurt way:

'I used to come here when I was a girl. I love it very much.'

He looked at her reflectively. She would have been a pretty colour and shape as a girl. (Would it be possible ever to fall in love with a woman? Could one hope to find one who did not prove tiresome sooner or later?)

She murmured:

'Did she suffer much, I wonder, over her lover? It must be very peaceful to be deaf—plenty of time to think over your whole life. I suppose it 's having had so much in the past that makes her so—ungrabbing. She 's the only person I ever knew who sees—human relationships in their right proportions.'

Suddenly, as she spoke, she felt how true this was, and how important to her. Why had she spent so many years away from all contact with her—walking, perhaps, down a blind alley till this moment?

It was awful to be so muddled and slow-witted. She felt like holding her head in her hands, so painful was the effort to collect and rationalize this kind of emotional disorganization which was assailing her.

'I don't know what to do next,' she whispered; and then aloud, to the young man:

'I must go and find her.'

Find her at once: she would hold up a lamp, without speech, in that way she had: show her that there was nothing wrong; or, if everything was wrong, make her see that too, clearly and with dispassionate acceptance.

'It must be dinner-time,' he said. 'I 'll come with you.'

The sun was gone now from among the tree-trunks; only the urgent throats of the birds still haunted the wood with shapes of sound. They walked in silence up the winding path.

He said, abruptly:

'Who is he, the man you brought?'

'The young one? Hugh Miller. Isn't he nice?'

Not a name he had ever heard. . . .

In silence they walked across the lawn; but, just as they reached the sunken garden, he turned to her and said with all the charm that youth, beauty, and natural simplicity could lend him:

'And you really will forgive me for being rude?'

She looked up at him, her smile broadening gratefully, but, he saw to his horror, a little tearfully. She nodded, tried to speak. . . .

Thank God, there was his grandmother, kneeling on the pavement in her flowered silk, shaking bits of earth out of the leaves of a tiny rock-plant.

'Cousin Mary!' cried Norah; and she ran forward.

He watched the embrace of the two women. How admirable she was, his grandmother, how he delighted in her! Kneeling to tidy the plants, holding out her arms in welcome, looking upwards, now, at evening star and crescent moon—her every pose and gesture graced the mind with images plastic or poetic. He would write her a dedicatory poem in his first volume, something that should capture and express her quality: (and tell her incidentally—but secretly, so that not even she should guess—how happy he was to have a home: how much he'd always missed one).

The other looked small beside her, yet she was as tall: small, ordinary, and in some way pathetic.

He wished again he had not made himself so unpleasant. Her cry of ' Cousin Mary ! ' still rang in his ears. What was the matter with her ?

And all of a sudden, for the first time in his life, it struck him how profoundly each individual life is concealed. In spite of all public indications such as faces, words, actions, the blank persists. Truth is at the bottom of a bottomless well ; so that not Shakespeare, not Proust himself, has done more than faintly to ruffle the surface of the waters. . . . And this commonplace reflection gathered in one second such momentum, assumed all at once such overpowering proportions, swept him along so straw-like in its wake, that he felt that never in his whole life would he be able to seize, reduce, control it, or demonstrate, even to himself, what he meant by it.

So that—since no other subject was worth writing on—one might as well give up writing at once. . . .

But his grandmother, moving towards the house, one hand laid lightly in Norah's arm, turned and beckoned to him; and despair evaporating he went towards her.

The three women moved about in the spare bedroom, washing their hands in the rose-patterned china bowl, examining their faces before a dressing-table draped with white-spotted muslin over pink chintz.

Norah, examining her nose in the mirror, glanced

out of the corner of her eye at the reflection of Grace beside her, and held up her powder-puff.

'No, thanks.'

'She never touches a drop,' said Norah, still peering. 'Can you imagine?'

'She doesn't need it with her skin,' said Clare, giving Grace a rapid, vague, admiring scrutiny. She combed out the coppery silk waves of her hair and readjusted them with delicate precision. 'I should look simply too ghastly for words. . . .'

'Mm. . . . So should I. . . .'

'Oh, I do occasionally,' said Grace, feeling embarrassed. 'I just can't be bothered.'

'You 're an idiot not to take more trouble,' murmured Norah, passing a finger carefully over her eyebrows. 'I always tell you. . . . 'Scuse me, ladies. . . .' She lifted her skirt and pulled down her elastic belt and refastened her stockings. 'What do you wear in the way of a belt?' she said to Clare.

'Oh, just one of those little things with suspenders.' She displayed a fraction of it. 'I have them made for me by a woman . . .'

'Not even elastic. . . .' Norah ran her hand over Clare's waist. 'Aren't you afraid of spreading?'

'Oh, I never seem to alter. I haven't put on an ounce for years.'

'Lucky thing. It 's babies that do the damage. You try it! I 've never been *quite* so thin through, since David . . .'

PART IV

'Oh, my dear, your figure 's marvellous! . . .'

'My dear, do you see how grey I 'm getting?'

They went on patting, smoothing, murmuring. . . . They answered each other absent-mindedly, engrossed in their own preparations, but sparing a look now and then, a word of praise, advice, encouragement. Grace felt the luxury of the atmosphere recede from her, enclosing the other two securely in their voluptuous feminine intimacy, and leaving her stranded with hands washed, hair made neat, and nothing more to say or do. It was no use pretending. Womanly instincts must be largely lacking in her: she was as ignorant as a man of the intricacies and amenities of the toilet. Poor Tom—perhaps he had found her bleak and disappointing. Perhaps his inclinations were beribboned and frilly. It was a wonder really that (so far as she knew) he had never been unfaithful.

She leaned against the wide Georgian window, and looked down at the blossoming pear tree just beneath her. Perhaps pear is the loveliest of all, she thought, so blurred and tender-looking, mingling soft green with cloudy white. . . . And over there, in the angle of the kitchen-garden wall, was a great bush of flowering pink currant. She fancied she caught a whiff of its special enchanting pungency.

She saw Hugh come out from the house and stand on the lawn, holding a cigarette and a glass of sherry. He sipped, looking about him. Gerald and the old gentleman joined him, and they all sipped together.

Why should one young man, drinking sherry and smoking, be so absorbing and mysterious?

He looked up and caught sight of her, and a smile spread over his face.

She smiled back, gazing down at him, feeling that she saw him in a dream; that this simple greeting had a poignant, dream-like quality of joy and meaning. . . .

She moved abruptly away from the window.

Clare was dipping her finger into a little round gold box full of red paste. She peeped into the lid, stretched her lips, and carefully re-shaped them in a brilliant bow.

'Gerald would murder me if I did that . . .' said Norah, watching.

'Would he really? How hopeless of him! Still—— ' Clare reiterated, somewhat mechanically, her message of comfort: 'You don't need it.'

'And yet obviously he finds it absolutely fascinating when you do it. Men are peculiar.' She laughed cheerfully; and, while she laughed, wondered at herself for having indulged so recently in a tense, self-pitying mood.

What a lot there was to learn! thought Grace. She felt lonely. She looked at Clare. It was no more possible to think of this perfected, shining creature as a fellow-woman than to claim kinship with an angel or a wax mannequin. There must be something about this gossiping and fidgeting very soothing to a true woman. The influence is powerful, creating sisterliness in strangers and causing life-long enemies to call a truce.

Norah was talking and smiling now apparently without reserves; yet all the afternoon she had seemed different; and this evening, when she came in from the gardens after her queer long absence, there had been secretiveness and strain in her usually clear face; so that one had asked oneself if she were alarmed by Gerald's obvious infatuation for Clare.

Supposing Tom started a flirtation, would one mind at all? Or supposing one were to tell him that it was all a mad and horrible mistake, this having married him, that one must leave him at once . . . and be free to start all over again, to go back to young womanhood, wiping out ten years as if they had never been. Time was not real, except as one made it so. Why not bind it to one's purpose, make it servant instead of master? It should be a simple matter to abolish ten years of nothingness. . . .

Ten years old, a person already shaped for her destiny, when he was born. . . . Ten years married, a person without a future, when he, with all before him, came in one day to tea. . . . It had seemed so unlikely, then, that they could ever meet again; yet, ever since, the thread of connection had held. In spite of her longing, she had forced nothing. Surely, she told herself, something outside herself—call it Fate—had not permitted her to forget him: had drawn her to the window to see him walking past; had caused that unlikely encounter in the Park, and its still more improbable sequel of this day. Yes, she thought with excitement, each meeting seemed purposed, an inevitable step forward, like the development of a play from act to act ; and herself at once actor and spectator. Where was she going, powerless, independent of reason, and so idiotically happy ? . . .

'My dear,' Clare was saying, 'what fun this is ! Cousin Chris is a lamb, isn't he ? I adore his beard. And you said he was so frightening ! Tell me, *who* is that mysterious young man ? '

And the gong boomed out, cutting short Norah's explanations.

The clocks were striking nine when they sat down to dinner. Tall groups of unshaded candles in five-branched silver candlesticks of elaborate Georgian design lit the long polished table. An ancestor by Raeburn hung above the mantelpiece ; and there were other portraits all round the room—portraits military, political, fox-hunting ; beribboned, satin-clad, waxen-fleshed, rounded of arm and breast, maternal or maidenly. Upon the far wall a vast Salvator Rosa storm and wreck made more tenebrous the shadows

Claret followed white wine ; the velvet fire of port was succeeded by brandy, aromatic and precious in its crystal goblets. Christopher Seddon had the rarest cellar in the county. The meal was of trout and chicken, salad, fruit and cream and cheese—all home produce, said Mary Seddon, addressing the company for a moment—then resuming her conversation with Gerald—leaning towards him, cupping her ear to listen to his answers, discussing with him recent archæological discoveries in Asia Minor. Her face, severe, intellectual, crowned with white hair, her person, erect, imposing, dominated the table ; and she was absorbed in her subject. And Gerald, just sufficiently flown with wine for eloquent self-confidence, poured out to her loudly, happily, his views and his knowledge. She listened to him, she desired to learn from him. She considered him, he thought, a scholarly and interesting person. And he thought : 'There is nothing in the world more impressive and delightful than an old lady of position and culture.' And he explained to her a thing he had not been able to bear to mention for years : how it was that the war had put an end to his hopes of a fellowship at Cambridge.

And Norah thought : 'It is as I always said : he should drink wine regularly.' And she wondered what vast series of culinary reforms constituted the difference between Cousin Mary's cook's way of roasting fowl, and the way of Florrie. And she thought : 'Why did I worry? It is all being a perfect success. Dear Clare, dear Hugh, dear gay, good-looking couple. As for me, I was peevish and morbid because they got on so well without me.'

She talked easily now to Ralph who sat beside her, about David's drawings ; but quite sensibly and modestly, so that he thought: 'This woman is all right really'; and was prepared to believe that the child showed promise.

And being young and healthy, he thought mostly about his dinner, and said to himself in a vague way: 'Let us praise fresh trout and liqueur brandy, far more than most things.'

And Clare turned her heart-shaped face, her yellow-green jewel eyes, now to Christopher Seddon, now to Ralph. She looked, as she sat up straight, still and smiling, like a sleek young animal of the feline tribe, though more good-natured. And she thought: 'I would look nice in a frock made something like that grey thing the Fairfax woman is wearing, properly cut of course, the bodice tightly moulded to show my grace and slenderness, the skirt flaring out below my hips . . . grey moirée, with a white organdi fichu—pretending to be demure . . .' And she thought too: 'If this young man continues to take no interest in me. I shall know he 's one of *those* . . .'

And Christopher Seddon, at the head of the table, answered Clare's small talk in wincing monosyllables, and talked (across Grace) to Hugh, discussing almost with animation the subject of wines; while Grace, leaning back in order not to hinder them, asked herself what it was about Hugh, apparently undistinguished as he was, which gave him his distinction—made one instinctively aware of his birthright of such rooms and meals as these. And it was this background which made his manner of life in the main independent of considerations of income. He might have a thousand a year ; but more probably he was penniless. . . . And she told herself that if she could but see him for ten minutes every day till she died, she would become the most contented person living.

And finally, when they were all drinking coffee, and lighting cigars and cigarettes, Hugh turned to her and said 'Do you know Rudolph Valentino ?' And he did a very funny trick with an empty match-box and two matches stuck in the top in such a way that, when lit, their heads clung together in an implacable close kiss ; and up flew one match madly into the air as if lifted off its feet by the frenzy of passion ; and everybody cried 'Let me look ! Do it again ! Let me try ! ' . . . and everybody crowded together to watch the joke, even the young poet, even the old gentleman, solemnly informing himself of the meaning of the term Rudolph Valentino and enlightening the old lady rapidly in finger-alphabet. And for a few minutes they were all dissolved, that diverse and fortuitously-assorted company — dissolved and mingled together in the unifying element of laughter.

At eleven o'clock, Norah started up from a cheerful game of poker and declared that they must go home.

She was appalled, suddenly, at her long absence, fancied disasters—the house on fire, the boys alone, the faithful Florrie neglecting to put them to bed and going out on the spree ; and in any case, Robin staying awake to weep for her. Conviviality crumbled at her words.

It was then that Christopher Seddon invited them all to stay the night : not so much politely as with obvious eagerness, almost with anxiety. They could borrow everything, he said ; there were always plenty of new toothbrushes in the house. He looked at Hugh. And Hugh said he would simply love to stay. And Clare, thinking of Norah's cramped spare bedroom facing the street, resounding day and night with the groaning reverberations of a defective pipe, agreed with him, appealing to Norah for corroboration.

'I *can't*,' she protested miserably (for it was terrible to spoil their fun) : 'I simply can't leave the boys all alone. They 're expecting me.'

'Of course you can,' said Gerald. 'Ring up and tell Florrie. They 'll be all right. It 's ridiculous.'

But she shook her head. She would not. It was like Gerald to choose the one and only time when his unsociability would have been a help to enjoy himself madly at a party and object to departure. His eloquent eye pleaded with her rather threateningly.

Grace said suddenly :

'I must go too.' She turned to Hugh and added : 'My husband will be expecting me.'

Unbidden and most unwelcome had arisen the

thought of Tom—his voice if she were to ring up and tell him she was staying ; his manner when she finally returned. Probably he had missed his Saturday-evening movie on her account, and was waiting up for her, uneasy, gnawed with envy and curiosity ; and somehow pathetic, shame-faced. She must go back to Tom, her husband.

In the end it was satisfactorily arranged. Hugh was to take both Grace and Norah home in the car, and then return himself, at full speed, to spend the night. It was his own idea.

'I shall enjoy it frightfully,' he insisted. 'I often whizz off at night when it 's fine, just for the fun of it.'

Norah went to look for Mary Seddon, who had disappeared, as was her wont, directly after dinner.

She found her sitting by the fire in her own boudoir —embroidering a flower-panel, she explained, for a screen.

'All from my last autumn garden. I picked some of everything and mixed them up,' she said, articulating delicately in the flat voice of deafness. 'Dahlias, yellow daisies, and some of the mauve feathery ones, zinnias, and several sorts of chrysanthemum: the tawny ones, and two of this exquisite spidery kind—look, pale pink and lemon—and some of the tiny raspberry-coloured button ones. They work in so well. Won't it be charming ? I intend a panel for each season, but I like an autumn garden best, so I started with that.' She smiled over her spectacles, a smile of enchanting peacefulness.

Norah came and knelt beside her. She sorted some silks and handed her a threadful of crimson for her dahlia.

'It 's a warm night for a fire, but I like it,' said Mary Seddon. 'Directly the sun goes I light the fire.'

Norah nodded. She liked it too. Domestic comforts were as inevitable a part of Cousin Mary as her rings, her flowered silks.

After a while, unwilling to shout, she took a piece of paper and wrote upon it with the tiny gold and purple-enamelled pencil that hung—and had always hung—on a long gold chain at Mary Seddon's waist:

Cousin Christopher has asked everybody to stay the night. But I am going home to Robin and David; and Grace Fairfax, the tall one in grey, is going too. May Gerald and the two young ones stay, and may I come out again to-morrow in my car, and bring the boys?

Mary Seddon read the message and smiled. 'Very nice,' she said. 'I shall like to see your boys.'

Yes, thought Norah, she would smile adorably at them and stroke their hair, murmur a few affectionate words, be to them something more impressive, tender, and alarming than they had ever known: so that to their lives' end they would not forget her. And she would make one think, by some divine idiosyncrasy of comment, that they were both distinctly unusual children. But she would approach no nearer from her remoteness. She had a way of making one feel that after all there were so many human beings . . . one could not expect anything particularly new or surprising; it was nothing much, one way or the other, to have produced two oneself.

'Christopher is happy to have young society,' she said. 'What pleasant looks and ways that young man has! Poor Christopher finds it very refreshing. I knew a Hugh Miller many years ago: this boy's father, I dare say. There is a likeness.'

Of course. She had known everybody—sailing through the worlds both of society and of social rebels and outcasts in some astonishing and successful way of her own.

'And have you talked to my grandson?' she said after a pause.

Norah looked at her, nodded again.

'He's a dear boy—most affectionate and coltish. Quite unlike his father. . . . I had a good deal of wretchedness and disappointment with his father. However, that's all over long ago. . . .' She paused. 'Ralph writes, you know, so he tells me. I dare say he has talent. His grandfather was a painter—an extremely handsome man. I have often noticed that painting and writing interchange from generation to generation. . . . Now, should there be leaves, do you think, or simply the flowers? I've drawn it very roughly.'

She examined the work critically, her head on one side. She had said all she wanted to say, and one could ask her nothing more.

'Simply the flowers,' said Norah. She got up. 'Good-night, Cousin Mary.' She stooped to kiss her.

'Dear Norah . . .' Mary Seddon laid a white hand on her cheek. 'It is so pleasant to see you again. You don't come here very often.'

Norah shook her head. No need to excuse herself, or say how much she longed to come oftener, and could not.

'I had a most interesting conversation with your husband,' she went on, stitching away. 'I was very much struck by his intelligence. What remarkable eyes he has! . . . beautiful. He seems such a kind man, so gentle.'

Kind. Well, perhaps he was. It was rather nice, the way he had talked on with as much enthusiasm and unselfconsciousness as if she had not been deaf at all. And she saw him suddenly, giving extra coaching night after night to penniless examination-candidates—would-be teachers who could not afford to pay him. Yes, he was a kind man.

She went back to the drawing-room and found him amid an applauding group doing parlour tricks: a strikingly unexpected sight. He was on his hands and knees, hands tied behind his back, a bottle on his head, in the act of taking a handkerchief in his mouth and lifting it from the floor. Even when she exclaimed he did not drop it. His eyes were fixed on Clare, proudly, eloquently. The handkerchief was hers.

They drove in silence, all three packed into the front seat. Norah threw an arm round Grace's shoulder, for there was not room for all the arms; but the gesture made them smile at one another, gently. They were two women, friends of many quiet years, going back to their homes after a brief holiday.

And Norah thought: 'I am a lucky woman and I despise self-pity.'

And Grace watched the pale hand moving on the wheel. The seal ring on the little finger suited its proportions, that had both strength and elegance. A well-bred hand it was, with shapely nails and fingers. Her eyes dwelt on it, fascinated. She wanted to put her own hand upon it; and, drowsy with the night air, half dreamed she did so, felt the touch; roused herself, pressing both hands into her lap. Her mind fastened upon the oddness of his physical proximity. Their shoulders were pressed together, their heads were close; but on the other side of a fragile wall of bone, he was immeasurably separated from her. How was it that this tingling physical awareness did not permit her secretly to enter through some crevice of his mind, and mingle with his thoughts?

In a moment, it seemed, the lights of the town were

about them, and they had dropped Norah at her door.

Hugh drove the car into a garage.

'I must fill up,' he said. 'Also there 's a little job of work on a plug to do before I go out again. I 'd like to leave her here if you don't mind walking back to the house.'

'Of course not. I 'll say good-night now; you mustn't come with me.'

'Rot; come on.'

He slipped his arm through hers, and they set off along the empty street.

'I like walking in a town at night,' he said.

'Yes. All the shapes look so important and unfamiliar—the buildings and the walls; and the footsteps you hear, and the people you pass. You want to ask them why they 're still about. . . . I feel by day the people in the street are just a crowd: they scarcely know where they 're going and why. But by night each person is by himself and has his own meaning. If I were a writer and wanted to get the whole picture of life I 'd be up and about all night. You 'd learn everything then that is of any importance.'

'Yes,' he said, puzzled. He thought it over: parties, cafés, night-clubs . . . paupers and tramps on benches and under bridges . . . prostitute, of course . . . what else? . . . lovers—burglars—a murderer now and then . . . night-shifts in factories

. . . people sitting up by sick-beds and death-beds . . . people knowing damned well in the night how unhappy they were and how queer life was. (Yes, he remembered about that. . . .) He had seen a lot of night life himself, in Europe and in a far continent ; had felt on the bridges of silent ships at night something of what she seemed to mean. He said again :

'Yes.' He added : 'I wish I were a writer.'

'Do you ?'

'Mm. Sort of get things out of oneself—couldn't one ?'

She looked up into the youthful face above her own, and said nothing. He still had his arm through hers.

They reached her door. The iron gate creaked loudly, as it had for the last ten years, when he pushed it open for her.

'Now you must hurry back,' she said. She took his hand. 'You have given me a lovely day.'

'It has been fun, hasn't it ?' he said, a little embarrassed. 'I hope you 're not too tired.'

'No, no. Better. Cured. Renewed.' She smiled. 'I shall have all this to think about now. It will keep me going for a long time.'

Extraordinary, rather worrying woman ! Her pale face looking at him in the lamplight moved him. His hand was still in hers ; and as it seemed rude to take it away, he tightened his clasp.

'We must have another jaunt some time,' he said.

But she thought: it will never happen again; and it did not matter—at least, not yet. She was all right by herself now; she had been set going again. Like her lilac tree, she thought, looking at the few white blooms which to-day's sun had unfolded fully, she was to flower again after many years. She reached up and picked a head.

'White lilac,' she said. 'I'm very proud of my tree. Do you like the smell?'

She wanted so much to give it him. . . . She held it out awkwardly.

'Thanks awfully,' he said. 'I love a button-hole. . . . Well, good-night.'

'Good-night.'

He went away at a brisk pace, whistling a little tune. She waited till he was out of sight before starting to throw earth at the upper window: for she had forgotten her key, and the lights were all out.

It was half an hour before Tom woke from his first slumbers and heard her; and after listening some time in great alarm, realized the situation and came downstairs. How annoyed she'd be, he thought, switching on the light in the hall. Serve her right. But she was smiling when he let her in. Her smile did not console him. He had missed his movie and spent a dismal evening with the account-book and his own meditations before betaking himself to bed with his grievances; and when she entered his house at one o'clock in the morning, fresh and sparkling with happiness and the night air, he felt so strongly that this, in some unformulated way, was absolutely the last straw, that he was stricken dumb at the sight of her. It was not until breakfast the next morning that he could bring himself to ask her if she had had a good time.

Hugh broke into a run. An hour to get back, going all out, and then perhaps another bathe—an icy plunge in the starlight, quick in, quick out again. He pictured the shock and the ensuing glow through all his body. Lovely! . . Lovely to wake up to-morrow morning in the country. Hurry, hurry! The old boy had insisted that he would wait up for him. He was a rum 'un, frightfully nice though. So was the old lady. She was a corker.

Rounding a corner, he collided with a small female figure.

'Sorry,' he murmured, hurrying on.

But a tiny exclamation, a glimpse of a face mournful as a monkey's, a little pierrot face, made him remember and turn to greet her.

'Hullo, it's Pansy, isn't it? Good-evening, Pansy. Do you remember me?'

'Yes, I remember you.'

'Haven't seen you for ages. Where 've you been hiding?'

'I 've seen you now and then,' she said. 'You never see me.'

'Where are you off to now?' he said. (Funny place to meet her.)

'Nowhere in particular.' She smiled at him.

There was a silence.

'Well,' he said, 'I'm in an awful hurry, I'm afraid. Going off for the week-end. Good-night, Pansy.'

Fixing him with her strange veiled stare, she said:

'I still go down to the Palace most evenings.'

'Right you are, Pansy. I'll come and look for you one of these days. We'll have another dinner together, shall we? Do a show.'

He left her hurriedly with a smile and a wave of the hand.

Poor little oddment, he thought, what was she doing in these parts, away from her habitual haunts and the more frequented streets? Had she an assignation?

She'd seen him now and then, she'd said. . . . Now where on earth? People were always seeing him without his seeing them. Pity he'd had to leave her in the lurch. He wouldn't have minded giving her a good supper. She looked as if she needed it. Besides, she was amusing, with her prettiness and her chatter. Not the most virtuous debutante in her first season could safeguard her modesty with more decorum. The pathetic thing was the obviousness, the elaborateness of the pretence. She had to kid herself as hard as she could, one felt. She'd have a yarn to spin, if one were to ask her why she'd taken to the profession. And, as usual, he thought, he would believe her. He simply could not help a soft corner for prostitutes, a natural inclination to be sorry for them, to be polite to them. (Gross sentimentalism, Oliver had called it.) Perhaps that was partly why he experienced such increasing disinclination for their services. Nowadays, he told himself, reviewing the sexual temperature of the last year or so, one felt fed up with all that sort of thing. Reaction, distaste set in almost as soon as desire. One wanted—oh! longed for something permanent now, something aesthetically, emotionally satisfying. . . . Love, in fact.

Pansy left the privet hedges, the clean pavements and Gothic porches of the residential quarter, and boarded a tram bound for the meaner suburbs where she dwelt.

She was worn out. Hours and hours she had been walking up and down that street . . . avoiding the policeman . . and then, there he was, like Fate, like a miracle,—and then gone again. Well, it was better than nothing: he had remembered her; he 'd been most friendly and polite. Perhaps he would soon come down to the Palace now. But being tired like this, she felt depressed. Wasn't it all a pretence, his hurry, to get away from her? One didn't go off for the week-end in the middle of the night. And who 'd been giving him white lilac to stick in his coat?

She saw him waving, disappearing round the corner,

and herself standing there, gaping after him ; and it really seemed as if he knew what months she 'd spent, what schemes she 'd laid, to find out where he lived, and was having a good laugh at her.

Hugh put away his car, and let himself into the great hall. His feet rang on the stone floor before the silence of the Persian rugs received them. The old tapestries on the wall, lit only by the central chandelier, seemed to tower above him, with their gods, goddesses, nymphs and satyrs, forests and fountains magnified, interwoven in rhythmical gigantic patterns. There was nobody about.

On the hall table gleamed a pale and solitary square of paper. He glanced at it in passing ; and the name upon it, minute but clear as print, started up at him from the dark wood like a menace. He stopped dead ; after a minute had to go back, look again ; read *Oliver Digby, Esq.*, and the London address.

So he was writing to him, this chap. So they knew each other. So Oliver had come back from wherever he was, lost, silent. So he was in London. And he had not let one know. He must have had both letters, then, and simply not bothered to answer them. So that was final.

And such an extraordinary and awful feeling—something he had never known before or dreamed of—swept through him as he stood there, that he had to hold on to the table for a minute. But the envelope stared up at him with spiteful mockery, whispering, ' You don't know what secrets are beneath this flap ' ; and he had to move away, before the temptation to seize and tear it open—yes, actually dishonourably to seize and tear it open—overcame him quite.

Damn him, damn him. . . . He had plotted it. If Oliver with all his cleverness and unforgivingness had plotted a way to pay him out to the bitter end, he could never have devised anything more cruel and more effective than this letter laid there, as if by the hand of an accomplice. ' I have passed on,' said the letter. ' Now you are naught.'

And to-morrow he would have to see this chap. . . . And what did he want : to avoid him, loathe him like the plague ; or take particular pains to make a good impression on him ? . . . It would need a desperate effort to shake off this business and enjoy to-morrow.

Grock dragged himself from the luxurious depths of a brocaded armchair and ambled to his side. But there was no enthusiasm in his faintly wagging tail, nothing to call forth the consoling reflection that at least one's dog would always love one. There was some sort of slime or foam on his black jaws, and his expression was meditative, oddly weighty. He retired again to rest.

The fact was that, demoralized by the day's sport, and having come, by mistake, at last upon a victim in the shape of an unresisting toad, he had recklessly swallowed it alive ; and the resulting digestive problem pressed upon him, heavy as lead.

Devoutly hoping that every one had gone to bed, he pushed open the library door and looked in. But Christopher Seddon was sitting up for him, the pen and ink drawings, the maps for his new book laid out on his desk, all ready to be exhibited and explained.

But Hugh stood at the door, nervously smiling, saying that he was so sorry, that he was so terribly sleepy, that he thought he would go straight to bed. . . .

And to make matters worse, the old boy seemed to take it as a piece of rudeness, or a snub or something—winced, jumped up, whisked away his papers, and conducted him to his room in absolute silence.

Coming downstairs again in a wretched frame of mind to extinguish all the lights, Christopher opened the drawing-room door and beheld Gerald and Clare, both of whom he had completely forgotten. Clare lay on the sofa smoking a cigarette, and Gerald sat on the floor, close beside her head. He heard her laugh and say :

'Oh, Gerald, you are delicious. I 've never had a compliment in Greek before.'

Now what should he do ? thought Christopher, his hand on the switch.

PART IV

'Well, I suppose we can't stay here all night,' said Clare.

'I wish we could,' said Gerald.

She laughed again.

'You 're getting quite human. I 'll say good-night, I think.' She gave him her hand. He raised it to his lips.

'Is that a Greek custom ?' she said.

But he could not answer lightly, he could do nothing but look at her. . . .

At this moment Christopher Seddon extinguished the lights and silently retired.

They were startled. They had to grope their way upstairs with the aid of matches.

When all the house was still, Ralph left his sleepless pillow and crept downstairs.

There was his letter still on the table : it must have missed the post. No matter. There were several unsatisfactory sentences in it. To-morrow he would write a better one. He put it in his pocket.

Out into the faint transparency of starry darkness. Run towards the dark belt of the trees. Stand among the huge tree-trunks. Be lost, be mingled in their vaster being.

From the strong convulsions of knotted root to topmost quivering shoot, the nerves tingle, the vital energy runs throughout the majestic organism. Life aches in the branches. Huge pangs of birth, growth, death, are within these sentient frames. Listen in the silence to the trees breathing.

Ye vastest breathers of the air. . . .

And all in a moment he was overpowered. The living giant trees were so strong around him that he thought, with panic : ' I am caught for ever ! . . .'

Chained in the earth, cased in his bark he stood. He was a beech tree.

PART V

PART V

Where her holiday was spent she never quite knew. She forgot to ascertain, either by map, or by inquiry, precisely in what direction and locality the village lay ; but travelling out by bus from the southern market town where she had spent the night, mile after mile, waiting to detect it, it revealed itself at last, as she had seen it in her mind's eye, basking in sunlight among cornfields and water meadows ; and she had found a thatched cottage, white-washed on the garden side, old pink brick where it faced the lane ; and walked up through a small garden packed with flowers and set with a few ancient fruit trees ; and there taken lodging.

From her square of window she saw the garden and a row of poplars, pond and village green beyond, and more cottages sitting squat and rosy in their gardens, and sending up threads of smoke from sprawling chimneys ; and she heard hens and ducks, sleepy-sounding, and the children coming down the lane to school and back again ; carter and cowman calling to their beasts in the fields ; and the anvil ringing from the forge at the end of the village.

And she heard, too, warning notes of a new order —the frequent rattle of a motor-bicycle, newly-acquired property of the young man at the public-house, and the roar of the daily bus as it passed to the town and back, picking up, setting down its handful of shoppers and cinema-goers.

But for a little longer there would be peace : no factory stack, no entertainment hall, no railway station, tram-lines, or golf-links. For a little longer time would move kindly here ; the changing seasons of all created things would follow one another imperceptibly and bring no change. Men and women, and apple trees, the great cart-horses and the corn, the rose-bushes and the swallows, were all gathered up together into one common harmony of the fruitful earth.

She fell into a summer trance.

Beauty is a visitor, coming without warning, transforming for an hour, a day—sometimes for longer ; crumbling at a breath, vanished again.

She wove herself into an iridescent web, linking small charm with frail enchantment until the shining fabric hid from her the commonplace noon, the ordinary night.

She was in love with her room, with its cracked pink crockery, its four-poster, whose mattress reversed every property requisite for rest and comfort, the texts, the wedding group, and the photograph of a grave on the wall. She was in love with the acrid smell of the damp old walls, with the square of window that let in the stars by night and the sighing rustle of the poplar trees, and the fragrance of meadowsweet from laden fields.

PART V

She heard the young swallows at daybreak, stirring in their mud nests beneath the eaves, greeting the light with a tender chatter.

She found upon her window-sill a moth of palest jade, with a lime-green wavering track across each wing. It lay there in the evening outspread in swooning stillness ; but later she saw its life start into consciousness and sharply quiver, spinning towards her candle before she blew it out.

In the garden were large poppies and strong, straggling plants of borage. She picked some of each, mingling their harsh stems, their pure flames of red and blue in a tall vase of sea-blue glass.

By the gate grew a bush of yellow lupin ; and later, when its spires began to tumble, delphinium raised its solider dark blue towers.

When the sun was hot she lay in the fret-sawed shade of an apple-tree wreathed through all its limbs with a creeping white rose. She watched a tiny kind of bird, a flycatcher, that flitted all day in the standard rose-bushes. A host of young birds, swifts, martins, wagtails, swallows, were in the garden, and sharp parent cries rang out, plucking in anguish on one urgent string, while the tortoise-shell cat slid from ambush to ambush among the flowers. Nothing in the world, she thought, can match for brilliance the wet wings of birds flashing in sunlight after a shower.

She found a young swallow on the path one evening. She picked it up and brought it into the house, thinking : ' It is injured and will die ; and when its eye glazes reality will return ' It sat in her hand and its eye was bright, without film of pain or terror, watching her. It would not eat the crumbs she sprinkled ; but after a while, when the sun was gone—making a single abrupt movement, a backward curve of the neck, a rapid burrowing—breast puffed, beak beneath wing, it slept. She sat still in her chair, feeling the strangeness of infinitesimal claws, the tingling of warm feathers upon her palm ; contemplating with delight and awe the diminutive life, unalienated in an alien contact, trusting its shelter. She carried it up and set it, lapped in unstirring infant sleep, in the fold of a woollen scarf by the open sill. She woke before dawn and discerned it still motionless there, dark and round as a ball. When next she woke the sun was up and all the birds were calling ; and it had flown away.

She took this for a message, a happy omen. For the first time, she told herself, she had touched something to save, not to destroy it. Now she too would be saved. And the little dream of the bird became mingled with the essential dream of the young man. She walked holding the thought of him lovingly sheltered in the hollow of her hand.

Later came the crimson ramblers, massed and full-flowering, making a midsummer pattern rich and heavy over the yellow-green warp, the blue-green woof of all the gardens.

The grass was cut in the fields, swathe after swathe

curving and falling. She sat beneath a hedge of bryony and dog-roses, breathing in the smell of the fresh mow, and watching the hay-makers at work in the sun. All the village was there in the evenings, men, women, and children ; and mothers brought their infants and nursed them in the shade.

She saw the last load gathered in and piled upon the scarlet and yellow hay-cart ; and the children scrambling up and riding home to the farm with shouts and laughter.

Morning and evening now she looked out from her window at the hay-stacks in the field, two shapes whose beauty of strong, balanced lines and volumes seemed not accidental but designed—the composition of an artist. Once in the dawn after rain, she leaned out and saw them floating in white mist, half shrouded ; and she heard the horse stamping in his stall. The chill river vapours had started again to haunt this valley of streams and marshes, shadowing forth October in the last days of July. Often now a vaporous opalescence lay over the meadows when the sun was sinking.

Pinks and hollyhocks, clumps of phlox, madonna lilies, came out in the gardens.

A row of hollyhocks bloomed against the fruit wall at the end of the garden. She fancied that their round heads were notes of music painted upon an outspread scroll ; chords and scales splashed down in tones of rose and crimson upon the green keyboard of the espalier. Soon, she thought, in the present heightening and harmony of the interplay of all her senses, they would strike audibly upon her ears.

The fragrance of night-scented stock blew in through the window now.

She walked through the cornfields. In the wind, something more bodiless than flame flickered and ran over the green grain and the blond. The spirit moved upon the face of the corn.

She climbed the slopes and lay at the edge of a crowning grove of beeches. She wished to be as large as the hill, to sprawl against its side from top to bottom, great limbs at ease, and contemplate the view with giant's eyes: eyes big enough to hold all, on every hand—fields, trees, downs, and the clouds above them, as far as the horizon.

The wind came in soft puffs, swaying the loose floating plumes of the border of beech-branches. She saw fat bees asleep in the thyme around her, and ladybirds crawling with infinite labour over thread-like blade and root. The clouds streamed over the sky, repeating in ashen white the dark masses of elm beneath her and the long shapes of distant woods upon the downs.

When evening came the tree-tops seemed to be sailing with slow majestic motion, launched all together upon a full flood tide, leaning bright-gilded into the west; and above them the clouds sailed too.

Into the furnace of the west flew the clouds; and

the sun tore down, burnt up their strong fabric to smoky shreds and tatters ; and around the fiery core the dying wind drifted their ashes.

Mrs. Crawley was the name of her landlady. She was a village woman born and bred, dark, small, and shy. She had a child called Frank, six years old, and her husband was a gardener. He worked all day in the Rectory garden, and then came home and tended his own till dark : a man of wood, silent, brownish, fibrous, knotted in the joints ; forty perhaps, or sixty. . . . Was it a vegetable quiescence, she wondered, or passion, that bowed his shoulders for ever with such patient tenacity above the soil ?

Mrs. Crawley, bringing the eggs and bacon, smiled good-morning ; laying the loaf, honey, teapot on the table, whispered that the afternoon was wet or fine ; called good-night as she set down the quart jug of hot water outside the door. But one day she brought a wild orchid, pressed by Frank, fastened with stamp-paper to a sheet of foolscap. For the excellence of this specimen, she explained, Frank had received a prize of half a crown in a competition at school. 'It 's nice to know that they get on,' she said ; and she stroked Frank's head as he sidled round the door—but did not wipe his nose, which always needed wiping.

The coin could not be framed ; to wear it on a chain as a medal would be, they felt, unsuitable. What was to be done ?

Grace gave him a round, cut-glass, silver-topped box, a small maternal relic designed but never used for pins, buttons, and such oddments. Within this shrine lay the coin, secluded yet visible upon the parlour mantelpiece. After this, Mrs. Crawley spoke now and then, offering fragments of her life and thoughts with a flitting, diffident smile.

She said :

' I 've never been to London, nor yet seen the sea. I 'll never go to London, but I 'd like Frank to see the sea. Perhaps I 'll take him this year, with the Band of Hope outing. But I don't know. These sharabongs don't look safe to me. . . .'

She stared wistfully. It was plain that the venture was more than she could compass, even in imagination. Yet Frank, he ought to see the sea.

The child was slighter and whiter than many a child of northern slums. The stock was poor, inbred, unproductive.

She said :

' He 's hardy, Frank is. The doctor examined 'im at school, and the report said no disease of 'eart or lungs. Only it seems they want to 'ave out something in 'is throat.'

Candour shone in her eyes, and a hint—no more—of something else in her, a kind of charm, caressing, playful, that had been buried and forgotten. For now she was all given over to the unchanging round of daily tasks and the shadowing doubts and hesitations of her shuttered and dependent spirit.

PART V

Frequently she spoke of her confinement, her one occasion, her own ; measuring time by that supreme event, as who should say : Before the birth of Christ or after. Remembering the ten days' rest in bed, the baby, the importance, the ministering district nurse, she smiled dreamily, re-living the miracle of the laying down of her burden, the bewilderment both of pain and joy.

'When 'e was born,' she said, 'the cord was twisted three times round 'is little neck. I nearly lorst him.'

And once she murmured : 'Happiest time of my life it was.'

She was not curious, asked no questions. Bringing Tom's weekly letter, she would hold it out with a dubious smile and glance, guessing perhaps : her husband—hoping maybe to see a gleam, a hand stretched out with eagerness ; dimly apprehending the negation in her lodger of all that such hope implied ; thinking this a pity, for she herself was lucky—Mr. Crawley was a good man to work, and never touched a drop.

Passing the open door of the kitchen one evening on her way to bed, Grace saw them all three sitting together in silence at the table. Empty plates and cups were set before them ; and the light of one candle modelled the human group in tender masses of light and shade, and illumined their calm and empty faces. She was moved by the simplicity of their wants, the pathos of their elementary possessions : the hard wood chairs, set side by side, to support such weariness, such repose ; the slice of bread to satisfy such well-earned hunger. The child was on her lap asleep. There was not a sound, or a movement. Out of the luminous obscurity emerged the domestic union of their figures, with the significance at once placid and poignant, illustrative and transcendental, particular and symbolic, of a Dutch painting.

Tom's holiday did not prove a success. He stayed away nine days, and then came back to the town. There was nobody to greet him ; the house was shut up and Annie was on her holiday, not due back till the end of the week. Pulling back drawn curtains, removing dust-sheets, hearing his own feet echoing up and down the stairs, peering into bare kitchen and larder—that larder and kitchen empty of her whose very presence had seemed to create comforting puddings and well-stocked shelves—he had a sense of desolation that was like a physical ache. He procured himself a raw-boned daily char who made his bed and cooked him smoky bacon ; for his other meals he sampled in turn every cheap eating-house in the town, hating them all. Annie would grieve, he thought, when she returned, to see his pass. Grace would be sorry too . . . would she be sorry ? Would she care that his holiday had been a gloomy, ghastly failure ? More than a month now she had been away on her own, scarcely communicating with him. . . .

PART V

Potter had lent him his motor-bicycle—supreme token of a friendship matured over many a whisky-and-soda and a game of billiards—and upon this unreliable machine he had travelled gingerly but hopefully to Scarborough, to see life and be a bachelor again. But it had rained at Scarborough; and been expensive and unprofitable. Never, he thought, would he forget the dreariness of the rain-and-wind-swept promenade, his half-hearted attempts to scrape acquaintance here and there, the bleak chill of his bedroom, his liverishness, a feeling he had had of being a figure of fun when he tried to dance foxtrots with unattached young ladies in the lounge: an old fool, a figure of fun, he thought they were whispering and giggling. Romance, intoxication, the kind of adventure he had heard about from Potter—nothing of that sort had come his way. He lacked Potter's recklessness. His frame of mind had been all wrong.

From the hollow mockery of Scarborough he had fled, travelling across England, still more gingerly and now unhopefully, to the outskirts of Chester, upon a pious pilgrimage. But he had found no satisfaction, no purging influence of memory and sorrow, in the laying of a wreath upon his mother's grave; no sense of filial duty adequately performed in the inspection of the newly-erected marble head-stone. It looked all right: nothing cheap about it: more tasteful than granite, and imposing enough even without the addition of the words, *Her children rise up and call her blessed*, which, in the first generosity of mourning, he had considered no more than was fitting. After all, perhaps it would have been a trifle much, applied to mother. She had not been exactly what you would call . . . Grace, he knew, would have risen up and called her something quite different, given the chance. There she lay in her coffin, the old lady, Bertha Fairfax, never a beauty: he could only wonder, with morbid detachment, what she must look like now.

But that night, in the house of an old friend of his mother's, family solicitor and executor, wakeful upon the inhospitable spare mattress, that epitaph rose up before his eyes and haunted him. *Beloved mother of Thomas Fuller Fairfax*—so ran the last line. And he bethought himself that he was the last of his family; that no one would ever write upon his memorial tablet *beloved father* . . . or even *beloved husband* (not if Grace had the job—not unless Annie were to remind her). Somehow he had always seen himself as a family man—slippers warming—children running to meet him—blowing on his watch—pouring out his tea—that sort of thing. And none of it had happened or ever would. He had been cheated, and would go to his grave childless. It was not fair, of course, to blame Grace: perhaps she had minded in her own peculiar way about the baby; but she had not seen it, as he had: whatever she had suffered through the supposed properties of the maternal instinct, she could not know, he was sure, would never know as he knew what it really meant to look down suddenly at that form without life, and think all at once, with a most unexpected, appalling and unforgettable pang : *My son !*

Not for the first time, but more rebelliously than ever before, he found himself stumbling over a point in Christian morals. There he was, tied to one woman, and so frustrated in his natural desire and capacity to beget. The unfairness of the system—the stupidity ! Of course, one must bear one's cross. . . . Why must one ? The only hope was for Grace to die ; and (though one could not altogether control dreams of a timely widowerhood) he did not want her to die : not Grace herself, no, no : only—(how terrible thoughts were in the night watches !)—only his cold and barren wife.

The possibilities of his holiday were at an end. What was he to do with himself ? And suddenly the answer was obvious : join Grace. Yes, he thought, in a rush of contrition, affection, and returning cheerfulness, send her a wire in the morning and jog along South to join her for a few days. Probably he would enjoy a taste of the simple life. They would go for some good tramps together and get fit. He saw himself entering into the spirit of the thing : saying good-day to rustics, supping off bread and cheese and beer, having a chat with a farmer, sitting on stiles—generally giving his attention, in fact, to rural conditions.

Surely by now she would have had enough of her

freak notion of being on her own. Probably in her heart of hearts she was as bored, as lonely as he was. He would pop down and see what she was up to.

And in the back of his mind swam some confused idea of starting again on another footing—trying to rub along better, to share, to understand more. She was a funny girl, Grace: moody, touchy, queer in the things she laughed at, and the things that upset her. She was deep, was Grace. Sometimes he felt he was positively afraid of her. The times she brought him up with a jerk, made him wonder where, how, why he had got it wrong again!—the times he had stopped himself flinging at her shut face: '*Now*, what 's the matter?'—and decided to take no notice after all. Women had moods. Anything for a quiet life. . . . And then there was a quality about Grace, in spite of her being so big and quiet looking—a woman with a presence, as Potter said—that made him think to his inmost self, 'Poor little Gracie,' as if he divined in her something he could not deal with, but only pity: a youthful spirit, pathetic, girlishly impulsive, too sensitive for him: something that could be fitted with endearing, foolish, small-girl's nicknames. The first year or so of marriage had been full of nicknames—extraordinary to look back on now. Perhaps he was to blame: he had absorbed himself in his business and his masculine recreations, and left her too much to herself.

He would send her a wire in the morning, and

make a good start by admitting how much he had missed her ; and she would say, smiling in the way that still struck him as jolly, ' I 've missed you too, Tom,' and there would be a general feeling of having blown away cobwebs and turned over a new leaf.

But Grace's reply telegram, received at the moment of his setting forth, had told him not to come. *Do not come, writing, Grace*, were her precise words. No reasons given. So he had wired once more, *Going home*—breathing into the curt message (but would she see it ?) all his forlornness, his disappointment and wounded feelings. Then he had taken the road North again. He was still waiting for that letter of explanation.

This was his third evening in the deserted home. Thank God, only another couple of days before going back to the office.

For the first time he knew the meaning of solitude in the midst of a crowd. Potter and one or two other pals were all away. He had even rung up Norah to suggest a game of bridge—a thing he had never quite liked to do before. In spite of her being so pleasant always when they did meet, there was a tacit understanding that the relationship was between herself and Grace, not conjugally inclusive. He had pictured himself, however, pleading with her in a jocular way to take pity on a poor grass-widower ; but Norah, so the caretaker had informed him, was absent with her family in Brittany. He laid down the receiver with a secret sense of discomfiture ; for the word Brittany seemed symbolic of an indubitable social difference. The MacKays, though badly off, took holidays as a matter of course in places that sounded correct as well as romantic. One could not mention Scarborough or Whitby with the same air as that with which one would throw off such names as Bordighera or Seville—or even, he thought, Ostend.

He stood at the sitting-room window and watched the traffic pass in the August evening sunlight, and heard, far off, the music of merry-go-rounds. For the annual fair had come to town ; and it was towards the common that all the feet and faces were so briskly set.

What was he to do with himself ? He had read the *Daily Mail* and the *Mirror* twice over from cover to cover and done all the puzzles. There was still the evening paper. He would go out and buy one, and browse in it while he ate his dinner. What restaurant, he wondered, should he try to-night ? A decent one for a change, and blow the expense ? Why not the swell place, Barnard's ? Damn it, he would go to Barnard's, and put a jolly good dinner inside him, the best the place could provide—and drown his melancholy in a bottle of wine.

The waiter set him in a corner at a little table adorned with a pink shaded lamp and a small metal vase containing artificial flowers—one rose and one yellow one, not classifiable. He felt, as he marched in with manly tread and took his seat, that he could hold his own in any assembly. His appearance, reflected from different angles in several mirrors, did him credit, on the whole. He could not, he thought, be called stout.

He studied the menu, and ordered sole *bonne femme*, a mixed grill, salad, trifle, a welsh rarebit ; and a bottle of Burgundy. Barnard's was all right, no doubt of that.

The orchestra sent forth the preliminary wail, neurotic, voluptuously provocative, of the latest sentimental song-hit. The broken rhythms poured down like syrup from the gallery. He had heard it among the palms and pillars of the Scarborough lounge, the merry-go-rounds were sending it down with the wind from the common. Here, the diners paused in their talk as they recognized it, whistled or hummed a bar or two, swayed their shoulders, looked dreamy, tapped with their feet. He found himself marking the measure with mouthfuls of fish. This sort of music gave one a funny jog-up, and no mistake. He wished once more that he had kept up with this modern dancing. In the old days, he had romped round in a rollicking waltz with the best ; but this syncopated jigging defeated him. He should have prepared for this freedom by taking a few dancing lessons.

He watched his own reflection, raising a wine glass to its lips with dignity and assurance. The large mirror presented all the elements of a restaurant scene in a film—lights, dishes, hurrying waiters—with himself as focussing point—the man of the world, distinguished, solitary, on whom romance was about to centre. Where was The Woman?

The wine stole warmly through his blood and he thought of himself with regret and self-reproach, as one who had not had the courage to seek and seize his opportunities. All that was changed now. Should adventure beckon to-night he was ready for it. The question was, where and in what manner to assume the offensive. He was ridiculously ignorant of the ways and means of the town.

He had reached the savoury before the behaviour of a group of young chaps behind him became distinctive enough to engage the attention of everybody else in the room. Staring eyes, knowing glances, expressions of indulgence, surprise, disapproval, were directed towards their table. Passing waiters paused in their flight, hovered over them with amusement.

He turned round. A celebration of some sort, by the look of it. They were all a trifle merry. He put on his spectacles and recognized with astonishment a couple of clerks from the office, several other local young fellows known to him by sight, and in the midst, surely—yes—young Miller: young Miller, somewhat flushed, to all appearances performing in dumb show upon the table, with the aid of knives and forks, cruets and rolls, and other objects. They were all leaning towards him. Gusts of laughter rose again and again above his head.

What was he up to now? He was a nice young chap, but he lacked stability. If the old boss himself were to ask him his opinion, that was what he would say: 'Your grand-nephew is a great favourite with us all, Sir Lionel. He 's got brains and to spare, but what he lacks is stability.'

He recalled one or two frivolous incidents in the office; shook his head, seeing the old order changing, and the direction of the firm passing from the venerable hands that had shaped it, and bullied it, and won it name and fame, and paid him year after year a fair salary for conscientious services, into the hands he saw now over there, so nonsensically skilful, so irresponsibly busy.

The orchestra was playing to Hugh now, to him alone. 'Bravo!' he shouted, as each tune came to an end. 'Now for another! Come on!'—and the meagre violins gathered tone, the pianist performed his most elaborate convolutions.

A strange current arising from the heart of that intemperate table began to spread over the room. Like the Gulf Stream, cutting a path of warmth through chilly seas, leaving a green hint in its passage past winter-bound coasts, the relaxing influence flowed. Or like a draught, stirring up stagnant air with an exhilarating breath . . . or like yeast working headily in a doughy mixture. . .

But multiplication of phrases is vain : there was nobody among that company to whom these similes would have appealed. On the contrary, the more one element expanded, the more the other contracted, withdrawing uneasily from the pagan stimulus, the convivial contagion ; and stiffening gradually into one frigid and solidly resisting mass of outraged orthodoxy.

But Hugh remained unaffected. Cold breaths might blow around him, but could not penetrate. He was at the top of his form.

'Now for the roundabouts and swings,' Tom heard him cry.

Threading his way a trifle unsteadily through the tables, he kicked against Tom's chair, and turned round to apologize ; recognized him, and greeted him with enthusiasm.

'Hello ; it 's old Uncle Tom. Uncle Fairfax. Mr. Fairfax. . . .'

He stopped and collected himself.

'How are you ?' he said politely ; adding, with a disarming smile, 'we call you Uncle Tom in the office. You don't mind, do you ? It 's a term of—what d'you call it ?—affection. Had a decent holiday ?'

'Oh, yes, very jolly, thanks, Mr. Miller.'

'How 's Mrs. Fairfax ?'

'Oh, very well, very well indeed. I needn't ask how you are,' said Tom, heavily jovial. It was impossible to help feeling a little flattered. There was no doubt he had a way with him. Old Uncle Tom, indeed ! But you couldn't take offence. . . .

'Oh, I'—he chuckled—'I am damned well. Going up to the fair?' (What was he up to, dining in state on his own?)

'Well—I rather think I will, just for half an hour. . . .'

'Oh, you ought to. Marvellous show. Penny a ride on an ostrich. Palace of Beauty—Indian dancer—fat woman, I believe—all sorts of thrills.'

He surveyed Tom with a twinkling eye, then added hurriedly (for, horrors! the old buffer had pricked up his ears—would offer to accompany him in another moment):

'Well, I must get along. Phew, it's hot in here, isn't it? Fresh air for me.'

He smiled, throwing over his shoulder as he moved away:

'It's Brown's birthday.'

Brown's birthday, was it, thought Tom: Brown, that meek and mouse-like clerk, incapable, one would have thought, of calling attention to his own existence, much less celebrating it. At whose instigation was he having champagne birthdays? Undoubtedly, he thought, there had been a new tone in the office of late: a tendency among the young public-school clerks to throw their weight about. Was it the influence, he wondered, of young Miller?

He called for his bill, checked the amount with a carelessness that masked dismay; and took his departure.

Pansy paid her sixpence at the gate, and was borne

along on the ever-flowing human stream into the grounds of the fair.

Aimlessly drifting, dazed in the kaleidoscopic confusion of sensory impressions, flares of lights assailed her, shouts of showmen ; moving bodies jostled her, bodies that would not move, lumpishly fixed, staring before some stall ; crash of china smote her, ceaseless knocking, wooden, hollow, ceaseless thump and bump of balls, ninepins, cocoanuts ; smell of trampled grass, of beer, cigarette ends, pervasive smell of people, whistle and shriek of sirens, shiver of tambourines, metallic, brassy blare of merry-go-rounds, mournfully trumpeting, hot-sounding. Above her the swing-boats creaked, shook, shot up, shot down, so fast, so giddily, she could not look. Over the top they 'd go, surely, surely. They 'd be tipped out. The danger of it ! And the switchbacks, whizzing downhill on their shaky wooden scaffolding, with that horrible roar ! Listen to the people yelling ! And those little motor cars bumping into each other !—didn't the people look silly sitting behind the toy steering-wheels ! Useful, though, so one heard, any of these jolting, rushing things, give your inside a good shake up—bring it on.

That music, how loud it was, it fairly hurt one's ears ! Round and round the couples rode, as quiet as quiet, smiling a bit, dreamy-looking ; and one little boy, been there all the evening, pennyworth after pennyworth, now on an ostrich, now on a horse.

He 'd be sick, he would, sooner or later. The whirl slackened, the tune stopped, lights ceased from spinning. E. Pettigrew's Grand Electric Leaping Animals, she read : all sorts of funny birds and beasts. They went on turning, turning, after the music, slower and slower, in a kind of sick way. That kid was off at last, feeling in his grubby pockets. Empty. No more rides.

'Here.' She held out a penny. 'Want another go?'

He took it, hardly looking at her, dashed back again just in time. Out blared the music. She saw him scramble on and go sailing away. Well, his stomach was his own look-out. Seemed a shame he should have to stop for want of pence, when he enjoyed it so.

What a nice tune—so gay, such a swing to it! But all this gave you a nasty feeling on the chest—suffocating, faint-like, as if there was too much of everything—too much life. A year or two ago you 'd have done anything, gone anywhere, for a bit of fun. Nowadays nothing seemed fun. It must be having that weakness in the chest.

'Like a ride ?' said some one.

Up went the pierrot face, gazing into his. She had noticed him there beside her for a long time : great, burly man, sheepish-looking, ruddy complexioned, heavy-featured, but handsome too, quite the gentleman—nice, refined voice.

Her lips lifted, decorously smiling, red against white.

'No, thank you all the same. I don't care for these whirligig things, they upset me.'

'Dare say they would me too. I haven't tried 'em for years,' he said.

'I 'm just the same on a boat. I went once on an all-day excursion—with a friend. Never again. Isn't the sea terrible ? Don't you hate it ?'

'No, I like the sea all right. I was in the navy once.'

'Oh, yes, were you really ?'

She gave him another smile. That sounded all right.

After a bit she sighed, moved away without another look at him. She felt so sad, somehow, all of a sudden ; the music, perhaps, or something about him standing there beside her, watching her so heavy and so hang-dog, blocking out everything with his bulk. It would be like pushing at a mountain or an elephant to try to push him away.

There he was, there he was ! Oh, what a jump her heart gave ! There he was, at last ! Just as she had expected : she 'd known he would be along some time. Lucky she had put on her black and white printed crêpe-de-chine, and her new hat. He was coming out of that Palace of Beauty with a lot of others, and laughing fit to burst. He didn't look as if he 'd admired them, anyway. No wonder. Beauty through the ages, indeed—Cleopatra, Helen of Troy, and all. Painted old tarts, she'd seen them. Ought to be ashamed of themselves in their tights and bits of bare skin showing, and sticking gold saucer things over their nasty great chests, to call attention.

Weren't his teeth lovely, and the way he smiled —oh! . . . Really, his head was lit up like as if he 's got a halo. If he only knew, if he only knew—there was nothing she wouldn't do for him. . . .

He was going to do the whole round of the side-shows, from the look of it. There he went now, knocking the ninepins down one after the other, never missing practically; quite sour the keeper of the stall looked, dealing out prize packets of Gold Flake. How he did enjoy himself, letting fly with those balls one after another, as fast as fast, whizz, whizz, whizz! aiming so sure and flinging his arm out so strong and free. Down clattered the ninepins. It was quite exciting.

Follow him. Never let him out of sight. Sooner or later he 'd be bound, be bound to see you, as he strolled from stall to stall, topping the crowd by head and shoulders, laughing, talking with his friends.

Now the shooting-gallery, next the dart-throwing. There was nothing he couldn't do. He beat every-body. He was giving back his prizes now: he didn't want them. He was joking with the dark, suspicious-looking owners, and they were smiling, watching him. He looked so careless, such a happy nature; like as not he 'd had his pockets picked, but that wouldn't upset him.

Now the cocoanut-shy. What silly things cocoanuts looked, sitting in their holders with their beards hanging down. Click, click went the balls. Down tumbled two.

'Oh, lord,' he cried, 'a couple of 'em!' He waved them in his hands, juggled with them. 'What am I to do with them? . . . Here, catch, you!' He threw them into the midst of an audience of urchins, laughed, went on his way.

Follow him, follow him. It was like something on the pictures, all the bustle of the fair, and him the hero going about so heedless, and you the heroine, creeping like a shadow after him. . . .

All sorts of funny games he stopped at—games with coins, and dice, and race-horse games; and a try-your-strength machine that gave him his money back.

Up came a gypsy woman with great gold rings in her ears, whining softly, gazing into his face, so soupy, out of her black eyes, wanting to tell his fortune. 'Come on, Brown,' said he. 'Here 's your chance. Have your fortune told on your birthday.' But it was him the gypsy wanted. You could hear her: 'Gentleman, dear,' she called him, the cheek of her; 'you 've got a lucky face, dear,' she said.

'A handsome wife and ten thousand a year, eh?' he teased her. He put a coin in her hand, shook his head laughing, passed on to the sweet stall. Ever so bright it was with its striped sugar-sticks under the dazzling jet, fruit-drops pink, green, yellow, butterscotch in silver paper. Would he buy any? Sweets were lovely, specially walnut toffee. Why not buy some, go and stand beside him. . . . The group had separated. Now was the moment: he was alone.

'Quarter of walnut toffee, please.'

Why, he was buying some of the same. He saw her.

'Hello!—what 's your name?—Pansy-faces. . . . All on your little lone?'

Excited his voice was, and she noticed his eyes, bright, the blacks of them dilated. He 'd had some drinks.

She stared up at him; and once more the small face moved him: the hungry eyes, blue-shadowed, the flawless china mask.

'Where 've you been hiding yourself?'

What he always said. . .

'Well, I 've been rather poorly.'

'Sorry to hear that. . . . Buying toffee? Here, let me get you some.'

He bought a bulging bagful, gave it to her. Somebody was calling him: 'Hugh! Hugh!'

'See you later,' he said. 'Tried the merry-go-rounds? We 'll have a ride.'

He hesitated a little, repeated 'See you later,' made a little gesture with his hand, ran off to join his friends.

Never, he thought, had he known any one take her pleasures so seriously, have so little sense of humour.

She saw them close around him, laughing, teasing

him very likely : ' Who 's your friend ? ' Oh, what would he say ? . . . What would he call her ? . . . Oh ! he 'd never say a thing to take away a girl's character, surely not, so kind he was, and courteous. . .

She saw him jump on to a horse, heard loud whoops and hunting cries, as the roundabout gathered pace. Round he went . . . round he went . . . wheeling away from her . . . towards her . . . away, away. Oh, God, that sick whirl, and him there, leaving her behind, forgetting her. She leaned on the barrier, gripped it till her fingers hurt. Look at him, turning round to shout and laugh. Always the way : dashing on to the next thing, some one to meet, somewhere to go : no time for her. No good waiting, really. They were all going out in a crowd towards another roundabout with little cars hung on to it, room for two, flying right out over people's heads as they went round : awful.

Lost, lost. What should she do ? Too much trouble, it seemed, to go on living, let alone walk about, or go home. Heartsick—that was the very word ; and dizzy with the shouting, the glare, the smell. Such a sudden joy, and now the disappointment. . . . Well, go on hanging about on the chance, she supposed. . . . She looked at her bag of sweets. The very sight of them made her want to retch.

She stood outside a tent, heard a man shouting over and over again : ' This way, ladies and gentlemen, for the Ugliest Woman in the World.' The crowd streamed in unceasingly. They went in eager, sheepish, came out solemn, not amused. Some made pitying remarks, some looked quite disgusted. What did they want to see such sights for ?—some awful deformity, most likely. And weren't people's faces horrid, really—their expressions ? She 'd noticed it often lately : like a lot of animals, goodness knows what kind, nothing so harmless as sheep. Difficult to believe we are all God's Children. . . . But all the same, what did the woman look like ? Might as well have a peep : something to think about ; anything was better than just standing waiting, being stared at, nudged by drunken brutes—waiting, knowing it was no good waiting. . . .

And as she slipped into the crowd, she felt that this, this queueing up, this paying your penny to see a freak penned up in the dirt and squalor of a tent, like a beast in a show, for all to make a mock and a byword of—this was, of all the things she had ever done, the most against her nature, the most shocking letting of herself down. How could she be so common ? . . . It was all his fault.

She was pushed forward into the tent on the surge of the crowd, shut eyes for fear of what she would see, had to open them.

It seemed silent in the tent, thought Tom, after the last he had been in, where a sort of nigger woman rolled her eyes and writhed in a dismal way : quiet, dark, one lamp burning, and there she sat, in a decent black stuff blouse and skirt, a little shawl on her shoulders, an elderly woman, grey-haired, knitting. A hush in the tent . . . a child burst into a wailing cry. People spoke in low voices, fell silent, went away soon, sorry that they 'd intruded on her, this poor old knitting granny in monster's guise : especially the men : it was not funny, not what they 'd expected. The men were ashamed for Woman.

Why, it was a disease, thought Tom: elephantiasis, that was what it was ; how could they let her ? . . . How could she ? . . . those hands, twice the normal size, that hump, those purple growths for lips, the monstrous length of upper lip and chin ; and, surmounting all, that infinitesimal pair of eyes, mildly twinkling, mildly self-conscious, as she surveyed the pilgrims to her shrine. It made him feel hot and guilty—ungentlemanly, he felt, to see her. He left the tent, strolled away, tried to forget her ; but his melancholy persisted, the face haunted him. He stopped, assailed by the most painful sense of responsibility. He must go back.

He gripped the barrier hard, leaned forward, cleared his throat. She laid down her knitting and came towards him. (Oh, that face, looming nearer and nearer !)

'Good-evening, sir,' she said. She had the voice

of a motherly old housekeeper, dignified and respectful. She waited.

What to say or do now ? He grew red. His voice burst out of him.

' I say, why do you do this ? '

Her story was not long, was very simple. It was an illness, came on when she was thirty ; before that she 'd been—well—a nice-looking girl. She pulled a little locket from her bosom, opened and displayed it : a nice-looking girl. She was a married woman (and she held her hand up, showing the broad gold band upon the finger)—had a son, a sailor now, a daughter too, an invalid. Well, then, this illness ; and her husband died ; not a penny coming in, her daughter worse and worse, on her back with spinal trouble, year after year. Nothing but the workhouse or the Home for Incurables. Well, that made the poor girl frantic, very nearly killed her. So then she said to herself, well then, she said, Sir, I 'll make my face my fortune—remembering the fairs and the freaks, as a child. She didn't mind the life at all, and sent home money regular : plenty and to spare there was to keep her daughter comfortable, her son's wife for company and all her son's children.

There was no way, thought Tom, in which he could possibly express to her such feelings as he had —disturbing feelings of pity, horror, admiration. God, he thought, what an eye-opener ! Life gave some people a dirty deal. That son now, the sailor, far away in foreign waters, thinking of his mother, not sitting waiting for him by her own fireside, but touring the country, year in year out, as a freak with a fair. Good God, a man's own mother! . . . and she herself, that good old woman, wandering from place to place with the appalling burden of her own body, forced, since the world would pay, to show the world that which, surely, she would have hidden if she could more secretly than a modest woman her nakedness. It was all wrong. . . . He realized suddenly that an audience had gathered round him, to gape and listen, hoping for another side-show.

'Good-night,' said Tom.

'Good-night to you, sir,' said she.

He fumbled in his pocket, held out half a crown.

'Thank you very much, sir.'

'Good luck,' he muttered gruffly. He blundered out of the tent, dark red in the face and furtive.

What had come over him to-night, making him feel and act in such an extraordinary way? It must be the wine at dinner . . . or being so lonely. What would they think of him in the office, if they knew? He 'd be thankful when he got back to work. It had been a most wretched, a most unsettling holiday.

He stood at the entrance of the tent, staring upwards at a sky full of stars. Funny thing: he had not noticed stars for years; had forgotten what a lot there were, and how they shone.

Pansy came out of the tent and stood beside him. He looked down presently and saw her.

'Were you in there?' he said.

'Yes. I heard what she said to you.'

'Hmm. Pretty awful, isn't it?'

'Perhaps she doesn't mind, you know. I don't believe she minds.'

'I hope to God not,' he said.

They stood side by side in the humming and populous solitude, not drawn to each other—not exactly—but inevitably together: the last two people left in the world. No need to look before or after. They had nothing to tell one another, and nothing to conceal. With their quiet exchange of words was no exchange of glances, no challenge or invitation.

'Anyway,' said Pansy, vehemently, 'she's not what I call ugly—not after the first shock. It came over me all of a sudden when she smiled, and I said to myself: *you're* not ugly—not as bad, by a long chalk, as some I've seen to-night. I wish I'd told her that.'

'Mm,' said Tom, wondering rather dubiously if he agreed with her.

They were both silent, thinking kindred thoughts: that beauty is only skin-deep (how true it was)—that handsome is as handsome does (how they came home, these sayings, when one stopped to think . . .).

'Well, I've had enough of the fun of the fair for one night,' said Tom. 'This sort of thing's wasted on me, I suppose.'

'A little goes a long way, to my mind,' said Pansy. 'Some people have a funny idea of enjoying themselves.' (That young Miller now, and all those others with him, rampaging around, playing the giddy goat; he had been watching them. They looked as though they 'd keep it up till midnight. Luckily they seemed to have disappeared. It would not do to be seen like this.) 'It 's all right if you 're young, I suppose.'

'You 're not old,' said Pansy. 'It 's just that one 's different.'

Different, they felt: wise, knowing life for what it was.

They were silent again.

He eyed her narrowly, thinking that he failed now to detect what, at first sight, had seemed to be written all over her: the rapacity, the proclamation of lips and eyes, the lascivious promise of her whole person. Now, in spite of himself, desire was lacking. This business of picking up a girl was turning out quite differently from what Potter had led him to imagine. It was not brisk, or bantering or business-like. It felt important; it disturbed him with emotions unconnected with physical appetite; it made him melancholy. He did not know how to proceed, or whether he wanted to proceed. It seemed to him likely that he had mistaken her calling, and that she would reject any advances with contempt and indignation. She was taking no notice of him now at all, but looking about everywhere, as if searching for some one: her mother, perhaps, or her young man. The minutes passed.

She stared in every direction : not a sign. It was getting late. He must have gone away.

Sick at heart she was . . . and it was plain now : it was all pretence, his friendliness. He loathed the very sight of her.

Well, then . . . this man . . . she looked up and met his mute, shame-faced inquiry and appeal. He was looking at her now with the look she knew, but pitiful really, more than greedy.

'Lonely ?' she asked, in a different, a faintly professional voice.

He nodded.

'I 'll bet you are. I thought to myself in there : What 's he want to go talking to her for ? He must be hard up.' She capped her sally with a brittle and unconvincing peal of laughter, shot him a glance and added : 'I 'm only teasing. It was a very kind act, I thought. I saw you give her something, too. I said to myself : He 's generous.' (Looked as if he had something to spare, anyway.)

He heard the sharp undertone in her last words. She was giving him a lead. Generous, yes, of course he was—within reasonable limits. Well, he was in for it now. He cleared his throat.

'You 're welcome,' he muttered, feeling choked, 'to what I 've got on me.' (The last of the damned holiday money.)

'That 's all right.' She smiled, encouraged him. 'Cheer up. What about a bite of supper ?' She held up her bag of toffee. 'That 's all I 've had since lunch,' she said. 'Ugh, nasty, sickly stuff.' With a violent gesture she threw it from her. 'I know of a very nice hotel where we could get something—very exclusive.'

'Right-o!' said Tom.

Supposing some one saw him. . . . He pulled his hat over his eyes, longed for a false moustache, any disguise.

'Come along, then,' she said gently, taking his arm.

When Grace had read Tom's wire, announcing his arrival, she knew it for the first warning, the first threat to illusion. Immediately she telegraphed; and silence followed. He did not come, or write. But in the days succeeding, the web wore ever thinner. It was going to let her out, after all. She calculated the period of her absence: five weeks, nearly six. Her money was all gone,—all save the amount of her fare back north. Hour after hour she had been moving on towards the town again, and the autumn rains and gales in the cold streets. It had all been a deception. How the Parish Ladies of old days would have gloated: husband and home abandoned, duty neglected, the vicar's daughter, always unreliable, given over to guilty love and gone away. Odd, how the thought of them, their falcon eyes, their bloodhound noses, their parrot tongues, affected her still with childish feelings of hatred, awe, and superstition. They were so powerful, these guardians of morality, these dictators of her duty:

from Parish Ladies they grew to Giants, and ruled the world. They were sending her back from the recaptured state of original sin, from flower gardens and idle solitude, from ecstatic egoisms and unrealities as of another childhood, from pangs of love that brought forth love unchecked, and fed on love alone —back to a numbered dwelling in a town, to a steady husband, and the domestic responsibilities of a married woman.

Yes, it was true, her husband had sent a letter weekly, giving such news as should engage her whole attention : for he told her what her life was. His message was authentic, the accent unmistakable. Useless to say, like a child in a game, ' I 'm deaf now,' and turn away. Useless to run back, panic-stricken, rebellious, for a last glimpse, foolishly crying : ' I 've been cheated. All that has happened is not true, has been against my will. I am a poet, almost—a suppressed creator—' (surely it was to be a poet, almost, to see hollyhocks as music). ' I should have been beautiful, had love fulfilled me—' (surely it had been about to be beautiful, her mysterious seventeen-year-old face in the glass, one day long ago ; about to take on the symmetry, the harmonious stillness of a madonna, dreaming on things to come. She had seen her own beauty coming to meet her just that once : never again. And now again this summer she had seen it, passing her in the distance and bidding her farewell). Useless to say : ' I 'll go back now, and take what is my due: take love, take happiness, take perfect emotional fulfilment: grasp all I had a mind for, use every talent, waste no opportunity.' That was the nonsense common to any dissatisfied woman, treading the dangerous, neutral, and shadowy territory between youth and middle age. 'It 's her age,' would whisper the Parish Ladies, excited, furtively amused. 'Give her no sympathy. Keep the young men away. She 'll settle down again.' . . . Was that it?

Let her remember why she had come here. She had come here, not to prepare for change, for further flight, for life and love, but for the resumption, after a little rest and change of air, of her duties as a housewife. Let her remember there was no escape.

How could a woman forget, as she had forgotten—permit herself entirely to forget ten years of married life? Such a woman, irresponsibly revelling in sham freedom, was a disgrace to womanhood. A good sell for her to wake up and find Tom waiting to let her into his home again, quite unaltered, his bowler hat on, and the latch-key fastened to his watch-chain. He would say, 'What did you do all day by yourself?'—and she would have to say, annoyingly, 'Nothing at all.' He would scarcely ask, 'What did you think about?'—so she would not have to answer, unconvincingly, 'Flowers, trees, birds, cornfields, and water.' Still less would he inquire, 'Whom did you think of?'—still less would she be required to reply, insanely, 'Entirely of young Miller.'

She lingered a few days longer, then packed her suit-case and consulted a time-table at the village inn. She left at the fullness of the year, the pregnant pause before the treasure is spilt. The corn was heavy in the ear, the moulded copper and tawny fields pressed up against the sky-line, bursting with their yield. The small green apples swelled upon the bough. The roses were ready to drop. The fat, pink clover crop loaded the air with sweetness.

The day of her departure, walking for the last time in the garden, she saw, half-hidden in the flower-bed beneath her bedroom window, the draggled skeleton of a young swallow.

So it had been there all the time, waiting for her: it had dropped down, of course, and been broken, and never flown away. There was no winged life existing through her care.

She had gone away for her holiday a little farther, a little more recklessly than usual; was coming back a little later, a little more restless and rebellious.

And now when she thought of the town she saw only the stretch of street and tram-line through the leafless lilac tree, from the sitting-room window.

When she thought of him, she saw nothing but a shadowy figure passing, never stopping, never seeing her.

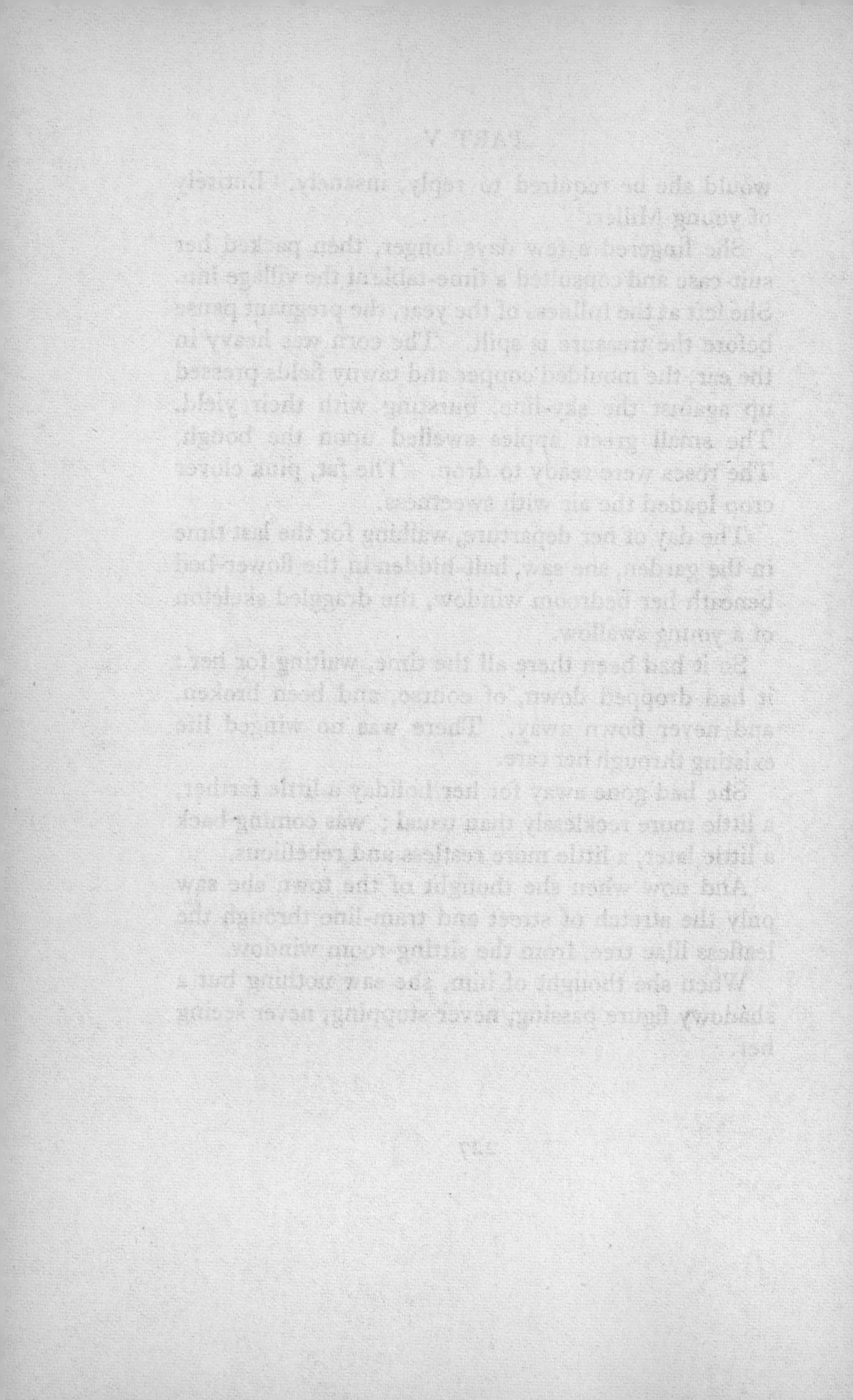

PART VI

PART VI

THE end of September. It is the time for autumn gardens. Michaelmas daisies are in the borders, and bright, lovely, free-petalled dahlias, asters of all colours, but formless and insipid ; and deep red and yellow zinnias, with their stiff-carved abstract painted heads. The asparagus beds are a feathery forest for children playing hide-and-seek. Cat-mint still decorates the edges of the borders ; the last crop of lavender throws up its many spindling lances ; and the lit autumn roses burn with concentrated glow, richer by far than their summer sisters. The lawn is drenched in soaking dews till midday, and the trees stare through sunlit mists with a metallic, bluish glaze. The rich rowan leans with its toppling weight of berries. The apple-pickers hoist their ladders in the orchard. The rooks are in the glittering stubble. Around the fields the hedges begin to smoulder and burn ; the green elms are patched with yellow, like a bold-patterned brocade.

In the town, at dusk, when the lamps are lit, blue essence sifts through the streets like shaken powder, and flocks of red cloud linger unstirring behind black chimney-pots at the end of every vista.

In the parks the browning trees shrivel, and the park gardeners begin to pile and burn the fallen leaves. Out of the heart of them the blue and acrid smoke is drawn in a thick rope.

What number was it, Hugh asked himself, wandering down the avenue on his last evening—31, 33, 37? All these house-fronts looked alike, the windows screened with mauve or yellow net. No, Number 37 was unveiled, and he caught a glimpse of brownish curtains. That seemed characteristic of her somehow: colourless and unadorned. Might as well look in for a moment: there was nothing particular to do. He rang the bell, reflecting while he waited that good-byes were a thing he particularly hated; thinking, too, how grim must be the lives of people who lived behind these façades of tile and stucco. But they would not realize, of course, that their lives were grim: so it was all right.

The stout maid beamed at him, in her eyes and smile such unreserved, angelic greeting, that he felt quite startled. She looked as if she had been waiting for years to welcome him as one coming at last with glad tidings from a far country. What a pleasant, peaceful-looking face and bosom; what comforting hips. He felt suddenly that not to have called would have been an unfriendly, inexcusable omission.

'Oh, yes, sir. Mrs. Fairfax is in. Please come in, sir.' Of course she was in, she seemed to imply, reassuringly: always at home, she 'd be, to the likes of him.

And triumphantly she flung open the sitting-room

door ; with soft and intimate emphasis she announced :

' Mr. Miller, madam.'

Grace cried out :

' Oh ! '

She was sitting on the floor in front of the gas-fire, and as she scrambled to her feet she felt a flush submerge her from head to foot.

' I wondered if you 'd be at home,' he said in his dual voice, diffident and assured, reluctant and sociable.

She heard her own cry ringing in her ears—the avowals in it, the greeting rapturous, breathless, and amazed, of a woman to her lover. She felt a nervous tremor start in her bowels, in every limb, and bent down, helplessly pulling a chair-cover straight, patting a cushion.

Why had he come ? Why this simple, awaited, this undreamed-of miracle ?

' Sit down,' she said.

What an awkward manner she had, he thought. How soon, consistently with politeness, could one get away ?

' Reading ? ' he said, looking down at the novel lying on the floor.

' More or less.'

' Do you read a lot ? '

' A lot of nonsense. I used to read all sorts of things—go to lectures—think myself cultured and superior. Now I can't concentrate.' She put a hand to her forehead.

'I used to read, too,' he said, 'at Oxford . . . quite stiff things.'

Oliver had given him a reading-list—poetry, essays, biography, goodness knows what—and he had ploughed through it zealously: given up cocktail parties and going out after Hall to sit in his digs and read; gone about ostentatiously with a volume of Blake or something in his pocket; felt an intellectual virtue uplift and sustain him for a season. He said:

'My trouble is—things go in and come straight out again. The moment I 've polished off the last page and shut up the book, I 've clean forgotten every blessed word.' He laughed.

'Cinemas are our undoing, I think.' She laughed too.

It was all right now. The usual ease was re-establishing itself. She stopped trembling. Why had he come? Simply because he wanted to see her—could it be?—because he liked her company; because all this time he had not forgotten about her after all. Perhaps another invitation. . . .

'Frightfully cold, isn't it?' he said.

'Yes. Summer 's gone. It would be nice in the country to-day. I was just thinking about it.'

Still harping on that theme!

'You always are—aren't you?' he said shyly, with a hint of chaff.

'Yes. I 'm a bore.'

She looked out at the misty, darkening street, made a grimace, leaned forward and turned up the gas-fire.

'Gas-fires are terrible,' she said. 'They haunt me in the night. Obscene little Molochs, squatting in every room, with their bland blind faces. . . .' She looked up at him, her eyes narrowed, twinkling, and said dubiously: 'I 've noticed people in this town with the same sort of look. . . . Faces like those pictures of insides—intestines, and things. . . . Have you noticed? . . .

He grinned, wrinkling his nose.

'However, as Tom says, they 're very useful and convenient. He had them put in everywhere. I told him once he ought to adopt one for his crest. He 's always talking about family crests and things.' She gasped and checked herself, lowered her eyes, a little ashamed. This was not playing the game, as Tom would say. At the time, he had been puzzled and suspicious. She added quickly: 'It would be very suitable for me. I sit over this one all day and breathe it in.'

Annie appeared at the door, in her best apron.

'Would the gentleman care for some tea?' Her voice was mild, reproachful.

'No, thanks,' he said hurriedly. 'I must be off very soon.'

'Not just a cup?' she said, tenderly persuasive.

'No, thanks.'

The door closed again with a disappointed, lingering click. (But she had accomplished her purpose. She had seen them both with her own eyes, sitting together as pleasant as could be, smiling at each other.)

'Ages since I 've seen you,' he said.

'Yes. Not since that day. . . . Oh, it was so lovely ! Oh, it 's so long ago.'

The sudden heightening and warmth of tone, breaking through the restraint of her habitual manner, took him aback. Had it really meant so much to her ? He seemed to catch an uncomfortable glimpse of empty and monotonous days.

'Yes, it was a good day,' he agreed.

But for his own part, he did not remember it as a striking success. He remembered only a general atmosphere of moodiness, unease—the old boy refusing to come out of his shell again ; and other more disturbing reasons for being glad when the week-end was over. In fact, he had refrained from dwelling on it ever since. He said, to change the subject :

'What have you been doing all the summer ? Been away ? '

'Yes, I went away to the South, by myself—just as I said I would.'

'Oh, yes, I remember.' He laughed. (She really was funny, like a child, her eagerness, her triumph.) 'You were determined to do a bolt.'

'Yes. And I did ! I found a little red village and the loveliest country—a real southern landscape

—just what I 'd wanted. I was very happy there. But that was weeks ago. It seems like a dream now—too remote and unreal to remember almost. I can't think about it. . . . Since I 've been back, I 've done nothing at all.'

Nothing but think of him and forbid herself to think of him ; nothing but trample on hope and feel it rear once more its sickly head ; nothing but look out of the window and never see him pass.

' And where have you been ? ' she said. ' I thought perhaps you 'd gone away for good.'

' Not yet.' He smiled. ' I 've been in Scotland these last three weeks.'

' And Grock ? '

' Yes, and Grock. He 's in grand form. I 've left him up there with my people.'

' You look as if you 'd been having draughts of moorland air.'

Like a sort of sun-baby he looked—so fresh, so glowing : he made her want to laugh.

' Never been so fit in my life.' He stretched himself. ' Do you know Scotland ? '

' Not in the least.'

' What—never been across the Border ? Try it next time you run away by yourself.' His look teased her.

' How 's your sister ? ' she said. ' Your lovely sister.'

He looked gratified by the epithet.

' I was forgetting you 'd met her. Oh, she 's all

right, I think. She never writes. I suppose I 'll be seeing her in a few days.'

'Is she coming to see you again?'

'No. In London, I mean. I 'm off to-morrow, you know.'

'Off? For good, do you mean?'

'Yes. I thought perhaps you might have heard. Though goodness knows why you should have,' he added hastily. (For it sounded as if he thought his movements should be of some importance to her.) 'I don't suppose you take a violent interest in my career—or anything else at the office.'

'Tom doesn't tell me much,' she murmured, adding slowly: 'He would, I think. He likes to talk about the office. It 's my fault. I—I don't encourage him enough.'

And less than ever since his return. A change had taken place: they were now less strangers than estranged. He had given up bothering to keep their evenings on an agreeable footing—seemed acquiescent now in the silences. Otherwise he might have risked a snub and mentioned changes . . . mentioned the departure of young Miller.

'No,' she said. 'I didn't know you were going away.'

'I thought I 'd just look in and say good-bye.'

'That was very kind of you. . . . I might never have known you 'd gone.' Her voice faded. It was very kind. Surprising, really. He must like her a little. . . .

'I've been sort of going round saying good-bye all day. It's a beastly feeling, isn't it?'

'Yes.' She paused. 'Have you seen Norah MacKay?'

'Not yet. I must try to blow in this evening.'

He had come first to her. . . . Was there any significance in that—any weighing and apportioning of their respective value to him?

What did it matter? . . .

'I haven't seen her since that week-end,' he said.

'Nor I.'

She got up, leaned her arms on the mantelpiece, and her head on her arms. Glancing at her drooping, unanimated profile, he told himself her whole attraction, such as it was, must lie in a smile she had, an occasional expression. For he had thought her quite attractive; but now she was positively plain, looked any age. Now, more acutely than ever, he had the feeling that he was being detained; as if in another minute she was going to ask him or tell him something which would make it awkward to get away without some sort of fuss. And he asked himself who before in his life had given him this feeling, so that he recognized it as a familiar experience. And it flashed on him suddenly: Oliver again.

'Well,' she said at last, 'I told you not to stay, didn't I?'

'Did you?' he murmured.

'I'm so glad for your sake. And now one can just go to sleep again. It was more comfortable.'

Her head was turned from him, and she spoke so low he scarcely heard her ; thought of asking her to repeat herself ; decided not to ; for the few syllables he had distinguished sounded so very odd.

'And now where ?' she said, looking round and smiling faintly at him.

'Oh, abroad again, I think. Back to the Argentine perhaps. Or I may get a job in Ceylon. I 'm afraid I 'm hopeless. Always have to be trying something new. . . .'

She saw sun beating down on burning sands, and sapphire seas lapping the coral reefs ; palm-trees waving over low white houses ; and brown-skinned people—brown women, graceful, soft-voiced, smiling, clad in bright garments, moving in the fields of rice and cotton ; and intensest sunlight always, filling the fierce blue sky, the thirsty land from end to end ; no clouds, no shadows at all. She saw him, standing in the sun, alone, smoking his pipe, the sleeves of his white shirt rolled up, looking about him with calm blue eyes. . . .

'And I shall go on staying in the same place till I 'm an old woman—like a limpet on a rock—as if I hadn't any limbs or senses. Why doesn't one just set out, and go on and on for ever ?

He laughed awkwardly.

'Because one prefers to settle down, I suppose,' he said. 'Have a home.'

'I don't. I 've got nothing to keep me,' she said harshly. '*Nothing*.'

He was at a loss. And he could only think that here again sympathy seemed to be required of him; and he was, as Oliver had told him, incapable of producing a morsel of it. Instead, a deep antagonism filled him, a desire to fly. He simply could not help despising, recoiling from any one who wanted pity. The more he tried to force himself, the colder he felt. Why should people moan? He never did so himself. He loathed any interference with his private feelings.

He said nothing, and presently she asked, quietly:

'Would you like to settle down, then?'

'I suppose I would, some time or other.' His voice was stilted, a little hostile.

'Wanderers always want a home. A place to come back to in between times and somebody always waiting. Isn't that it?' She smiled.

'Perhaps.' He smiled too. This was better. After all, she was not going to tell him (as more than one woman had) what a failure her married life was: how coarse, unsympathetic, bad-tempered her husband was. He was not going to be forced to mutter 'Bad luck,' and offer a handkerchief (or, as upon one ghastly occasion in London, a most reluctant shoulder).

'I feel,' she said, flushing and looking at him in a shy, deprecatory smiling way (and now, he thought, she looked quite pretty again)—'I can't help feeling I should like you to get everything you want.'

'Thanks awfully,' he said, taking up her jesting tone. He added: 'I always seem to somehow. It 's awful.'

'You always will,' she cried. 'You 're the person I 've been waiting for all my life. . . .'

He looked at her startled. She leaned towards him and continued eagerly:

'I always felt there must be somebody who was perfectly happy. You 're happy, aren't you? You 're not afraid of anything; and you 'll always be lucky. Good luck's the greatest talent in the world. . . .' She paused. Her expression was exalted.

'I do enjoy life, I suppose,' he murmured, overcome. 'All the same—I get pretty blue sometimes.'

For truth must be served, he felt. This was not he. A lot she knew about him! What would she say if he tried to explain to her what happened whenever he stopped to think: how he felt stirring in the depths of him his potent legacy from Oliver: that sly and secret draining of his self-confidence? If only he could explain, without her thinking he was asking for sympathy, it might be a comfort. . . . But no. He could not. Silence and secrecy were the only remaining links, as it were; the only loyalties he could offer.

'Do you get blue?' She smiled at him, softly, teasingly. She thought it was a joke. 'I can't believe it. As long as I'm alive I shall think of you somewhere in the world, still gay and lucky. . . . So you must promise me you'll be so always.'

His smile faded as he caught her tense expression. She seemed to be serious, to be willing him to speak: to say, as he now said, quite seriously, obediently, looking at her and repeating after her like a child:

'I promise.'

She told herself that he was armoured now in her love. This must be her faith, in future, if she was to endure life. She must make herself believe in the spiritual efficacy of her love.

He was moving, looking at his watch. He was going.

'I must be getting on,' he said.

'Will you stay a little longer?'

'Well——' he said, feeling, for some reason, he really could not think of any excuses.

'Please do.'

She had not yet dragged herself to the uttermost peak where she could shake his hand and say a simple good-bye. She must be allowed a few more minutes to shape herself a lasting image of this meeting. She must make it endure in the infinite void, with inward reality, for the rest of her life; so that his absence, his silence, his forgetfulness—which were to start in another half-hour at most and continue for ever more—should be mere facts of earthly time and space—terms artificial and of no account.

She saw him relax, lean back again in his chair, and she felt the cord of her anguish miraculously loosen, and a fragile joy emerge. He was here. He was now. . . . Holding this here, this now, every fragment of it, with all her being, she must reach always.

She smiled.

He felt that some sort of concealed crisis was at an end. Perhaps she 'd had a pain. . . .

'Been to any good movies lately?' he asked cheerfully.

'One or two. But I haven't properly started my winter season yet.'

'We ought to have done one together,' he said. 'Two fans like us. What a pity we never fixed it up.'

'Yes, what a pity. . . . Tom and I have such different tastes.'

'I should think you had a good many different tastes?' he ventured, feeling a little reckless (but really she was a nice woman—could be trusted not to moan).

'A good many.' Her eye twinkled faintly.

He plunged.

'I 've wondered . . .' He stopped. He was being an idiot. He felt obliged to go on: 'It seems funny, though I don't know why—I mean you and him . . . I don't really mean that . . . I mean . . . You seem so different. . . .'

'Yes. I know. Why did I marry him? . . .'

PART VI

She bent her head in her hands, considering. (She was not like others, who had popped out with an explanation before you 'd thought of asking for one.)

'I must think,' she said.

And with a sharp return of memories long-buried, she saw herself, fourteen years ago, in the first year of the war, a dreamy young woman with awkward, unmanageable limbs, and that face that was not, but might have been, like that of the Luini Madonna with the full, pale, delicate lids, the parted hair, the mysterious lips with upward-curling points in the Medici print on Father's study wall. And she saw Tom—Tom, muscular and well set up, not heavy, in the uniform of the Royal Naval Reserve—coming ashore from his mine-sweeper one summer afternoon, leaning over the gate and very politely asking Father the way to the golf-links; and Father, ever hospitable, straightway inviting him to tea. And after he had gone, feeling very happy; and after that seeing him nearly every day: waiting on the beach for him; walking with him on the chalky downs, up to the Fort and the wire entanglement, up to Tennyson's Monument; picnicking in the heathery part, high above the sea (she could feel and smell the heather now, taste the strawberry jam in the sandwiches, see herself pick a chance white spray and give it him—'for luck'; blush to hear him vow he 'd keep it always. . . . Where was it now?). She saw herself following him round the links with his clubs hour after hour contentedly; having a lesson from him one day, and being so hopeless, and he so patient and encouraging. They had laughed a lot at some of her shots.

She remembered her beating heart when he had said good-bye, ordered to the North Sea; her anxious heart that winter; how she had waited for his letters and kept them in a locked attaché case to read and to re-read till the folds fell to pieces. She remembered how he had never failed to come for a day at least, on each short leave, to visit them; how his return had grown to be her only beacon, as the war went on and Father got weaker. She saw him being gentle with her father, giving him an arm up the steps, along the village street. Together they had watched him in the last year of the war, narrowing his life down week by week, uncomplainingly, shuffling ever more feebly to the final armchair and rug, the Bible, and herself or Tom reading aloud to him from the works of Sir Walter Scott. And Father had said, very soon before he died: 'He 's a good man, my dear. He 'll look after you'—with these words sanctioning an engagement that had never assumed the definite pre-marital status of an exchange of vows and rings. And he had looked after her. He had come down the moment he got her wire and made all the funeral arrangements; and taken her afterwards to his mother for consolation; and hunted for a job that would enable them to marry at once; and by that time, of course, she had known it was all a mistake ; and all the same, of course, she had married him.

'But then,' she said aloud, following the train of her unspoken thoughts, 'I was so packed full of unspent, undirected emotions when I was young, that I 'd have married almost any one.'

She tried to weight the blame, to sort the early truths from the distortions of memory, the prejudices, the frigid judgments of the present : to see Tom as he was, not his reflection in the diminishing mirror of unkind habit.

'I was very fond of Tom,' she said. 'We had some happy times at first.' She recalled times of being very close to Tom in tenderness and companionship : the time he had shown her his boyhood's collection of birds' eggs, and wondered if he wouldn't take it up again ; the time he had put his head down on her shoulder and whispered to her how bitterly he minded not having been able to go to the University . . . other times. . . . 'It was lovely to have a person of one's own—you know. I felt important and proud, being a married woman, and I determined to help Tom get on. I did help him—at first.' (Given him incentive and confidence, helped him to become the efficient machine she now disdained.) 'Then I had a baby, and it died——' She stopped short, painfully wishing her words unsaid : for that really did sound like asking for pity. It was real sob-stuff—just the sort of thing to engage the unthinking sympathies of a good-hearted normal young man. 'Tom minded very much,' she added. 'But by that time I dreaded producing something like him—or his mother—or like me. I didn't want a child. I thought perhaps it was just as well.'

He looked at her and was silent—grateful to her: for she was tiding them both over that distressing confidence of hers—deliberately sparing him, he supposed, some expression of condolence.

'It was a shame to marry him,' she cried. 'I used to know it was a shame. I used to remember it every day.' (Tell herself, every day, she 'd cheated him of all he 'd hoped for, starved his domestic virtues of their food.)

'Tom 's so nice. . . .'

'Awfully nice,' he agreed quickly. (A decent old buffer, genial and warm-hearted; a joke in the office—but they liked him all right.)

What unexpected force was this, she asked herself, driving her irresistibly to spend her last moments with the man she loved in wiping the dust, the mould, grey and corrupt accumulation of years, with care and tenderness off the portrait of her husband? It was inevitable. Truth, which she must obey, was lifting her to its own incorruptible heights.

'I was brought up to believe in matrimony,' she said, 'and monogamy, and pure womanhood waiting for pure love to come and lead it off to a pure home. A spade was called—anything except a spade. I was a very slow developer. By the time I started to wake up and think for myself, it was too late : I 'd lost my chance. I don't mind paying for being dishonest, and for swallowing all the ready-made sentimentality and hypocrisy. I can laugh at myself for being so easily taken in, and kick myself for being so muddled and spoon-fed and sluggish : and that 's some comfort. The pity is, to have harmed for life a person who trusted you.'

He had found her speech difficult to follow, disturbing in its kind of matter-of-fact despair : but the last words came home to him with startling force : for he too had wrought harm where he had been trusted. He had damaged Oliver for life, so Oliver had told him. So he said gravely :

'Yes—I know.'

But it would take a good deal, surely, he thought, to harm a tough-hided old hippopotamus like Uncle Tom.

'I expect it 's all right, really,' he said, vaguely but earnestly. He wanted to reassure her, tell her she was taking it all too seriously, reproaching herself unnecessarily. It was really very upsetting—though refreshing—to find her taking all the blame. And to divert the subject from the personal to the general plane (for she looked so very serious, sitting bolt upright and staring in front of her), he added, as man to man :

'Then you don't believe in marriage ?'

That made her laugh.

'In marriage? Oh, yes! *And* in bachelors and spinsters. And in having a hundred lovers, or one, or none. And in everything else you can think of, according to individual wants and capacities. . . . Oh, what would Tom say if he heard me? Tom 's a man of principle.'

And she thought to herself: 'After all, one can never get away from one's husband.' One asserted one's personal importance with such extravagant anxiety, saying to oneself: 'In spite of outward bondage I am free.' But it was not so. The edges got worn away, and independence slithered out.

'Freedom for the individual,' he murmured, remembering discussions at Oxford.

'Freedom. . . . Yes, I suppose so. Nobody interfering with anybody else's life. That 's why I—what I like about you—you 'd never let any one manage your life for you, would you? Not even somebody you loved. . . . Oh, Hugh! . . .' (What joy to say his name at last!)

She laid her hand on his, and he took it quickly, nervously, and squeezed it. Now, she told herself, she could say anything to him. She was so filled with the truth that she could not err in judgment; need not draw back, qualify, regret her reckless words.

'I 'll tell you,' she said. 'When I first saw you, it flashed on me I 'd seen you before. It was in a cinema the first night you arrived. You didn't see me. . . .' He listened to her, watched her, looking solemn and boyish. 'The next time—that time you came to tea—I wondered again. Your face seemed so familiar. But I know now why. Though I'd never seen you before, I recognized you at first sight. You were the person who was going to mean so much to me.'

He bent his head, was silent. This should be classifiable, he thought, as a tight corner; yet for some reason he did not feel embarrassed. Something in her manner convinced him she expected nothing of him. But he wished to goodness she would realize the truth about him.

'You know, you're all wrong about me,' he said earnestly. 'I'm simply hopeless.'

She smiled, shook her head, looked dreamy.

'I shall think of you . . .' she said.

He wished, he told himself, really wished he could be helpful. He was going away for ever. And she would have to stay. He was distressed for her.

'It's simply rotten for you,' he said blushing, 'having to stay here—when you hate it so. I wish you hadn't got to. I wish you could have the sort of life you like . . . .'

She opened her eyes wide.

'It's all right,' she said, smiling radiantly. 'It doesn't matter. You mustn't be sorry for me. I can't bear to be pitied.' (Really, he thought, she was extraordinarily nice.) 'I can stand *anything*. I 'm very tough.'

And she thought : there was something in her that was not herself ; something that seemed to prevail even beyond her own resources—an inheritance of strength, of endurance, of a religion that had no faith or hope. 'You 'll be like your mother,' Father had often said, smiling or shaking his head. Her mother had been in her grave these many years ; the photograph was lost, and the features had vanished from memory, and there remained of her only the image of the fashion which had surprised her childish eye—the fringe and the hour-glass figure, high collar, cloth buttons, and bustle. But she would be like her mother. . . . Yes, as one grew older, it happened thus. The moulded contours, the animal impulses, the flesh and blood of youth might differ from generation to generation ; but, beneath, endured a portion of the shape and structure, the bone of one's ancestors.

He was getting up. Now she must let him go.

'Well, I 'm afraid I really must be off,' he said.

He held his hand out.

'Good-bye, Hugh,' she said. 'Be happy. You've promised, remember.'

'Yes.' He grinned.

'Love some one. Marry her.'

'Oh, I 'll never marry,' he said gaily.

'No ?'

'Never find anybody to stick me.' (Any woman

would find him out in two twos—his nothingness.) 'Not for more than a month or two.'

'I think somebody might. . . .'

They smiled at each other ; and he thought again what a good sort she was. He was quite glad she 'd taken a fancy to him.

'Well, good-bye.'

She did not answer this time, and for a full moment their eyes met. There was something more, he felt, he ought to say. He would really like to say it ; but what was it ?

'I 've told you the story of my life,' she said. 'That 's a thing I 've never done before. You must forget it.'

'No, I won't do that,' he said soberly.

Perhaps that was part of it : he would not forget her. He was sure of that. She had impressed, affected him. He liked her. He looked at her helplessly.

She led him out into the hall and opened the door ; and he wrung her hand once more, ran down the steps, waved and was gone.

It was over.

It had not been loss, but gain—as she had purposed. The Parish Ladies could never point fingers, hold their sides, whisper behind their hands. With her integrity, she had dealt them their death-blow, and was free of them for ever.

She had told him all . . . and nothing.

A NOTE IN MUSIC

It could not have been better, she told herself . . . feeling her agony rise . . . it could not have been a more satisfactory parting.

She looked along the lamp-lit street and shut the door . . . then opened it again, left it open.

Tom would be home, very soon, now.

PART VII

PART VII

THE end of November.

The gale came shrieking across the common from the sea, driving straws, leaves, papers down upon the town. The swollen clouds heaped themselves across the sky from end to end; down came the rain. Those abroad in the streets leaned, struggled in tortured attitudes against the wall of wind, straining to place one foot before the other—suffocated, battered, blinded. Then all at once a lull; bruised light tore a way out; ached, pallid for a while between the stormy rifts—faltered once more and fainted. Wind roused with a roar from its caverns, whipped the rain again, rallied a million million stinging arrows, slapped them in rattling volleys on the windows.

She could not bear the groaning voice in the wind. She went to the kitchen, needing to see Annie.

'What a gale, Annie.'

'Yes, madam. Think of the poor sailors . . .'

She asked herself again where Annie had learnt her punctilious and respectfully elegant mode of address. It was not in the North that one was taught to call one's employer 'Madam.' It must be Annie's romantic imagination: setting a flourish as of stately homes upon the simple annals of the *bourgeoisie*.

'What have you got there, Annie?'

She had her back turned, was stooping down with a saucer of milk. A small black object was before the stove : a very wet kitten.

'It 's a little stray, madam, but it looks quite clean.'

She straightened herself with difficulty, leaned against the table. They watched the tiny creature curved over the white rim—deep, already, in a voluptuous lapping trance.

'I opened the door, and there it was on the step. It means luck, you know.'

She smiled, but briefly, mournfully. What was the matter with Annie lately ?

'Annie, I thought you might make an apple pudding for Mr. Fairfax to-night. You know, one of your special ones.'

'Very good, madam.'

No more. No lighting of the eye, no resolution to excel herself to-night in apple puddings. Her voice was flat—bored, almost. Was it possible that she had acquired some secret grief or grievance ?—even Annie ? Was she going to give her notice ? She bent down again with the milk-jug.

'You 're shockingly thin,' she murmured. 'Have some more, my piccaninny.'

As she raised herself and turned away, Grace decided that it was no fancy but a fact that for a long time now Annie had been trying to avoid her eye. She looked tired, had lost her colour.

'Annie, are you feeling ill ?'

'Not at all, madam.' Her tone was wary, almost sullen. She looked attentively at Grace under her eyelids: the picture of guilt, thought Grace, astonished. No child, or puppy, conscious of inevitable impending retribution could have looked more stubborn, more stricken, more composed.

'You don't look very well.'

'I 've had a little indigestion. . . . It 's this kitchen.' She looked resentfully at the stove. It was quite painful, quite shocking, to hear Annie suddenly turning against her kitchen. What could it mean?

'Would you like to see a doctor?'

'No, I 'd never see a doctor. I don't believe in doctors . . .' she said defiantly.

What a lie! She adored doctors. Next to consulting one herself, she enjoyed nothing more than the ceremonious—but conversational—ushering of one into the sick-room. She must be in a thoroughly bad temper. Perhaps her friend had jilted her.

'Well, I 'm sorry. . . .' Grace turned to leave the room. Annie burst into loud sobs.

'I won't deceive you, madam,' she cried. 'To tell you the truth, I 'm in trouble.'

'Are you really, Annie?' said Grace blankly. The phrase brought back Vicarage days, Rescue and Prevention Bazaars, Parish tongues wagging, her father shaking his head. But Annie could not mean that? . . . Yes, she meant that.

'I knew I 'd have to break it to you. . . . I said

to myself: " She 'll never catch on." You 're not very sharp, are you ? . . .' After several sobs she added ' Madam . . .'

' I 'm dreadfully sorry, Annie.'

She was conscious that she was not saying what was expected of her. Annie was awaiting immediate dismissal.

' I 'm very sorry indeed to have brought this on you. You and Mr. Fairfax—always so good to me. How ever will you manage ? . . .' Sobs choked her.

' Why, I couldn't manage without you, Annie.'

' If you could see your way, then—to let me stay on till near my time. It 's many months yet. I must earn . . . I haven't any home. . . .'

' Of course you 'll stay, you silly, silly Annie. . . .' Grace came blindly and stood beside her and put her arm round the broad, plump, heaving shoulders. Tears that had strained in vain for many weeks to find release, started from a heart grown rigid with its pangs—poured down her face. Annie was laying on her the last load of the futile misery of existence, and she could raise herself no longer. Cruel Annie had broken through her last defence—(to be as stone before the world, to tell no one ' I also suffer ').

' Do stop crying, Annie. It 's quite all right. It 's bad for you to cry.' She shook her, repeating sharply ' Stop crying '—frightened of her own pain—of the slipping of control.

The kitten vibrated, swelled over its saucer at their feet.

'I 've felt so sadly. . . . I haven't been able to take any pleasure in my cooking. The sickness is something shocking.'

'I know.'

It was all she could remember of child-bearing.

'Still, that 's gone off now.' She wiped her eyes on her apron. 'I 'm quite fit for my work, madam.'

'You 're not—thinking of getting married ?' Grace asked shyly.

'No, madam.' Her sobs burst out afresh. 'To tell you the truth, madam, he 's a married man. I knew it all along. He didn't deceive me.'

'I see.'

But she felt quite startled, she told herself. Annie's code was more lax than she had imagined.

'He 's a traveller, madam, with a van. His home 's in London. Somehow it didn't seem like he was a married man—being always on the move. . . . I shall never see him again.'

'Does he know ?'

'No. I never told him. I didn't want to put him to any inconvenience, or cause any trouble, not if I could manage by myself. I 'd rather not give you his name.' She looked anxious and obstinate for a moment, so that Grace realized she was expected to insist on this revelation. 'He 's only young. And got two children to keep. . . . Last time he came, I went straight to the door, and "Hullo, it 's you," I said, like that. "Don't you come bothering me any more. I 'm fed up." He was that upset . . .

wanted to know what he 'd done. Poor Arthur.' She cried a little, but not bitterly. The situation, though painful, had obviously not been without a saving dramatic grace.

'I suppose you loved him.' (Another improper remark, she thought. Annie would consider her thoroughly immoral.)

'Well, he was very nice, madam. If he hadn't been I shouldn't have let it happen.' She added delicately: 'Of course, it was an oversight that caused this. Somehow, not being as young as I was, I never thought it would occur.'

Annie, with her fund of physical wisdom, was not the one, of course, to let her own ripeness wither unplucked: to deny the needs of her body in the pagan amplitude of its middle years. Love was a term foreign to her vocabulary—an emotion not exploited in her world. He was young, he was nice. They had suited each other. Rather than harm him, she had let him go—did not miss him much. It seemed so simple and right: right, too, that this symbol of matronly qualities should be in truth with child. Annie was a triumph for unchastity.

'We must think about a hospital for you later, Annie. I 'll find out——'

'Oh, thank you, madam. I haven't slept for weeks thinking whatever should I do. It 's the baby that worries me. Who ever would take it for me? . . .' She repeated: 'I must earn. I haven't a home.'

She hid her face in her apron—straining her ear for the words that would not—might—must come.

'Well, you can have the baby here. . . . As long as it *never* cries.'

'Yes, madam.' Annie saw the joke. She beamed, though faintly. 'Oh, madam, you shall never regret this—never. You 'll never notice there 's anything funny in the house. I swear I 'll give you every satisfaction. . . .'

She had planned it all—where he 'd sleep, how she 'd fit in his feeds and all. Many a time since the final loss of hope in the last pill and dose, she had rehearsed the scheme, when thoughts of the river, the gas-oven, the workhouse had stared at her so uncompromisingly that she must cheat herself with an improbable happy ending. Now it had come.

But Mrs. Fairfax was not one who liked a lot of talk. Deeds, not words, should prove her gratitude. All the same, she would just like to say . . .

'All the same, madam,' she said, 'I 've often thought I 'd like a nice chubby little boy.'

'Yes, Annie.' She felt that, whatever the sex, the chubbiness was certain.

'People are very narrow-minded, aren't they?' she ventured, with a deprecating sigh.

'Yes, very.'

Annie, free now to think of other people's troubles, looked with her usual solicitude at Mrs. Fairfax. That tear-stained face, pale, apathetic, worn, those sunken eyes. . . . Ah, poor soul ! . . . She guessed, well enough, what ailed poor Mrs. Fairfax ; how salt, how barren were the tears of her life. Yes, it was for herself she wept. Mr. Fairfax was a good-hearted gentleman, he meant well ; but no use to her, not as a man, as you might say. What she needed was the same as what every woman needed. She 'd seen it coming on bad of late. She had put two and two together. . . . But he 'd gone away now, left the town for good. Listening—only for a very few minutes—at the keyhole, she 'd heard him say so.

What was the use of Mrs. Fairfax being so broad-minded ?

'Well, then, the apple pudding, Annie.'

'Very good, madam. I 'll put the rind of a lemon in : it takes off the tartness and makes a lovely flavour.'

And as Grace left the kitchen she heard her addressing the kitten :

'Here 's another drop, then. Have a nice blow-out and a good sleep afterwards. I knew you was lucky, you little black love.'

'Good afternoon, then,' said Norah at the door of the cottage, smiling cheerfully and telling herself it was no good pretending this was an agreeable old woman. 'Now let 's see who 's next on my list.' She consulted a notebook. 'Number 15. Miss Roberts. That 's your next-door neighbour, isn't it ?

A sudden stiffness shot into the hitherto unresponsive, collapsed face of the old woman. A spark animated her eye.

'If you take my advice, you won't go there.'

The smile faded from Norah's lips.

'Why not?' she said, quite coldly, she thought, for her.

'I 'm saying nothing.' Arms folded, head shaking with senile emotion, she looked at Norah. Her eye was stony, lidless, unwinking as a reptile's. 'We 're all respectable people in this street. We don't have no dealings with Pansy Roberts. Good afternoon.'

She banged her door.

'You 're a nice one,' murmured Norah.

She stood still a moment, discouraged. Should she give up and go home? . . . and write to the bishop's wife to-morrow, resigning once for all from the committee? Social work was no use at all. Yet, instead of giving it up, one let oneself be flattered and bullied into doing more and more of it every year. And all the time there was a part of her that hated and disapproved of every committee and board and institution, social or religious, ever founded. Gerald would not believe her; but it was so. It was the people, she told herself, that made one go on: the fascinating human contact, the discovery here and there of a revivifying drop in the unpalatable ocean. But her reception in this new district, whose housing and health conditions she had undertaken to help investigate, had not encouraged her to believe in her success as an apostle of social welfare. And she thought of the last house, where a woman had shouted to her from an upper window that she was behindhand with her washing and could not see her ; and the one before where the mistress of the house, in gaping petticoat and bodice, and a filthy shawl wrapped round her head, had informed her with tipsy tears that she was far from well and must be permitted to return unvisited to the sofa ; and the first house of all, where, besides a woman and some children, several men, in rags, long workless, sat all together by one relic of a fire, stared at her dumbly out of starved eyes in animal faces ; and her set speech of a Visitor had died on her lips ; and she had given them money to buy food (which was against the rules and precepts of the society) and gone quickly away.

Yes, she thought, she could report want and sickness, drink and defective sanitation, bad manners, ignorance, malice, and uncharitableness . . . the way of the world, in fact. And now for another sinner, to season the slice of life ; and if she failed here to make herself acceptable, not as a Worker but as a person, she would resign to-morrow and leave this inquisition to spirits more combative for good, to skins made tougher by missionary fervour.

She went up to the door of Number 15 and knocked, reluctantly. After a time she observed a familiar agitation in the thick lace curtains of the front room. Somebody was taking a good look at her. A long pause ; then the door was grudgingly opened, and the face of a girl peered out at her ; a face unreal in its delicacy, its glow, its look of wasting.

'Good afternoon. Are you Miss Roberts ?'

The face did not return her smile. It gazed ; then as if assailed by a dreadful conjecture, it froze. A voice said :

'Did you want anything ?'

'Only to—to pay you a little call—if you 're not busy.'

'I 'm not very busy, but I 'm not at all well—I wasn't expecting callers. . . .' Her pale blue gaze, bright with fever and suspicion, explored Norah minutely.

'I 'm so sorry. I 'll go away.'

The mask confronting her made her feel guilty, helpless.

'One of these church-workers, are you ?' remarked the voice from an infinitely remote watch-tower.

(For she 'd heard of them coming poking, prying —rescuing, they called it. You had to be careful, with Enemies everywhere.)

'No, no !' cried Norah. 'Nothing to do with any church.'

'Oh, I see. I thought I 'd just inquire . . . not being a church-goer myself—not regular, that is . . on account of my health.'

She drew a black velvet jacket closer over her small chest. She was charmingly dressed, Norah noticed, in an unsuitable little frock of black crêpe-de-chine with white lace collar and cuffs, stockings of finest silk and high-heeled patent leather slippers: the get-up of a hostess at an urban 'At Home'. How could one address such a creature on the subject of drains?

'I only wanted to ask if—if there 's anything I can do for you. You know, we visit, some of us . . . try to help . . . But——'

Faced with her last, her worst failure, she turned to go. One might as well offer to help a bird, explain one's object to a squirrel. She had the desperate recoiling dignity of an animal; the hauntingly lonely look of a being irreconcilably divided from oneself by difference of species.

'I see,' said the voice again. 'Well, I don't think there 's anything I want, thank you. I can manage for myself. If you 'll excuse me . . . this draught . . . I 'm quite an invalid.'

'I 'm so sorry,' said Norah, opening her umbrella. 'Please take care of yourself. Nobody so young and pretty has any business to be an invalid.'

The face thawed all at once, a mournful smile lifted the lips.

'It 's my lungs,' she said. 'Dear me, the rain! Won't you come in till it stops?'

She ushered Norah into the front parlour. A smell of room, thick, unventilated, filled the nostrils; green plush, antimacassars, photographs, an aspidistra, made suitable display in the meagre space; a fan of pleated white paper concealed and adorned the empty grate.

'Please take a chair,' she said. 'You 'll excuse the fire not being lit. It 's a trifle chilly. . . . As a matter of fact,' she conceded lightly—for we ladies, said the smile, all have our whims—'I was sitting in the kitchen this afternoon.'

'Oh, let 's sit in the kitchen. I always think it 's far the cosiest room,' said Norah, corroborating, suggesting comfortably that all ladies have this whim in common.

She opened another door and called out gently but authoritatively:

'Will, put your coat and scarf on, dear, and take a turn. Sister has a visitor.'

It sounded as if she were speaking to a child. But a man, indistinct in the obscurity of the tiny room, rose from an armchair and shambled out silently by a back entrance.

'It 's my brother,' remarked Pansy, setting another chair by the stove. 'He 's just a trifle backward, but he means well. He 's very good to me. He looks after me when I have a bad turn. But it upsets him, poor fellow, to see the blood. Of course, he remembers mother. She died of it, you know.'

'The blood?' inquired Norah, aghast.

'Oh, yes,' said the voice, primly. 'I 've been spitting blood off and on this autumn. I 've been obliged to give up my work, of course. I 'm a coiffoose and manicurist.' She tossed her fly-away top-heavy cloud of ash-blond hair, glanced at her polished nails. She said :

'The doctor thinks I 'll never get well again.'

And she continued to describe the variations in her temperature, her night sweats, her cough ; mentioning each fatal symptom with decorous restraint, with a little shrug ; with that delicate, precise degree of under-emphasis that is the difficult, the supreme achievement of the professional actress.

They parted an hour later.

Pansy stood at the door watching her walk away. 'Yes,' she told herself, 'I like your style.' Good tweeds but shabby, good low-heeled shoes but old. Powder but no lipstick ; just the gold band upon the wedding finger—no other jewellery. Nice teeth, pleasant smile, the right sort of voice. *His* sort of voice. . . . Funny thing, to have got it into one's head all of a sudden as she sat there that she knew him. Like telepathy, something had seemed to say : 'She 's got him in her mind.' . . . More like sick fancies. . . . But you could almost see her entertaining him to dinner, calling him Hugh, telling him to come again soon. . . .

Anyway, it would be quite a pleasure to have somebody like her coming to pay a visit now and then. The interest she 'd taken ! . . . but not a prying sort of interest. And to think how nearly she 'd had the door shut in her face ! It couldn't be helped. One had to think of one's self-respect.

'You 're much too pretty to be ill,' she 'd said. She was quite upset to find how bad it was—wanted to make inquiries from the doctor. She must be prevented somehow from doing that. . . . It wasn't quite true, of course, not strictly, about the doctor. 'Not serious yet,' he 'd said, 'but it 's the first warning.' He 'd told her to report herself at the clinic. A few months in the sanatorium would cure her, so he said. She knew better. Why, she 'd got ever so much worse in the last week. She was dying. She 'd die like Mother in a fit of coughing—blood everywhere. Then whatever would Will do? . . .

No; of course, she 'd be all right for years yet. She must look after herself. She 'd soon be back at work . . . get a new hat and coat . . . go down to the Palace one evening . . . see him coming in to look for her, to take her out to dinner.

No, he would never come. Something told her she would never set eyes on him again.

So die . . . But not alone, oh God, not alone. . *She 'd* be there now to look after her at the last. *I've just come from the death-bed of our own little friend Pansy. . . . Good God, not little Pansy? . . . Yes; her last words were a message for you. . . .* Then he 'd remember; then he 'd be sorry . . . come and kneel beside her, lay flowers in her cold hands, where she lay dead. . . .

'Pansy!'

There was Will, back from his walk.

'Pansy!'

He was shouting up the stairs . . . so hoarse and silly-sounding—panicky.

'Here 's sister, Will.'

She took a last look up the dim and squally street. Out of sight.

Come again soon, as you promised. Come again.

She shut the door.

Norah hurried through the streets.

Another storm was piling in the tormented west, spreading across the sky. The gale was growing wilder. It would howl now all night through. She told herself it would mean a midnight visit from David, creeping from his bed to stand beside hers and whisper that he thought he had a little pain. He was frightened of the sound of a storm: expected, in spite of Robin's scorn, and all she could do to reassure him, earthquakes, tidal waves, the end of the world. She must leave a night-light burning for him.

Well, the afternoon had not been altogether wasted after all. That little creature rose before her eyes, standing at the door of her cottage looking after her attentively from its mournful animal remoteness. What was the clue to such unreality? 'I cough blood,' she 'd said, as one might say one felt rheumatic in wet weather. 'I wasn't at all surprised to see the blood,' she 'd said. 'I was expecting it, really.'

PART VII

Was it that artifice — dramatization — was the essence of her existence . . . her way of escape from reality, as the psycho-analysts would say? Did she practise an absolute self-deception—seeing herself, in one perpetual day-dream, as the heroine of a series of interesting and pathetic situations?

Or was it the pathological hopefulness of the consumptive which made it so impossible to rouse her to a sense of her own danger? . . . Or what?

Never did anybody so disguise herself, so reveal herself in a variety of obvious but impenetrable shams.

But, what about her profession? thought Norah, waiting for her tram at the street-corner. Would one have guessed, without the evil hint? Was it in her eyes, with their fanatical stare and lightness?—in something dreadfully discreet, avid and secret about her whole expression? Or was that simply imagination?

Would any man recognize her at once for what she was?—take her—describe her afterwards to his friends? For they did tell each other (so Jimmy had said) about their casual experiences (though never about their wives). . . . She felt a kind of pressure in the brain, sweeping her away on a tide of images and conjectures: the old abscess of sex throbbed again, still festering, never properly healed. It was hard still to take the physical importance, the emotional unimportance, for granted. A nice boy like Hugh, for instance—how would he treat a prostitute?

He had such charm, such good manners ; answered in every particular to the prescription for a clean type of young Englishman. Candour and kindness shone out of his blue eye ; no sensuality was apparent in his features. But would he also . . . without a qualm of conscience before or afterwards ? Surely, such serenity as his, such healthy roundedness of character, must come partly from having got his sex-life regulated to his thorough satisfaction. She wished she could have asked him about ideals, and sowing wild oats ; what point of view he 'd recommend for the boys. Really, it was the first, the most important and interesting thing to know about any one ; though Gerald would not agree. He thought, or pretended to think, one wanted to know what sort of books people read.

There was Gerald, now, she thought, jumping on to her tram and settling herself in a corner—Gerald, so fastidious and high-minded, abhorring all forms of bodily indulgence—but Gerald was not free, not calm and balanced : quite the reverse—a tangle of passionate conflicts and repressions. What good to anybody was his idealism ? First, the boys would be alarmed and alienated ; then, by the force of reaction, plunged into excesses ; then immediately disowned. . . . Oh dear ! . . . .

She wished Hugh had not gone away—dear Hugh, so happily at home on earth, looking outward, not always at himself ; encouraging one to believe that the gaiety of life had not perished from the world, nor the flavour departed : but had only passed out of one's own reach.

It was extraordinary (seeing how rarely one had seen him), but an undoubted fact, that since his departure there had been a change for the worse in the texture of existence, a failure of elasticity, an onset of aridity. If one listened when one woke up in the morning, one could hear as it were the sound of a prosaic voice, hollow, droning on. . . . Yes, he had made a difference. He had been most unsettling.

She experienced a sudden anxious pang, a momentary misery and void, thinking that only herself knew how near she 'd been to—being silly about him ; in spite of having thought herself long past such disturbances. Well . . . but one needn't feel too guilty and unfaithful. Gerald had quite lost his head over Clare. Did he ever think of her now? He never spoke of her. Yet sometimes one wondered. . . . Wasn't there a new—a rather horrid—expression on his face ? Wasn't he behaving as if—as if he 'd scored somehow, without one's knowing it ?

The tram stopped. She roused herself and saw that she had reached the top of Grace's terrace.

On an impulse, she jumped out, suddenly wanting the queer stimulus of Grace's presence, her odd sanity, her impersonal smile. They had not met for months.

It was Grace herself who opened the door. Her face was altered somehow—worn down, transparent.

If it were not so very improbable, one would have said she had been crying.

'Norah!' Unwonted pleasure and affection rang in her voice. Her face had lit so suddenly that one realized, thought Norah, how sad it had been before. 'I'm so glad to see you. Come in and talk to me.'

And she took her arm and led her into the sitting-room, saying, as she pushed up the armchair:

'You're the very person I wanted. Tell me the nicest place to send a person to have a baby.'

It was nearly supper-time when Norah started to walk home. The rain was over, and the sky was fairing—wind-swept, starry, dramatic. The gleaming white mast of the crescent moon went tossing and dipping through hurrying rollers of dark and pallid cloud. A lovely night.

As she hurried home, she thought of Grace: how fond of her she was, how enduring it had been, if never intimate, this bond between them: so that after ten years it was plain truth to say, as she had said at parting—putting on her hat again and sighing comfortably:

'Well, good-bye, Grace. You're a great comfort to me, really—very soothing. I often wonder what I'd do without you.'

To-night they had got on better than ever before—made, as it were, a sudden step together. In fact, they had had a good old gossip.

PART VII

They had discussed everybody : first Annie, with Grace giving an imitation of her, and being funny about her as well as sympathetic ; then Hugh and Clare, and all the people and the incidents of that far-off day in summer. Norah remembered remarking, with assumed carelessness :

'By the way, Hugh 's gone for good '—and Grace answering in the same offhand way :

'I know. He came to say good-bye.'

A pair of old pretenders they were, thought Norah ; for surely the way Grace had added 'Have you heard anything of him ? '—trying unsuccessfully to conceal a blush—surely that went to show that even unsusceptible old Grace had felt a flutter. . . . It was an amusing thought.

Then, Norah remembered, she had told her about her afternoon—described her experiences, tried to give her a sketch of Miss Roberts.

'Norah, why do you do these awful things ? ' she 'd said.

'I suppose to keep myself from the unhealthy habit of thinking.'

'Mm. I suppose I ought to, too. But I shan't. I 've never yet disciplined myself, and I 'm not going to start. My vices are my only consolation. You 're a much more moral character than I am, Norah. I should think the chastest star might peep.'

'At its peril ! '

And they had laughed, saying how like a chaste star it was to peep—and gone on from there to talk of literature, and regret their ignorance of it ; and agreed to go to some lectures together this winter.

Grace had said, too :

'Secret thinking 's as bad as secret drinking. It makes one a living falsehood. But what 's a person in my position to do ? '—giving thus the first definite hint she had ever given that her personal life was all awry.

'But perhaps we 're all deceivers more or less,' she 'd said. 'I 've even wondered once or twice lately what goes on in Tom's head. I dare say his dreams are all disgraceful. I couldn't blame him. I 'm so awful to him '—which was another glimpse, never before vouchsafed. She had added reflectively : 'Should I mind, I wonder, if he were unfaithful ? ' And they had gone on in a quite unprecedented way to speak a little of their husbands, and of married life. Mysterious creature ;—from the way she 'd talked, it almost sounded as if she must have more concealed in her life than one had given her credit for. It was a pity she had not married somebody less uninteresting. She had such possibilities.

She tried to cast her mind back to the young woman of ten years ago—seeing her as she had first seen her, wandering into the cookery school as if she had lost her way—large, mild-browed, dreamy-looking ; silent and self-conscious ; easily the most bored and inept pupil in the class. When the instructress had said acidly one day, 'I am afraid,

Mrs. Fairfax, you have no gift for cookery,' how amused she 'd been! Her smile, broadening mysteriously, but a little dismayed and guilty, had seemed to spread humour over the whole solemn, painstaking class. They had caught one another's eye; and made friends after that.

She had afforded one, thought Norah, a lot of entertainment in those days. She had been so teaseable, with her adolescent awkwardness and seriousness, her laziness and cat-like love of comfort, her funny bursts of energy and eagerness; so nice, with her dreamy sort of unworldliness, her intelligence, her dry little jokes.

But somehow she had not developed as she might have; she had grown more and more reserved, and dull; or else it was that motherhood coming to one and not the other (had she minded that at all?) had arrested the progress of their friendship. For, undoubtedly, it had remained a mere beginning—promising, but with no subsequent fulfilment.

But to-night it had seemed as if, in her funny way, she was asking for affection. She had seemed pleased—really pleased—to be visited; even a little grateful and pathetic.

'Oh, don't go,' she had pleaded. 'You needn't go yet.'

She looked run down—as if she needed a change.

And only about her holiday, thought Norah, reaching her own front door, had she been uncommunicative: had said, idiotically, characteristically, that she didn't know where she 'd been or what she 'd done—and changed the subject.

Yes, she must see more of her this winter.

She shut the door behind her and stood in the hall. There were the boys' overcoats thrown down in a heap—the kitchen door open again and the smell of onions stealing towards Gerald's study. As it was in the beginning, she thought, is now and ever shall be. . . . But why did the images of Hugh and Clare come suddenly, sharply, to mind ?

She heard the boys giggling together upstairs. Well, that was all right. But there was a funny feeling in the house.

Noiselessly she opened the door of Gerald's room. He was sitting at his desk, writing, an open letter by his elbow. He did not hear her.

She said softly :

' Hullo, darling ! '

He jumped violently, and made a movement to cover the blotter with his hands.

' Why do you come in like that ? ' he said petulantly.

' I didn't come in like anything. I didn't want to disturb you.' She came and stroked his hair in the way he liked. ' Angry tom-cat,' she murmured (for that sometimes made him smile). But he shook her hand off and said :

' You startled me.'

He waited with his head bent, lowering and watchful, for her to go away again.

She caught sight of the letter beside him, recognized the sprawling hand, read : *Gerald darling* . . . She said :

'I didn't see how busy you were. I must apologize. . . .' Her voice was rather shrill. She added : 'Letter from Clare ? When did that come ? May I read ? . . .' She stretched a hand out.

Very slowly he took up Clare's letter, folded it and put it in his breast-pocket.

'No,' he said, finally. He added after a silence : 'Why should you read my letters ? I never ask to read yours, do I ?'

'No,' she said. 'Because you don't need to. I give you them to read—any that could conceivably interest you. I 've nothing to hide.'

'How do I know that ?' he shot at her.

She might have known, she told herself, that he would not simply remain on the defensive ; that he would attack at once, thrusting, as he always did, with weapons so skilful and unkind that doubtless he counted on her retiring now, as usual, from the unequal contest.

A small voice said reasonably in the back of her mind : 'His question is pertinent. Have you nothing to hide ?' But no. Time enough to see his point of view afterwards, when the worst of the disaster was known.

'Gerald,' she said, 'I don't wish to make a fuss, but I would like to know what is going on between you and Clare.'

'May I ask what exactly you mean by that phrase?' His withering voice accused her of vulgarity, made her feel ashamed. But she retorted:

'It 's no good treating me like that, Gerald—not this time. You can't get out of it this time by trying to make me feel a fool.'

He raised his eyebrows, stared at her with fixed, bright, pin-point eyes, smiling a little.

'If you would kindly control yourself,' he said politely, 'I could follow you better.'

She went a violent red, then white; waited some moments and said, in a flat monotone:

'Will you show me that letter?'

'No.'

'Why not?'

'Because my letters are private and do not concern you.'

'I see. Now I know what to do.'

'And what is that?'

'Write to Clare. A letter that does not concern you.'

'A truly dignified resolve!' He added, still smiling: 'Personally, I should prefer not to give myself away. Jealousy 's not a very pretty emotion.'

'I don't care what you say.' Her voice rose hysterically. 'I 'll say what I like, and I 'll shout at the top of my voice if I like. I 've stood it long enough. . . .'

He laughed—a series of dry, cackling sounds.

'Go on,' he said softly, 'go on.'

'I will go on! You want to drive me mad—you

want to . . . I 've stuck it for years—tried to put up with your temper, your meanness, the way you 've treated me and the children. . . . But you shan't make a fool of me—having affairs with my friends behind my back . . . I won't stand *that* . . . I 've finished with you.'

Still he sat at his desk, playing with a paper-knife, watching her with glittering cat's eyes.

'So now we know where we are,' he said quietly. 'As you will. This is the end.'

Well, now they had both said it. The issue was forced, the crisis reached. Was it true, what he said—that this was the end? It had come so suddenly. . . .

He leapt up, hurled back his chair, sent books and paper-knife flying and crashing, faced her, whispered through thin lips:

'*I 've* had enough too. *Wonderful*, it 's been for me, my married life, *wonderful!* "Such a good wife! So patient! So unselfish! So self-sacrificing! Such a lot to put up with from that man—and always so cheerful!" Can't you hear them? Oh, yes, you 've heard them all right! Trust you! "I 'll do my duty to the bitter end!" Loud applause! But nothing to what you 've given yourself. Such conscious virtue! Never was such virtue! *You 've* nothing to reproach yourself with! . . . not you! Never had an undutiful thought. Have you? Nothing to hide!' He came closer, said with soft, icy emphasis: 'You think I don't know who fills your thoughts, your dreams . . always, from the beginning. . . .'

'No,' she gasped, out of a nightmare.

'Have I ever been necessary to you—ever ? No ! I 've had your duty to me—your *duty!* What 's that worth ? You 've never been unfaithful—no !—you 'd never go to another man's bed. Because your whole soul 's bound up in me, I suppose ! . . . Why shouldn't *I* have something for myself for once—something of my own ? You 've always left me out. I 've seen your plots and your conspiracies ! But as you say, the worm will turn ! It doesn't really matter, does it, whether the object of one's passion is alive or dead ? ' He laughed loudly. 'Dead ! What a loss ! We must all pray to be like him. Though who could hope to emulate such virtue ? So fine, so noble ! So faithful to you, I 'm told—so devoted ! . . .'

She flung herself at him, shrieking :

'You devil ! You devil ! I hate you ! '

He caught her arms and held her away from him with a grip that made her speechless with pain.

'That 's right,' he said. His face was livid. 'Louder ! Tell the servant ! Tell your children ! Do ! '

She started to collapse, and he let her go. She ran out of the room, up the stairs ; called briskly on the landing : 'Get to bed, boys. I 'll come later ' ; reached her own room, sank weeping on to the bed.

PART VII

Hours passed. She lay in the dark, hearing the cathedral clock strike eleven. She began to wonder what she was to do. Lie as she was till morning? She was chilled to the bone, shivering with cold and nausea. Fill a hot-water bottle and undress as usual and go to bed? . . . And there were the children to see to. Life left no room for crises. Time was flowing on without a check, bringing the day's last round of habitual duties. Who would perform them, if not she? Who would tell her gently to rest, to cease from worrying—if not Gerald? No one could be so comforting as Gerald; no one—paradox!—bore so tenderly with foolish tears.

The door creaked open. She did not move; but knew he was standing near her in the darkness.

After a while he sat down beside her on the bed. He said nothing.

She sniffed, caught her breath on the tag-end of a sob.

'You 're shivering,' he said quietly. 'Go to bed.'

'No, I can't move,' she whispered.

'Poor girl,' he said pityingly. 'You 'll be all right.' He covered her with the eiderdown.

'I suppose I must go and see the boys. . . .' She sighed.

'They 're all right. I 've been in. They 're both asleep. I left a night-light in case David wakes. Was that right?'

'Yes. Thank you.'

Thoughtful of him. . . .

He groped for her hand and took it, started to stroke it.

'I 'm so tired,' she whispered faintly. 'I don't know what we 've done. . . . Is everything finished?'

'Anger is finished.'

'And forgotten, I suppose!'

'And forgotten.'

'How can it be? As if we could forget. . . .'

'We could, you know.'

'It 's easy for you to say . . .' She sobbed. 'When you 've smashed everything for ever. . . . The thing is, what to do now—for the best. I don't think I can go on living with you, Gerald. Perhaps you don't want me to, anyway.'

He did not answer, but went on stroking her hand with the sapient, soothing touch she knew.

'I don't know if Clare . . . Will she . . . Oh, God! . . . to think of *Clare*—my friend . . .'

'It 's all right,' he said softly. 'You 've nothing to reproach her with. I fell just a little in love with her. I told her so. That 's all.' His last words seemed to stab and strangle her. She tried to snatch her hand away, but he held it and went on: 'She doesn't care for me at all. She writes to me now and then—perhaps out of kindness—she 's not unkind, you know; or possibly she 's a trifle flattered: she 's very vain. There 's nothing in her letters—she dashes off half a dozen of the same sort in a morning, I expect . . .'

'And you 've been writing her long letters—all this time? . . .'

'Yes.'

'Love-letters . . on the sly. . . .'

'Just letters—to the person—the symbol, rather—that she was to me. Quite harmless. You might call it a recreation. I wrote her little verses. There was nothing in my letters that is yours, Norah. No disloyalty.'

'Oh!' she cried out reproachfully, in bitter disbelief.

But he repeated softly:

'Nothing that is yours.'

How cruel he was, she told herself, wounding her so calmly with blunt facts. But he sounded so sad one had to listen to him, so wise one had to let oneself be persuaded.

Now and again, not often, in the ten years, she had come to this hidden spring in him, this irresistible wisdom of sensibility, this truth of his nature which cancelled—though only at the worst of their need—all the perverse distortions of the surface. It had led her through their strange, happy, unhappy honeymoon; through child-birth; would lead her, if she died first, through the last extremity of death. It was something that lay deeper than the sympathy learnt from experience—something born with him, one felt, whatever it was: perhaps the tragic sense of life; . . . so that one told oneself, whatever he might do, he had a noble spirit.

She moved, turning her face towards him, and said in a different, a rational voice :

'Why didn't you tell me, Gerald ? Couldn't you trust me ? That 's what hurts so.'

She knew that he was smiling in the dark.

'Ah, why not ? You 'd have been so glad to assist me, wouldn't you, if I 'd appealed to you ? You 'd have been charmed to give my little affair your patronage. "Poor dear," you 'd have said to yourself, "he does so depend on me. He can't even manage his love affairs without me." Wouldn't you, now ? Didn't you try to, in the summer ?'

She was silent, hurt. But he was right, she acknowledged secretly. She recognized the attitude as her own this summer.

He went on, steadily, holding her hand in his :

'I was foolish enough to want to try for something on my own. I needed to prove to myself that I could be acceptable—as an individual—apart from you. I wanted Clare's feeling for me at first hand—not just as a reflection from your relationship—which is what 's generally considered, isn't it ?—as much as I can possibly expect.'

'I didn't know you minded . . .' she murmured. 'I thought you generally hated everybody.'

'Yes,' he said. 'Sometimes it 's difficult, living always with a person, to be perspicacious.' He pressed her hand. 'Perhaps I wanted to spite you a little, too. However, as I said, it had its roots in unreality, so it was bound to fail. And anyway, she much prefers you. She said so in her last letter. So, you see, you've scored again, as usual.'

She put her arms round his neck and held him.

'Do you mind dreadfully?' she whispered.

'It's galling to one's self-esteem,' he said, lightly. 'However, there it is. You must forgive me, because all it comes to is . . . that I find I do depend on you. I do need you—only you.' His voice shook. 'So you can feel quite safe. I shan't rebel again.'

'Don't put it like that,' she said. 'You make me feel so ashamed. I'm afraid I've always been a very jealous character. It was such a shock—to feel like that about you. You've never made me jealous before.'

'And you've always made me jealous.'

'Oh, Gerald! . . .'

'He's always been between us. . . . Hasn't he?'

'I suppose so,' she whispered. 'I got the proportions wrong. I did love him so. You never helped me to forget him. You would never let me talk of him—or even cry about him—in a natural way. Even though when we first met you knew I was sore and raw and aching for him.'

He had driven the poison inwards, to feed upon and corrupt the healthy body of their relationship.

'I know,' he said; thinking how, even after all these years, he had been compelled to ask Clare about him, had gloated and suffered over the hints she'd dropped. 'I wanted you for myself, *because* of myself. I'm a diabolically jealous character, too. However, I never got more than a little bit of you, I know, and never shall.'

'You have, Gerald. You must believe it. I need you too, permanently. Jimmy's unreal too. At least—I must make him so. . . .' She went on slowly: 'It s quite true poor Jimmy wasn't what you'd call a fine character. He had every vice, and . . . he didn't care for me *nearly* as much as I for him.' She stopped, overcome by the pain and the truth of her words. 'I suppose Clare told you . . .' she whispered. 'It's good for me, of course. It's the truth. But I wish she needn't have. . . .'

'It was my fault,' he said, gripping her hand again. 'I asked her. She was very reluctant. She hardly said anything.'

One would not have expected Clare to have such scruples. It must be that she had forgotten Jimmy; or else it was true, what one had long ago suspected: that she had been in love with him herself.

But Jimmy had died, poor boy, many years ago; had been killed in the war, like George and all the others. That had been his end.

She sat up, sighed, leaned against his shoulder.

'You make me feel very unconceited,' she said. 'I sometimes think, Gerald, you're my only enemy.'

'Do you wonder?' he said. 'You pleasant, popular woman.'

'You unpleasant, unpopular man. . . . We suit each other, don't we ?'

'Yes. Yes.' He sighed.

After a silence she said :

'But you will go on writing to Clare ?'

'There you go again ! Not I. You 've spoilt it all.'

'Do you . . . have you still got a little passion for her, darling ?'

He smiled.

'Hardly even a little one—so long as I don't set eyes on her.'

'I'll see you don't. . . . But she is lovely, isn't she ? . . . Did you write her some nice little poems ?' (And, waiting for his answer, a worm of jealousy writhed again, irrepressibly.)

'Just some appropriate trifles. They pleased her. You know the sort.'

'Tell me some.' (For he liked to recite his little compositions.)

'There was one that came off a little better than most :

Sunlight you are, but shadow I ;
Fetters I wear, but you are free :
Sing, laugh, the more, the more I sigh ;
Let me love you, but love not me.'

'Very neat,' she said, thinking : No wonder Clare had been pleased. It was very . . . Clare had never had anything to put up with. . . . That 's why she 'd kept her looks, her youth. . . . The worm wriggled dreadfully. . . She said quickly : ' It rather expresses her. Him too—Hugh, I mean. Don't you think so ? ' Very secretly, she told herself she must not think about Hugh in this silly way any longer. Sometimes of late—yes, it must be acknowledged—Hugh had appeared in day-dreams—mingling with the other, and wearing his face. . . . She was a person of most undisciplined imagination. She must try really hard. . . .

Through mists of drowsiness she saw them both, brother and sister, two bright heads, far away for ever. ' They were an attractive pair. . . .' So far out of sight they were, the past tense had already claimed them. . . . ' That was a happy day, wasn't it ? ' But very far. . . . They would not go there together again and feel enchantment. ' Really, you know, he had the nicer character. He 'd feel sorry, I think, for making havoc . . . but she was quite unscrupulous.'

He murmured absently :

' The female of the species . . .'

The worm ceased from its agitation. He was not thinking about Clare's beauty any more.

' The gale 's died down,' she said. ' Thank goodness, David won't get religion to-night. Look at the moonlight on these roofs ! What a lovely night ! '

' A Lapland night,' he said.

And he sat on in silence beside her ; thinking that soon he would go down and heat up the soup that he had told Florrie to leave for her in a saucepan ;

thinking that if the final relinquishing of all that one had wanted could continue to be so graceful, so simple and serene as now it seemed ; if one could go on holding one's wife's hand in peace and weariness, and never be made jealous, never be enraged by her any more—then age might lose its sting, the grave its victory.

Saturday afternoon of mid-December. The football crowd streamed one way across the common, the whippet-racers another, their curving, knife-pared hounds quivering on the leash. The pale blue sky was cloudless from end to end, the air windless, soft and chilly.

It was one of those late autumn days when, above purple hedges in the country lanes, the tree-trunks are disembodied, stand up ethereally in shining essence—shapes built of intersecting shafts of coloured light and shadow.

Seeing them in her mind's eye, gazing over the vast and treeless space of brownish grass, Grace walked across the common with her husband. He had foregone his game of golf to take her for a walk this fine afternoon. She had not been well.

They came to the end of the path, at the far end of the common, where iron railings divided it from the last suburbs. All was quiet here, deserted. The sound of the town came muffled to the ear.

'I must rest,' she said. 'Let 's sit down.'

'There 's nothing to sit on,' he said anxiously.

'The ground,' she said.

She took her hat off. He spread his burberry doubtfully—but there was no arguing with her—and they sat down on it side by side, their backs against the railings.

Presently he took his hat off. It was a risk; but the sun was really very pleasant.

When she looked at him, she laughed.

'We look very bank-holiday,' she said. 'It seems so funny to see you sitting on the grass.'

The incongruity of Tom in relation to the rural, the picnic, had always been marked.

'Too stout these days to get down so far and up again,' he said, encouraged by her smile. (For lately she had been so low, so silent, had had such shocking neuralgia.) 'I 've put on weight again this year, you know. Can't seem to be able to stop.'

'Give up weighing yourself,' she said. 'And then it doesn't matter.'

'Don't you mind?' he said.

There was something so timid, so wistful in the question, that she felt touched—sorry to have exhibited her indifference to his appearance.

'Only if you do,' she said gently.

'Couldn't you restrain Annie in the matter of soups?'

'I can't restrain Annie in anything. She 's going to have a baby.'

He was incredulous, then correctly horrified; but

not for long. Soon, it was plain, he was permitting himself to think as regards her lapse, rather lewdly, rather admiringly, 'Good for Annie!' and as regards the consequence of her lapse, that it was rotten bad luck. And he commended Grace's decision to extend the hand of pardon. It would cause talk, he said; but, everything considered, if Grace didn't mind, he didn't. Annie was a necessity.

After a silence he said timidly:

'Is that what's been on your mind, Gracie?'

She paused before answering, pityingly:

'No, Tom.'

She would have liked to be able to say yes—give him the satisfaction of cheering her.

'I thought it couldn't be that. . . . I do wish you didn't get so down in the mouth, Gracie. I suppose it's . . .'

He stopped. He knew that she would never let him help her. She did not give him credit for any perception, any understanding.

'It's just being run down, I think, Tom.'

'You ought to have a change. You wouldn't like to pop off again . . . by yourself, I suppose?' He swallowed hard, added firmly: 'I'd gladly pay your expenses.'

And he looked away, dreading to hear her greet the proposition with breathless eagerness. He had never been able to forget the sharp, egotistical insistence of her manner over that confounded holiday.

Her one thought then had been to get away from him. She had not shown the slightest interest in his plans, the slightest regret at the prospect of the separation. It had been a pill.

But she said, in the same gentle, resigned way—which was worse than sulks, it made him feel so wretched:

'No, Tom. I don't need a change. Besides, I don't want to go away from home.'

It occurred to her that this must be the first time she had referred to the town as home. A childish obstinacy, a sentimental loyalty to the Vicarage had always prevented her. But now she said it deliberately, adding:

'I don't want to leave you.'

Just to stay where she was was best. Never again would she be able to go away alone for a summer holiday. To be alone would be too sharp a pain, too haunting a contrast. Nothing would be nothing now, instead of the illusory expectation of the whole fullness of life: as if herself were great with all creation. Never again would she be dissolved, poured through the universe with the insubstantial elements of light and colour, reunited with the component forces of vital energy. Rhythms that had stolen on her senses, informed her person, would be lost now in the nerves' sick jigging, heart's jagged beat. The perpetual *I want*, creeping and coiling across her life in a harsh and dirty growth, like ivy, little by little would choke the living pores, and batten on the ruin of her. How could she save herself now?

But her words, her tone consoled him: made it easy to say:

'Well, I'm sure I don't want you to go. It was damned awful this summer, dragging around alone.'

The resentment of months rose in his voice—and a chokiness, a tremor that he could not suppress. He wanted to cry, to complain and be comforted.

'Was it awful, Tom? I'm so sorry.'

She had never asked him for a precise account of his trip. He had bluffed to her, assured her he had had a topping time; and she had left it at that, secretly recognizing the false enthusiasm of his manner—she admitted to herself now—and unwilling to let him undeceive her openly. She said:

'I'm afraid I guessed, Tom. But I didn't want to think about it. It made me seem so wicked—to have been so happy myselt.'

She felt him wince at this. She said: 'We won't think about it any more. I was on a wild-goose chase. It won't ever happen again.'

Now what did she mean by that, he wondered. She was always saying things he could not follow. But he would not ask her to explain. Instinct told him the answer, if any, would be painful and disturbing: and the last thing he wanted was to probe deeper: only to cover up again roots dangerously exposed. In another minute he'd be blurting out —that thing he was trying so hard to put out of his mind, to dismiss as an improbable and distressing dream; that incident which had been a fraud, a failure, a mistake, from beginning to end.

He said:

'It won't ever happen again in my case either . . . I can promise you that.'

His voice, sheepish, weighty, and ambiguous, might have made her wonder; only she was not listening. She failed to note that her husband had confessed intimacy with a prostitute; had expressed remorse; had vowed her future constancy. She was thinking how strange it was that she was able to keep her secret from him—that she would know in a minute if he had anything to conceal. No doubt, men were more honest and transparent than women.

He lit a pipe and leaned back, his anxiety relieved, his sense of guilt appeased. Now he could indulge in something of the purged, unburdened feeling of confession, without the general upset attendant on it. He sighed comfortably.

'It 's jolly here,' he said. 'Peaceful. Almost as good as the country.'

'What a shame to miss your golf!'

'Oh, I wasn't keen on golf to-day.'

But she knew it had been a genuine sacrifice.

'You 're a kind man, Tom. You deserve a better wife.'

'I 'm quite content with the one I 've got.' He put an arm round her, self-consciously, and said with a jocularity that trailed off suddenly into a return of the chokiness :

'We rub along together all right—don't we ?'

They really did, he thought, when all was said and done : as well as most.

'Yes, Tommy.'

And all at once the grey future appeared before her in a reconciling sunset light. 'Be good to Tom,' she told herself. 'Resolve to make the best of him. Do this for Hugh's sake.' (How easy, how consoling, if Hugh cared what one did ! . . .)

A yellow mongrel terrier, wearing his ears briskly askew, came bustling along the path. Grace put out a hand to him. He hastened up to greet her. Beneath his tousled fringe his eye was bright and liquid. After a few moments he sat down beside her, head cocked alertly, his chocolate nostrils twitching. Now and then he growled under his breath, aggressively, hopefully, at some fancied phenomenon.

'Nice dog, that,' said Tom. 'Good watch-dog, I should say.'

'He 's a busy-body,' said Grace. 'I can see nothing 's allowed to happen without his permission. I 'm glad to say that means he 's spoilt at home.'

'He 's taken quite a fancy to you,' said Tom, encouraged once more by her smiling face. 'Look at him guarding you.'

'It 's just that he 's out of a job for the moment,' she said, stroking him.

After a time, scenting a disturbance on the sky-line, he excused himself with an ingratiating wag, and disappeared.

'Good-bye,' she called.

'They 're faithful animals,' Tom observed. 'I suppose—' he hesitated, for the subject had been taboo ever since that unfortunate business of the puppy; and one never knew, with women, what secret inconsolable refinements of sensibility they nourished; so that one was always blundering, and being made to feel callous, gross. 'I suppose you 'd never care to keep another ?' . . .

'I 've been thinking I 'd like to,' she said. (For the first step towards improving the present and future is not to be morbid about the past.) 'Dogs do so enjoy living with one, one really must—— Besides, I 'd be compelled to walk round the park every day, and that would be very good for me.'

There were practical remedies against despair that must be tried: exercise for one.

Presently he said:

'Talking of pets, I 'm thinking of keeping one myself.'

From his tone, she judged that a joke was impending. His jokes depressed her—irremediably, she feared. But she answered in the same vein:

'What, a white mouse ?'

'No. Guess again.'

'I couldn't.'

'A motor car ! ' He looked at her triumphantly.

'Oh, Tom! Not really?'

'Potter knows of a second-hand Singer, going very cheap. It seems an opportunity. I thought I'd go and have a look at it.'

'How thrilling!'

'I dare say I might manage to beat them down, too.' He meditated, planning a little sharp practice. . . . 'Of course, we'd have to go slow on petrol, etcetera—not take her out too often. But what price jaunts on Sundays—eh? You'd get into the country regularly!'

She averted her imagination from the prospect of jaunts with Tom on Sundays. He was so happy—doing his best for her. She must be grateful, eager.

'I don't see why you shouldn't learn to drive yourself—in time.' He had the air of one who adds the last drop to the brimming cup.

'I'd love to try.'

Yes—she must try. Driving would be a remedy . . . if only one could take it. But there before her was the hopelessness of her character, exposed with deadly clarity. There was the country within reasonable reach at last: her life's longing dependent for its fulfilment simply upon a little effort of competence and the price of petrol. But were petrol ten times cheaper, were she ten times more anxious to escape from the town and Tom, she feared that never would she be seen setting out for the country alone in a second-hand Singer.

He leaned back in great contentment, puffing at his pipe.

'I don't mind telling you,' he said suddenly, with a confidential inflection, 'I 've had a stroke of luck over that little legacy of Mother's I invested.'

'Oh, good.'

There seemed no end to the benefits he was conferring. This was a supreme mark of his favour—almost embarrassing. As a rule he was financially secretive, and kept her short, alluding to rainy days, and looking with pardonable distrust upon her household economy.

'Not so long now till I 'm thinking of retiring. Then for that little house somewhere with a garden—eh ?'

'When shall you retire ?'

'Oh, when I 'm sixty, I dare say. It all depends,' he added, nudging her jovially. 'If you 're a good girl and don't go blowing all the pennies as fast as I make 'em.'

'I wish I managed better.' She sighed. 'I don't know what it goes on. It must be Annie. . . . Or buying hats and jumpers I can never bear to wear.'

'Cheer up,' he said. 'You look all right to me.' And he thought to himself she 'd had her share of looks. She 'd been a sweet-looking girl, not strictly pretty, but unusual. A sweet-looking girl.

They sat on, side by side, in silence.

He put his hat on again.

'It 's getting chilly.'

She pleaded :

' Just a little longer. The sun 's so lovely. Probably it 's the last we 'll get this year. Wait till it goes right off us.'

' If you swear you 're warm enough—— '

' As warm as toast. I feel so much better, Tom, for my fresh air.'

' Do you honestly ? '

He was immensely cheered. She had never been one to complain ; but she was sleeping and eating so poorly he often felt quite worried.

' I suppose,' he ventured dubiously, ' you wouldn't let the doctor overhaul you thoroughly ? '

' No. There 's no need. I 'm quite all right.'

An alarming, an intoxicating thought recurred to him. Could it be . . . could it possibly be—another baby . . . and she was keeping it from him, or wasn't sure herself yet ? There were so many symptoms : the distaste for food, the tiredness, the banishing him to his dressing-room. . . .

He said, very gently :

' I 'm afraid, my dear, you 've never been quite as strong again since the—since the child—— '

That would give her a lead. He waited, looking in front of him.

' Perhaps not quite, Tom,' she said shakily.

It was odd, she thought, how any explicit reference to the child seemed to cause a somersault in some inmost part of her ; for it was not as if she really minded any more, or wanted another. It must be sheer sentimentality.

'Shouldn't you think——' he said, 'if only—if you were to have another, it might be an excellent thing—for your health, I mean?'

'I don't know,' she said. 'I never shall have another.'

He nodded.

Well, there it was. . . .

Presently he got up and helped her to her feet.

'Still, there's Annie,' she said, looking up at him with an expression, he thought, that begged him to smile too.

He did so.

'Yes, by Jove!' he said. 'A ready-made heir. She would, wouldn't she?'

She put her arm through his. Slowly, they started to walk home.

She looked far across the common into the misty distance. The reconciling sunset light was everywhere, transfiguring earth and sky.

'A touch of frost to-night,' he said. 'I shouldn't be surprised. Doesn't the sun look rum?—like an orange. Christmas will soon be here.'

'So it will.' Her heart sank. And then soon the January snows, and then the hyacinths on the barrows, and then . . .

After a while she said:

'How are things going in the office?'

'Oh, pretty well. Things look a bit brighter now, but it's been a shocking year. The old man got the wind up. Ah, he 's failing a bit. It makes him crotchety. You can see it 's hard, at the end of your life, to fall on bad times like this. . . . It was a blow to him, you know, that young relative of his chucking it up.'

' I suppose it was.'

' Oh, yes. He had great hopes of that young chap. It 's more than we had.' Tom chuckled. ' He was a regular demoralizing influence among the clerks. He was *able*, I grant you—very able when he applied himself—but he hadn't the temperament. I always said it.' He wagged a finger. ' The first week he was here I said to Jones : " Mark my words ! That young fellow will never make a business man." ' He chuckled again. ' But he was a great lad ! You couldn't help but take to him.'

' Yes, he was very attractive.'

Arm in arm, they passed through the public gardens, where beyond the asphalt and the railings the empty borders were raked, the grass made trim for winter ; and turned their feet towards the lamp-lit terrace.

He fell asleep, after supper, in his armchair. She watched his loose lips puff out and in, his head fall forward, jerk up, collapse again. He looked old, sensual, and forlorn. He snored.

He is betrayed by sleep, she thought. He was too vulnerable thus to be exposed. It was wrong to look on while sleep made cruel sport of him—held up to mockery the assumptions of his waking self; his self-respect and anxious dignity ; his simple faith in his immortal soul.

She thought of Hugh asleep ; saw him as she would never see him, lying in calm beauty, like a sleeping child.

He woke up with a start, yawned, stretched himself. ' I 'm beat,' he said.

The week's work told on him. Saturdays and Sundays he fell asleep off and on all day. The habit was growing on him rapidly. She had noticed it with coldness and distaste. Unjust, she told herself. He was no longer a healthy man. He worked too hard. He needed rest.

' I 'll turn in.' He yawned again, cleared his throat loudly. ' Coming ? '

' Soon.'

She heard his ponderous tread mounting the stairs.

Afterwards Annie, rustling and creaking, going slowly with her burden to her attic room.

She sat on alone, listening to the breath of the gas, hearing the tram, the wounded one, come limping and groaning past.

Now for another night, restless, sleepless, thronging with fantasies.

She turned out the lamp and the fire, and went to bolt the door.

Hugh had decided to come back after all—was waiting on the other side—about to ring the bell. If she were to open the door she would find him there, smiling, holding his hands out, saying : ' I 've come back to you. . . .'

A tremor of bliss possessed her for a moment. Her hand crept out to the door-knob.

No. Folly. Lock up. Lock up this house, this cage, and stay within it. Shut doors and windows. Thieves might break in; or rain, or wind. Draw the curtains close against dawn, against peering eyes, against waking up too soon. Fasten chain, draw bolts. He would never, never, never come to the door again.

She went to her cold room, undressed, got into bed, clutched her hot-water bottle. What months, she thought, of wintry sheets stretched out before her !

Not a sound from the dressing-room. He must be asleep already. Had he minded, she wondered, her request that they should sleep apart ? She remembered his face when she had suggested it—pleading insomnia—after the summer holiday. Searching frantically still for independence, for some way in which she might dedicate herself—she, a married woman beneath her husband's roof—more fittingly in spirit to another, she had asked him : might she sleep alone ? Yes, he had minded, while he acquiesced and pitied ; no doubt was waiting dumbly to be told he might come back.

Presently she got up, opened the dressing-room door and called in the darkness :

' Tom ! '

' Yes ? '

She heard him stir alertly. He had not been asleep.

'I 'm so cold, I 'll never get to sleep.'

'Want me to come ?'

'Yes, please.'

'Right you are !' he said happily, jumping up.

He came and lay beside her and put an arm over her (the habit of years).

'Soon warm up !' he said. 'Poor old iceberg! What a cheap circulation !'

And soon, drowsily :

'Drop off to sleep now, there 's a good girl.'

He slept.

She whispered to herself, over and over again :

'Peace. Peace. Peace.'

Let me stop thinking, dwell on little things.

To-morrow I get up, eat breakfast, read the paper, tell Annie to order stewing steak for lunch. . . . Annie who, caught in the trap of creation, swept, dusted, cooked the dinner for Mr. and Mrs. Fairfax ; knew there was no way now to cheat nature, or escape from Time. Time was dragging her without respite to the day when she must bring forth a living being.

No, that was the wrong kind of thought again. . . .

To-morrow I take my winter coat to the dress-maker to be turned ; to-morrow I pay the plumber's bill long overdue. To-morrow I 'll have chocolate shape for supper. To-morrow . . . .

But what were they—these activities ? These were not life. If one could but think cosmically, keep one's mind strained to it even for one minute without collapsing—then one would be brushed by a fleeting intimation of what life was.

All that one took for granted was a mystery, all day to day experience delusion. Truth, could one but remember it, wrote naught with everlasting impersonality on all that seemed important. Even love—love that is God—was nothing; would vanish with the beings it had beguiled? For life is scientific—chemical, mathematical, exact.

The world is . . . is gases blown off the sun and cooling, clotting into systems; and life is infinite millions of atoms and electrons, collecting themselves into millions of shapes of living objects. Life was in all things. Dead stone, dead wood was all one mass of vital energy.

First rocks and mountains; then the green, the forests springing over them; then beasts, birds.

And man came out of the sea. . . . Man came out of the sea and stood upright; and thought.

And what was man, standing and thinking? Who were these infinitesimal specks, accumulating knowledge and possessions, assuming the lordship of understanding over earth and sea; who dropped too far, too swiftly, and earth broke them; who sank too deep, too long beneath water, and water choked them? Who were they, precariously balanced in immensity, whose eyes beheld the little sparks that were the planets; whose minds could plunge through space to observe and measure them with instruments; whose lips could name them, record their scientific attributes ; or else record them with another tongue and eye : worship the sun, fear or love moonlight, praise the stars. Who were they, these self-conscious organisms reproducing their kind at will, but perishing inevitably after brief agitation ; and wishing never to perish ? But laws impersonal, biological, governed their coming and their going. They did not live through joy, that seems to give life, nor die of grief, that seems to kill.

Yes, and who am I . . . *I* ? What is I ? What is *knowing* ? And what is *dying* ? . . . *Christina Grace* . . . *daughter of* . . . *wife of* . . . *born* . . . *died* . . . That is *I*.

Yes, but that 's not it. What happens to *me* ? How can that cease ?

That bouncing rhapsody of childhood recitations :

You are more than the world though you are such a dot ;
You can think and speak and the earth cannot.

Well, was that it ? Was there anything in that ? Was it going anywhere, this anxious, ignorant, inquiring *I* ? . . . (To future life, whispered old childish habit—to the reunion with all we love and lose. . . .) To Hugh.

. . . All gone, leaving not a trace—Grace Fairfax ; Hugh Miller (wandering over the world all his life long and causing women to love him) ; Norah (the good wife, the loving mother, watching her offspring pass through man's stages one by one towards death) ; people asleep in bed now ; wakeful in passion, in child-birth, in sorrow or excitement ; people dancing, drinking ; family groups, and friends, and lovers sitting by the fire now, laughing, talking, whispering to each other ; people sitting alone in empty rooms ; people destroyed in swift disasters by land or sea or air ; or, inch after inch, of cancers, in hospitals ; all gone—the strong, the weak ; the fortunate and the unfortunate; the loved, the hated . . . all, all gone?

Oh, Hugh ! . . . Is this all ? Must you too come to dust ?

Run, kneel at his death-bed. *My darling, I will save you* . . . clasp him, breathe life into his lips, till the heart beats again, the lids unclose. . . .

No, he would die in his own time ; some one would wash him, fold his hands, arrange the funeral. Hugh would have a funeral, a burial service, wreaths. . . . In his coffin, his body would fall into corruption . . . and some one would be busy in his room, sorting his clothes, putting away his pipes, his books, reading and burning his old letters. . . .

And that was that.

Tom moved in his sleep, turned over. His chest was pressed against her hand ; she felt his heart.

This was life—this steady beat, beat—she was touching the mystery with her finger-tips.

Go back to the beginning—to the seed, the embryo, the heart's first beat, the blood's first flow. But that was not far enough to reach him. Go back beyond the beginning, through his progenitors, back through the generations. Behind the living pulse another living pulse. . . . Where was the beginning of life? Where would it end?

No, it was not clear yet, not analysed, dissected, labelled--the nature of this heart-beat. The vital spark was still enshrouded: not ever to be captured in the laboratories of earth. The germ that was life still wrought in the darkness secretly: but only to be separated, sealed at last in a tube? At the rending of the last veil, one day, would all be demonstrable, visible for ever under an inextinguishable Arch-Laboratory light? Would there be no more silly old birds then to catch by their jaunty tails with a pinch of salt? No faiths, no superstitions? Would doubt be banished, fear routed? . . . hope routed too?

Or would the veils disclose,—in eternal prospects, infinite solutions.

No, it was not clear yet.

Tom was unfathomable mystery.

The street lamp underneath the window made a faint glimmer in the room. She turned and looked at him. She saw the outline of a head upon the pillow—a man's dark head beside her, perfectly still. . . . It might be Tom. It might be Hugh. It might be a stranger.

She lay down softly, drew closer to him, shut her eyes; felt thought's harsh fever fade gradually out, a slow tide start to drown her.

From a square of cottage window she looked out for a moment upon stars and haystacks and a row of poplars. The smell of mist came in sharply; the smell of earth and leaves. . . .

The poplars started to shake, to make a dizzy whispering. . . .

Tom moved in his sleep, gave a little groan, half woke.

'Can't you sleep?' he muttered in dim dismay.

'Sh! Yes!' she murmured. 'In a minute.'

They slept.

The first night out. Quiet starry weather, no moon, calm sea.

Hugh wandered into the bows after dinner, and stood alone, leaning over the rail, staring at the water.

He listened to the throb of the engine, the unmistakable dull wooden thud of feet tramping round the covered deck. The walkers had started to walk, with brisk and regular tread, in their burberries, their leather coats and veils, round and round, morning, noon, and night, till they reached land again.

The ship rolled ever so slightly. Laughter came out from the smoking-room. He must join them soon, look around, scrape acquaintance with his fellow-travellers before turning in.

Well—there was always a time of loneliness, depression, after the first excitement of the start, the bustle of departure. Hours now since Clare had vanished, standing waving on the quay. Ripping of her to come and see him off—looking her best, in a marvellous black coat and skirt, and a queer little cap with turned-back ear-flaps, like a Mercury's helmet—queer, but just right. Her face had sparkled and glowed out of dark furs. She 'd been in such good form. Every one had looked at her. Lovely Clare—dear Clare. How long till he saw her again ? He hoped to goodness nothing boring would happen to her : that she 'd have no bothers with any rotten sort of chap.

A damned awful mood had come over him, amounting to : *Why live ?*

He stared at the water. If one were to go quietly overboard. . . . A lot of trouble saved, an end of getting up in the morning, shaving, wondering what to do next—all the dismal rigmarole.

The cold foam churned in the water, flashing and falling behind, flashing and falling behind. . . . The *darkling* water . . . Oliver had called it so, murmuring to himself, resting on his oars, staring out from the fishing-boat one night. The darkling water . . . funny word.

The gulls still followed the ship, calling and complaining, a hundred raucous voices. . . .

The gulls wheeled and fell down the sky all day on motionless wings, cutting a whole arc of blue in one long, slow, white fall. They had lain on the rough Cornish beach and watched them circle and squabble—hundreds and hundreds of them ; settle a moment in their fouled rock crannies—swoop off again.

By day they were birds, with ravening fierce bird-habits, beautiful in their flight ; but by night . . . by night the gulls were the last voices of humanity, after the end of the world ; the unappeasable sick protesting echo of all the desolation. He had thought so all at once that night, that last night when every sight and sound had seemed to reflect, enlarge, sharpen his own pain ; when climbing the tremendous cliffs in the late twilight they had both paused with one accord, listening in silence to those voices, querulously complaining, mocking—stressing the breach, the final failure with infinitely cruel, with diabolical relish. By then, the quarrels and struggles were all over. They had nothing more to say to one another. The gulls were saying the last word on their summer holiday—crying that everything was wrong, for ever.

Oliver's face (his terribly attractive, crooked face) rose up before him, pale, haggard, with a terrible expression : saying something that in one moment, so it seemed, had changed the very face of July, and all the warm, rich, serenely shining landscape. . . .

Diving from a rock, swimming under water right round the bend, coming up finally out of sight of Oliver, wondering cheerfully if Oliver had missed him, floating idly back, enjoying himself most frightfully, and finding Oliver. . . . No, it didn't bear thinking of—his face, his low voice saying in such stony anguish 'I thought you'd gone'; saying: 'What a good joke, so typical' ; saying that it was only one more instance of his utter lack of sensibility and consideration, and going on to say . . . to plunge them further and further into a miasma of stored-up grievances, of accusations that one would never, never be able to deal with, or quite forget.

Where was Oliver now? Whom was he making miserable? Or had it really been, as Oliver said all one's own fault?

That boy, now, that young Seddon . . . what about him? It might have been the merest formal note, of course, which that envelope had hidden. Why should one have been so convinced that it was intimate, important?

He was a clever chap, of course, artistic, cultured—all that Oliver was, and that one had tried for a while, quite uselessly, to make oneself. . . . But was Oliver really attracted, taken in by such a ghastly prig? And then his conceit, his pompousness, his affectation: the things he wore, the colours; his hair; the book of poetry he would carry about with him. . . .

Still the looks, the charm—one had to admit that to oneself. One had been drawn to him reluctantly, hostile and fascinated, the unspoken name of Oliver weighing the air between them. For that had been the queerest thing: one could have sworn that the chap recognized him, was on his guard—interested. Probably Oliver had told him the whole story, exhibiting one's own behaviour in the most unfavourable light. . . .

Stop thinking about it, once for all. There was plenty to look forward to. Months of freedom before one, no compulsion to take a job before the summer. Father had really been very decent—much more amenable than most parents. But of course he must keep his promise : to stick to the next thing, wherever he landed up.

What was it she had said about him ?—' always gay and lucky. . . .' She 'd made him promise. Fancy promising ! Funny idea she 'd had of him : exaggerated.

That had been a queer time altogether.

He saw her looking at him with her peculiar smile. . . . The thought of her would keep on coming back to worry him. Wasn't there something more he might have done or said ? She seemed so peaceful, so large, so quiet—like sculpture almost—but she wasn't peaceful. He had felt that strongly. There she was for ever, hating it—saying that she 'd think about him. ' As long as I live.' How extraordinary ! Could she have meant it ? He should have said something in return—something complimentary or a bit affectionate. Was that what she 'd wanted ? At one moment he had thought it was going to be a tight corner. . . . But surely, it couldn't have been that ? . . .

No good thinking about it. He had failed again ; bungled it somehow. He had never been able to understand himself—much less anybody else. He was a person who would never be able to find any one to confide in—or to love him.

Time to turn in. But first a drink, perhaps a chat.

Laughter came out again from the smoking-room. It sounded as if the ice was already broken. Perhaps there was some one specially amusing on board. It was time to start enjoying the journey.

Ever so slightly the ship rolled, creaked, vibrated; the strong bowels throbbed.

For a moment longer he watched the great bows plunging majestically; spinning out of their prodigious iron austerity delicate ruffles, ephemeral films of foam; white laces, ruffles of foam blown over a dark breast; blown over a swelling breast . . . a vanishing breast.